Égalité

Égalité

TIMOTHY EVES

Contents

Chapter 1: What's for Dinner?   p. 1
Chapter 2: What Is Speciesism?   p. 11
Chapter 3: What Is Equality?   p. 18
Chapter 4: Are All Human Beings Equal?   p. 30
Chapter 5: Are All Animals Equal?   p. 38
Chapter 6: What Is Good Health Care?   p. 47
Chapter 7: Are Animal Experiments Justified?   p. 59
Chapter 8: Can a Vegetarian Utopia Exist?   p. 71
Chapter 9: Should People Be Vegetarians?   p. 80
Chapter 10: How Should People Treat Companion Animals?   p. 96
Chapter 11: What Should People Wear?   p. 108
Chapter 12: How Should People Treat Wild Animals?   p. 120
Chapter 13: Is Anything Wrong with Zoos?   p. 133
Chapter 14: Are All Animals *Really* Equal?   p. 145
Chapter 15: How Can One Person Make a Difference?   p. 163
Notes   p. 177

Chapter 1
What's for Dinner?

"We hold these truths to be self-evident, that all animals are equal ..."

What on heaven and earth is going on? A moment ago I was standing in the ample light of Mrs. Shoemaker's living room; now I'm in pitch darkness. Straining my eyes, I peer in every direction, but I see nothing. I can't even make out my fingers two inches from my face. Where can I possibly be? As panic grips my chest, I back up a pace. Bad move. I bang the back of my head against something hard, some sort of rocky protuberance. In pain, I crumple to the ground, which also appears to be rock.

"... that as sentient beings they are endowed with certain unalienable rights ..."

The voice that's talking about unalienable rights—reedy, like Mrs. Shoemaker's voice—isn't far off. Massaging the back of my head, I call to the voice, but I produce only an inarticulate wheeze. I call again, with the same result. Calling, I decide, isn't going to help me, so I try crawling toward the voice. Groping blindly, I turn one corner, then another. A single ray of light, barely detectable, falls into my eye. I peer again in every direction. A cave. How did I get in a cave? When I turn one more corner, I see the entrance to the cave. Still crawling, I scramble toward the entrance.

"... that among these are life, liberty, and bodily integrity."

I tumble out of the cave. The air is tropical, the light so bright that I must shield my eyes. A gnarled hand touches my shoulder. When my eyes sufficiently adjust, I look up into a bony black face haloed by a wispy white perm. The face, which smiles at me warmly, revealing a set of pearly false teeth, belongs to Mrs. Shoemaker. In her reedy voice, she says, "Welcome to the twenty-fourth century, son!"

o o o

Just like that, I'm back in Mrs. Shoemaker's living room. Mrs. Shoemaker is sitting on her sofa, her walker to one side and her telephone pressed tightly against the less deaf of her ears. She's speaking with Sophia, to set her up on a blind date with me. Sophia is reluctant, but Mrs. Shoemaker assures her that she'll love me to pieces, that I'm a good boy, as gentle as a lamb. The conversation has precious little to do with self-evident truths or the twenty-fourth century.

I whirl around three hundred sixty degrees—everything seems normal enough. So what just happened? Was I daydreaming? Uh-uh. The cave felt too real to be a daydream. Maybe I was hallucinating? Strange hallucination! I hope I'm not losing my marbles.

I plop down on the sofa next to Mrs. Shoemaker. My hallucination—if that's what it was—worries me for thirty more seconds, until I'm distracted by the pizza that Mrs. Shoemaker and I ordered from Giovanni's. The pizza reclines seductively on the coffee table in front of us, emitting undulating fingers of steam that caress the surrounding air. The aroma of bacon and hamburger penetrates my nostrils. I inhale deeply, hungrily, lustfully.

As I pick out a slice, Shirley Temple, Mrs. Shoemaker's toy poodle, hops on my lap. The dog gazes longingly at the pizza in my hand. I stroke her behind the ears; she waggles her stub of a tail. Today Shirley Temple is wrapped in a pink tutu. Garish costumes, according to Mrs. Shoemaker, enhance a dog's cuteness. Mrs. Shoemaker fancies herself an animal lover—especially if the animal is a poodle. The words "I ♥ POODLES" emblazon the T-shirt she's wearing.

I fold my slice of pizza in half, and then in half again. After cramming the whole thing in my mouth, I let Shirley Temple lick my fingers. She licks systematically, making sure she doesn't bypass so much as a molecule of pizza. I wipe my fingers against my sweatshirt and reach for another slice.

I've been visiting Mrs. Shoemaker every Saturday afternoon for the last six months, ever since that frigid winter day when, on her way to her mailbox, she slipped on the ice and shattered her left hip. Each week, I bring her up to date on the latest town gossip, and in turn she tells me stories about her childhood—the bad old days in segregated Alabama. Her stories are much like the latest town gossip: far-fetched, but just plausible enough to make me think there's a kernel of truth to them.

In recent weeks, Mrs. Shoemaker has developed a genuine, if meddlesome, concern regarding my bachelorhood. One Saturday, as she tilted her head upward and peered at me through the bottom lens of her trifocals, she told me that, now that I was thirty years old, it was high time I settled down. She added, lowering her reedy voice as if to let me in on a little-known secret, that men were like puppies: if no one kept an eye on them, they'd run wild and get into mischief. Every man needed a woman to keep an eye on him. Behind every good man was a woman.

Doubtful, I replied that, once a year, I riffled through the pages of the swimsuit issue of *Sports Illustrated*; once a month, I nursed a few beers with Blake and Chaz, two of my longtime buddies; every day, as I drove to work, I exceeded the speed limit by five miles an hour. This was as wild and mischievous as I ever got. Yet no woman was currently in my life. If men were indeed, as Mrs. Shoemaker thought, like puppies, wouldn't I be wilder than I was and get into more mischief than I did?

Mrs. Shoemaker, however, dismissed my argument. A woman, she said, *was* currently in my life—I was forgetting about my mother. It was my mother who, all these years, had kept me on the straight and narrow. But a man my age should no longer depend on his mother. He needed to find a wife. It just so happened, she went on to say, that she knew someone who would be perfect for me, a nice young lady she had met eight months ago in the produce section of the local health food store. When I inquired who this nice young lady was and what made her perfect for me, Mrs. Shoemaker answered only, "Never you mind, son. You'll find out when you meet her."

The nice young lady turned out to be Sophia. Still on the phone with her, Mrs. Shoemaker rattles off a list of virtues that she claims I embody in the utmost degree. I blush. Certainly I try to be a good person. I donate old clothes to Goodwill, I collect money for cancer research, and between Thanksgiving and Christmas, each time I walk out of the supermarket, I give a dollar or two to the Salvation Army. I wave hello to my neighbors, run errands for my mom, and patiently assist customers at the sporting goods store where I work. I don't lie, cheat, or steal. I'm gentle, calm, and polite. Although I tend to be shy when I'm among strangers, I lavish affection on those I know and trust.

But I also have faults. For example, I've never had a great love of learning. I managed to graduate from high school, but my grades were mediocre at best. Only rarely did I receive a B, and—with the exception of a course about computers, for which I had, if not a passion, at least an interest, a result of all the hours I spent on my computer socializing, playing games, and snooping around—I never got an A in any subject. One day, when I brought home a particularly dismal report card, I overheard my dad (may he rest in peace) mutter to my mom, "I swear, if that boy's head weren't attached to his shoulders…." A few years later, Mr. Bhayq, my high school biology teacher, expressed a similar sentiment. Taking me to one side, he said, "You have a good head on your shoulders, Phil. It's too bad you hardly ever use it." Mr. Bhayq had all the tact of a charging bull.

Furthermore, I dislike confrontation, so much so that I sometimes let people take advantage of me. Once, when I was sitting through yet another dreary Sunday school class—I must have been nine or ten years old—my teacher, Brother Bell, expounded on turning the other cheek. He told his fidgeting pupils that, according to Jesus, we must never hit people, even if they hit us first. He went on and on about not hitting people, and about how the meek shall inherit the earth. I marveled how he could fill an entire hour talking about this one topic. As it happened, a week later, I ran into a bully during recess. The bully slammed a fist into the right side of my face and demanded that I give him my lunch money. Recalling Brother Bell's Sunday school lesson, I complied with the demand and invited the bully to slam a fist into the left side of my face. It would be nice, I thought, to inherit the earth. I never did, though. All I ever got were two bruised cheeks.

Finally, like so many Americans, I'm overweight, exercising too little and eating too much. Although I love sports, I spend too much time watching them and not enough time playing them. Every now and again, I eat a healthy vegetable or piece of fruit, but all too often I eat junk. I enjoy Egg McMuffins, bacon, and sausages; Big Macs, Whoppers, and KFC chicken; macaroni and cheese, spaghetti and meatballs, and fettuccine Alfredo; French fries, potato chips, and popcorn; Coke, Pepsi, and Sprite; Ring Dings, Twinkies, and Krispy Kreme Donuts; ice cream, crème horns, and chocolate cream pie.

Mrs. Shoemaker puts down the phone and takes a sip of her tea, some herbal blend that the sales associate at the health food store insisted would help her live to a hundred four. Turning to me, she says, "Be at the public library tomorrow at 5:00 PM. Don't be late."

◦ ◦ ◦

Mrs. Shoemaker keeps me in the dark: I know hardly anything about Sophia, not even what she looks like. When I enter the public library, I see a woman sitting at a table, lost in the pages of a book, her chin resting in one hand like Rodin's thinker. Her hair, as black as a raven, is tied up in a bun so tight that the skin on her forehead stretches upward in defiance of gravity. She wears black high-heeled shoes, a gray skirt, and a blouse covered with black triangles and white squares.

In contrast with her creaseless outfit, my T-shirt and jeans are badly rumpled, and clinging to my tennis shoes are several blotches of beige paint, lingering evidence that I painted my living room walls two years ago. Having no comb with me, I attempt to smooth my hair with my fingers. I walk up to the table and ask the woman if she's Sophia. She glances up from her book, appraising me with penetrating steel gray eyes. She scowls and tells me I'm twenty minutes late.

I ask her where she'd like to eat dinner. She says that an Indian restaurant would be fine. I've never eaten Indian food, but every day, on my way to work, I drive by a restaurant called "The Sacred Cow," so I take her there. The restaurant, however, turns out to be a beef joint. I order the veal parmesan, Sophia a salad with sirloin tips— except that she asks our waitress to leave out the sirloin tips. The waitress—a plump, pimply teenager who repeatedly blows bubbles with her bubble gum—furrows her brow. "I'm a vegan," Sophia explains. Bursting a large bubble, the waitress returns to the kitchen with our orders.

I look at Sophia, admiring the whiteness of her teeth and the healthy glow of her cheeks. Leaning forward, I stretch my left arm across the table to offer Sophia my hand. She folds her hands in her lap. I tell her that I didn't realize she's a vegan. She says she is. I ask her several questions. She answers that her name isn't Sophia, as I had thought, but Safiya, an Arabic name meaning "pure." Her parents, devout Muslims, named her after one of the Prophet's wives. She herself, though, drifted away from Islam when she was a teenager, and now she's an atheist. She's twenty-eight years old and an oboist who prides herself on her technically proficient, mathematically precise playing. In her spare time, she reads utopian literature and the great works of philosophy. As a student of philosophy, she values the truth above all else. Consequently, she never tells lies, not even white lies. I'm unable to distinguish an oboe from a clarinet, and I've never read utopian literature or great works of philosophy. Rather than risk revealing my ignorance, I stop asking questions. A long silence ensues. I clear my throat. I say that I work at a sporting goods store. Safiya expresses surprise. I ask her why she's surprised. She says she assumed that people who work around athletic equipment are athletic, and I don't look athletic. She quickly adds that looks don't matter to her. Another long silence. I stare down at my left arm, still stretched across the table.

Finally, our food arrives. The salad is in a tiny bowl; the veal is on a huge platter. The veal is too much for one person to eat, but I eat it all anyway. As my plate steadily empties, I think about Brussels sprouts. Once, when I was six or seven years old, I left three Brussels sprouts on my plate. I was full, and I didn't much care for Brussels sprouts in any case. My mom noticed the little green globes. Her voice low, she pointed out that there were starving children in Africa, that Brussels sprouts were a treat their parents couldn't afford, and that I was lucky my parents could afford such a treat. She urged that I always finish what's on my plate. I felt bad about the starving children. So I forced down the three vegetables. Ever since that day, I've been unable to leave food on my plate, at first because the starving children gnawed at my conscience and later because the habit had become ingrained.

Our waitress gives us the check, still blowing bubbles. We pay. We leave. I drive Safiya to her house, a modest but immaculate ranch surrounded by an immaculately manicured lawn. From behind a bush trimmed in the shape of a perfect cube, a black and white cat gazes at me furtively. It has the same steel gray eyes that Safiya has. I don't ask if I can come in. Nor do I attempt a kiss, since Safiya and I don't seem to be hitting it off. I say goodbye and speed off to my apartment on the other side of town.

Like Safiya's house, my apartment is modest, consisting of a living room, bedroom, kitchen, and bathroom, all of them tiny. The apartment, however, isn't immaculate. Strewn everywhere are unmatched socks and autographed baseballs. They're in every room, and on every floor, every piece of furniture, and every shelf. The baseballs number well over two thousand. An avid collector since childhood, I'm hoping they'll one day be worth a pile of money.

When I open my apartment door, I smell the chicken I ate a day ago. I must have inadvertently left the bones on the kitchen counter. I dump the bones in a trash bag and throw the trash bag into the dumpster outside. I feel dirty, so I take a shower. The cool water feels good as it rains down on my body. I soap myself and work shampoo into my hair. The soap and shampoo feel good too. Much refreshed, I step out of the shower and get dressed. I wander into the living room, brush a few baseballs off the couch, and plop myself down. I turn on the TV. I flip through the channels. Nothing interesting is on. With one hand, I absently finger a worn spot in the leather fabric of the couch. With the other, I unbuckle my belt and unbutton my pants, relieving the pressure on my full stomach. I yawn.

An episode from a popular science fiction series, set in the twenty-fourth century, is showing on the TV. An earth vessel arrives at a planet to transport some aliens to another planet. En route to the other planet, the ship's first officer and one of the aliens discuss dietary requirements. The first officer reminds me of Safiya, insofar as he too abstains from meat. He says, "We no longer enslave animals for food purposes." The alien, who does enslave animals for food purposes, objects, "But we have seen humans eat meat!" The first officer replies, "You've seen something as fresh and tasty as meat, but inorganically materialized out of patterns used by our transporters." The alien is mortified. He says, "Sickening! Barbaric!" The first officer furrows his brow, exactly as the plump waitress did.

After that, I stop listening. My eyelids grow heavy. I fall asleep.

o o o

A murmur tugs at my ears. A voice? Am I hearing voices again? Yes, it's a voice. The voice is familiar, a woman's voice, but not—this time—a reedy voice. The woman speaks slowly and softly, as if she's mourning something. Accompanying the voice is music, a single instrument, its tone color nasal, its playing as slow, soft, and sorrowful as the voice. I don't bother to open my eyes. I'm too groggy to investigate. Gradually, however, the woman's words filter into my consciousness. This is what I hear:

"A sentient being is chained in a crate. He has lived there his whole life. He knows nothing of the outdoors, nothing of his family. He doesn't know that his mother cried for days when, shortly after his birth, he was taken from her, and he doesn't know that he has siblings who were also taken from her.

"His crate—the beginning and end of his universe—is six feet long by thirty inches wide, too narrow for him to turn around or comfortably lie down. The wooden slats that make up the floor of his crate hurt his feet, but they allow his urine and feces to fall through to a concrete floor below, so that he doesn't have to lie in his own waste.

"Though his caretakers give him plenty to eat, his food consisting of milk replacer fortified with vitamins and minerals, they carefully restrict his iron intake, with the result that he's anemic. At no time do they give him solid food. Because of his diet, he develops chronic indigestion, ulcers, hair balls, and diarrhea.

"Other than eat and sleep, he has nothing to do. He's prevented from even seeing, much less interacting with, others of his kind, and he's tethered to his crate so tightly that he can scarcely move. Overwhelmed by boredom, he spends his day rolling his tongue or licking and biting his crate. Because he's unable to exercise, his bones and muscles are underdeveloped.

"When he's about twenty weeks old, he'll be removed from his crate and transported to an unfamiliar building. He'll be jittery as he's forced along a chute. At the end of the chute, a stranger will stun him in the head with a captive-bolt gun. Another stranger will shackle and hoist him by one leg, while a third will cut his throat.

"The sentient being is a veal calf. He suffers and will die because human beings enjoy eating pale meat."

My eyelids snap open. I realize who is speaking. It's Safiya! Sitting bolt upright, I try to get my bearings. I recognize my couch, the beige walls of my living room. Is Safiya in my apartment? I don't remember inviting her. How did she get in? I notice that my belt and pants are still unfastened. Fumbling, I refasten them. I look at the TV. It's still on, but the science fiction program is over. On the screen is a veal calf. It's hunched in its crate, turning its head back toward the camera. It looks at me accusingly. I hear Safiya again. Her voice is coming from the TV! Why would Safiya be on TV—especially this evening, the first evening I've spent with her, an evening on which I've eaten veal? I wonder if I'm still asleep, having an unsettling dream brought on by an unsettled stomach. Perhaps this dream is the veal calf's version of Montezuma's revenge.

Safiya stops talking about veal calves, turning her attention to chickens. She distinguishes between two types of chickens: broilers (the kind people eat) and laying hens (the kind people get their eggs from). Broilers are commonly housed in sheds, tens of thousands of birds in each shed, well under one square foot for each bird. The extreme overcrowding has consequences. The chickens peck each other's feathers and, on occasion, even kill and eat one another. Poultry farmers don't like these consequences, because they can't sell damaged goods. To prevent feather-pecking and cannibalism, they trim the beaks of the birds. Beak trimming is painful. It isn't like clipping fingernails.

The broilers leave their droppings on the floors of the sheds. Nobody cleans. The birds walk through and sit in the droppings, and breathe air saturated with ammonia. Many of them suffer from ulcerated feet, breast blisters, and respiratory disorders. Many also suffer from leg deformities, because, as a result of the growth-promoting hormones mixed with their food, they become too heavy for their legs to carry. They live in the sheds like this for six weeks. Then they're slaughtered.

As Safiya speaks, images flash on the TV: a shed holding thirty thousand broilers—a chicken that has had many of its feathers pecked off—a chicken that has been half eaten by another chicken—the blue box with three holes that trims beaks—ulcerated feet—breast blisters—leg deformities—chickens hanging upside down in a slaughterhouse. Could all this be true? Are the conditions in which food animals live really this bad? I think about the bones I threw into the dumpster. Are they the corpses of creatures that suffered their whole short lives just so that I could please my palate? I feel queasy. I don't want to listen to Safiya, or the accompanying nasal music, anymore. I don't want to look at any more graphic images. Grabbing the remote, I change the channel. Nothing, however, happens. Safiya still speaks; the music still plays; the images still appear.

Safiya moves on to laying hens. They're kept in battery cages. The TV shows a battery cage. It's about the size of a drawer in a filing cabinet. It holds eight hens. Two of the hens have lost most of their feathers, because in such cramped quarters they can't help but rub against the wire of the cage. A third hen appears to be dead, its head flopping awkwardly to one side. My queasiness increases. I change the channel again. Again, no new program comes on. I go through every single channel. There are no sitcoms, no ballgames, no movies featuring car chases and explosions—only Safiya's voice, the music, the images of laying hens. As I flip through the channels, my ears pick up scraps of what Safiya says: "fifty-two square inches"—"aggressive"—"unable to stretch their wings, exercise, or dust bathe"—"no privacy to lay their eggs"—"half starved"—"forced molting"—"ammonia"—"gas mask"—"slaughtered for cat food or soup meat." When I reach the last channel, Safiya wraps up her commentary on broilers and laying hens: "About nine billion chickens are slaughtered in the United States every year."

I'm dumbfounded. I press the power button on the remote, but the TV doesn't turn off. (Safiya: "Pig farmers …") My thoughts race. Is the remote malfunctioning? Dropping the remote, I kneel in front of the TV and hit the power button on the TV. Still no luck! I hit the power button repeatedly. No effect! (Safiya: "… confinement of sows …") Growing frantic, I reach behind the TV, grab the plug, and yank it from the outlet. There! That should shut Safiya up! But it doesn't. (Safiya: "… castration of males …") I stand, backing four or five paces away from the TV. What on heaven and earth is going on? (Safiya: "… dock their tails …") Turning, I flee from the living room. (Safiya: "… porcine stress syndrome …") I don't know where I'm going. I know only that I have to get out of my apartment. I fling the door open. (Safiya: "… we no longer enslave animals for food purposes!") Leaving the door open behind me, I run as fast as my legs will carry me.

Almost immediately, though, I stop short. I have no idea where I am! I should be just outside my apartment. To my left should be the dumpster where I threw out the chicken bones. In front of me should be my car and a parking lot and, beyond that, across the street, Mrs. Shoemaker's house. To my right should be the rental office. But I see none of these things. Instead, I find myself on a footpath in a wooded area. The sky is a soft, hazy blue—day has replaced night. On one side of the footpath, a small river flows peacefully. On the other side, where my apartment should stand, a jumble of rocks lies on the ground like rubble. Where the door to my apartment should be, a crack in the rocks opens into a cave. Not far from the rocks, a rabbit is munching on clover. I hear music, a single instrument with a nasal tone color. However, unlike the mournful music that came from my TV, this music is cheerful and serene. I turn toward the music. There is Safiya, standing on the footpath, not ten paces from me. She stops playing her instrument, smiles at me warmly, and says, "Welcome to the twenty-fourth century!"

Chapter 2
What Is Speciesism?

I stand on the footpath, gaping at Safiya. A swarm of questions swirls through my mind, but I'm unable to articulate any of them, much as a hunting lioness, confused by the stampeding herd, is unable to zero in on any individual.

Safiya approaches, still smiling. She places a hand on the small of my back and starts ambling down the footpath, gently urging me along. "Come," she says, "I have much to show you." Her voice is so soothing, her manner so disarming, that, in spite of everything that has happened, I begin to regain my composure—at least a little. I follow her along the footpath.

As we walk, I look Safiya over. In some respects, she's the same as she was at the restaurant. She has the same white teeth, the same healthy cheeks, the same gray eyes. But I observe differences too. Her black hair, which was earlier wrapped in a bun, now flows freely over her shoulders. In addition, she's changed her clothes. Gone are the high heels, the gray skirt, and the blouse covered with black triangles and white squares. These are replaced by sandals and a creamy yellow robe. The robe has no zipper, no collar, no cuffs, not even a logo or brand name—only a sort of pocket in which Safiya deposits her musical instrument. The robe reminds me a little of a Greek toga. Furthermore, Safiya wears a necklace with a pendant. I've never seen anything like it. Could the pendant be a communication device? Or perhaps a camera? Or does it serve no function beyond beautification? I can't tell.

I notice one other thing as well. At the restaurant, Safiya seemed cold and distant. Now she's warm and affable. She has even clasped my left hand in her right. I can't help but wonder if she's the same person I dined with a few hours ago. I struggle to formulate a question. After stammering incoherently for several seconds, I finally spit it out.

"Are you Safiya?"

"Hmm. Safiya.… Not as appropriate as Sophia, but I suppose it'll do. Yes. You may call me Safiya."

I'm not sure what to make of her response, so I try a different question: "Do you know who I am?"

"Let's see. Your name is Phillip, you're thirty years old, and you work at a sporting goods store. Aside from being a speciesist, you're a decent fellow—soft-spoken, friendly, generous. That's pretty much all I know. I guess I don't know you very well."

I quickly review the conversations Mrs. Shoemaker and I earlier had with Safiya. We revealed to her my name, age, and occupation, and, while praising me over the telephone, Mrs. Shoemaker used the words "soft-spoken," "friendly," and "generous." Beyond this, we said almost nothing about me. So far, so good—the woman in the creamy yellow robe walking at my side seems to be Safiya. However, I don't know what a speciesist is. I decide to ask.

"Speciesism," Safiya says, "is analogous to racism and sexism. I suppose you must know what racism and sexism are? Though widely condemned, they were still practiced in your century."

"Of course I know what they are. Racism is a prejudice in favor of one's own race and against other races. Sexism is a prejudice in favor of one's own sex and against the other sex."

"Exactly. Similarly, speciesism is a prejudice in favor of one's own species and against other species."

For a moment, I fall silent. We pass two squirrels chasing each other around the trunk of a tree. A heron, gangly yet elegant, wades along the edge of the river. Suddenly, I feel a surge of resentment.

"Are you telling me that I'm prejudiced?"

"Yes. But you needn't take offense. In your time, the overwhelming majority of human beings were speciesists. It's only to be expected that you'd be among them."

"So not only am I prejudiced, but my whole culture is?"

"I'm afraid so, Phil. Like most people of your time, you're a speciesist because you consider the lesser interests of human beings to hold more value than the greater interests of nonhuman animals. Take, for example, your belt."

"My belt?"

"Yes. Why do you wear it?"

"Because I need something to hold up my pants, and the belt looks nice."

"So you have an interest in holding up your pants, and you have an interest in looking fashionable?"

I glance down at my rumpled clothes. Never before has someone accused me of having an interest in fashion. Nonetheless, Safiya is right. If I hadn't thought the belt was fashionable, I would not have bought it. I say, "What if I do? Is anything wrong with that?"

"Not at all. Do you know what your belt is made of?"

"Leather, I guess. Probably cowhide."

Safiya touches my belt with her fingers. "Yes, it's cowhide. Did you know this when you bought the belt?"

"I might have. Usually, when I buy clothes, I don't pay much attention to what they're made of."

"Do you know anything about the cow from whom your belt was made?"

I start to laugh. Who investigates the history of their belts? But when I see that Safiya is serious, I stifle my laughter. I say, "I don't know much about cows."

"Then you don't know how, in your time, cows were raised and slaughtered?"

I recall the veal calf on the TV, hunched in its crate. The queasiness in my stomach returns. How are cows other than veal calves treated? I have no idea. I ask Safiya, "Did my belt come from a cow that suffered?"

"In all likelihood, he or she suffered a great deal."

I stop walking. Safiya stops with me. Ahead of us, a stone bridge spans the river. Halfway across the bridge, a bench looks out over the tranquilly flowing waters. I ask Safiya if we can sit on the bench for a bit. She agrees.

After we sit down, Safiya continues. "So what do you think? Are your interests in holding up your pants and looking fashionable greater than the cow's interest in avoiding suffering?"

"Uh-uh. They're lesser, even trivial by comparison."

"Could you have satisfied your interests in some way that didn't involve the suffering of nonhuman animals?"

"Uh-huh. I could have bought a cloth belt."

"Then what conclusion may we reach?"

"Evidently, I'm a speciesist."

o o o

We sit on the bench in silence. The air is warm and moist, like the air in a greenhouse. Beads of perspiration gather on my forehead. A mosquito lands on Safiya's arm. She carefully brushes it off. When it moves to my arm, I too brush it off. For a moment, it hovers near my neck, until a breeze blows it elsewhere. The breeze is refreshing.

Before long, a woman approaches the bridge, heading in the same direction we're headed. She looks familiar. Isn't she Mrs. Shoemaker? Like Mrs. Shoemaker, she has a sweet, grandmotherly face and skin as black as night. But no, she can't be Mrs. Shoemaker. With countless creases that cut into her face like cracks in a sidewalk, she must be at least a hundred years old, a good twenty years older than Mrs. Shoemaker. Moreover, with her bad hip, Mrs. Shoemaker can't limp from her living room to the kitchen without the help of her walker. In contrast, this woman strides with the surefootedness of a mountain goat. She wears sneakers, shorts, and a T-shirt displaying the words "I ♥ BRUSSELS SPROUTS." From her withered neck hangs a necklace, its pendant identical to Safiya's. When she reaches the bench, she greets Safiya, embracing her. To my surprise, she also embraces me. Then she continues on her way, saying, "Go with love and wisdom." "Go with love and wisdom," echoes Safiya.

After the old woman disappears around a bend in the footpath, Safiya takes her instrument out of her pocket and plays a cheery tune. I look down at my tennis shoes. They're made of leather, just as my belt is. Safiya, I notice, wears no belt, and her sandals are made from a material I don't recognize. I suppose, though, that no animal was sacrificed for the sake of her feet.

I count the leather objects I have in my apartment. There are my wallet, my couch, my jacket, my autographed baseballs, my.... When I get to my baseballs, I think about the sporting goods store in which I work. It sells all sorts of athletic equipment made of leather, everything from baseballs and footballs to running shoes and soccer cleats. Do any of these things really need to be made of leather? Can't people play their sports without the killing and suffering of animals? How can I deny that the manufacture, sale, and use of leather products are speciesist activities?

Then I think about the images from the TV—the veal calf, the chickens, the pigs. Are the raising and slaughtering of food animals, and the selling and eating of meat, also speciesist activities? I've been a meat-eater all of my life. Never, until now, have I questioned the practice. Do I need meat to survive? Uh-uh. Some people are vegetarians, and they're clearly able to survive. If they can survive, so can I. Do the animals I eat suffer greatly, as did the animals I saw on the TV? I don't know. Does my ignorance of animal suffering excuse my meat-eating? Uh-uh. I could easily gain the knowledge. All I have to do is run a few searches on the Internet. Why haven't I done so? Perhaps I'm afraid that, if I do, I'll spoil my appetite. Does my appetite for meat excuse my meat-eating? But what if the animals I eat suffer greatly? Isn't my interest in tasty food lesser than the animals' interest in avoiding suffering? Besides, can't I find tasty food other than meat?

I let Safiya's music relax me. I can't tell whether it's mathematically precise, as Safiya explained at the restaurant, but it's certainly beautiful and full of feeling. I stop thinking about leather and meat and speciesism, and enjoy the view. The water below us is as clear as glass. Despite our distance from the water's surface, fish are easily discernible. There are lots of them, some skulking along the sandy bottom, others swimming lazily near the surface. Lining each side of the river, stately trees stretch their boughs toward the sun. Under them grow wildflowers, a profusion of colors. The scene is idyllic. It contrasts with the dumpster, parking lot, and brick buildings that surround my apartment. I ask Safiya a question that has been on my mind since I first saw her on the footpath.

"Where am I?"

Safiya stops playing her instrument. She smiles at me. "We call this place Égalité. By your calendar, the year is 2376."

"Am I really in the future? How do I know I'm not dreaming? Or hallucinating? Is Égalité real?"

Safiya pauses. For a split second—a time so short I might be imagining it—she averts her eyes, as if she has something to hide. Then she looks back up, her warm smile returning. "Ah! A philosophical question. I love epistemology!"

"Epistemology?"

"Theory of knowledge. It's a branch of philosophy. Haven't you ever studied philosophy?"

"Not much." I signed up for a philosophy course my first semester in college. The professor overwhelmed me with names and terminology. Aristotle, Berkeley, Camus, Descartes. Axiology, brain in a vat, consequentialism, determinism. I dropped the course after a week. A year later, I dropped out of college.

"It's fascinating! Some philosophers, called skeptics, claim that we can't know anything about the world around us, not even apparently obvious things, such as that we're sitting on a bench. Some of them would say that, for all we can tell, we're just dreaming that we're sitting on a bench. Others would claim that it's possible that the bench is nothing more than a drug-induced hallucination, or a suggestion some hypnotist planted in our minds."

"Is that right?"

"It is. There are other hypotheses too. For instance, imagine a mad but brilliant scientist who removes our brains from our heads and puts them in a vat. After hooking them up to life-support machinery, she or he stimulates the parts of them that control vision so that we think we see a bench when in fact there is none. How can we know that no such scientist exists?"

"You don't say." Agh! The last thing I want to hear is another lecture about brains in a vat.

Safiya must sense my lack of enthusiasm. She says, "But we'll have to discuss this another time. I didn't bring you to Égalité to study epistemology."

"Why did you bring me here?"

"I brought you here because I want to show you my world. I want you to experience Égalité—to see how we live and to learn why we live this way."

"As simple as that, eh? But why show me Égalité rather than some other place, and why bring me to the year 2376? What's so special about this place and time? For that matter, what's so special about me? If you wanted someone from the twenty-first century, you could have chosen any of seven and a half billion other people. Why did you choose me?"

"But you're not the only person from the past who has visited us— some have come before you, some are here now, and some will come after you. We've invited each of you because, deep down, despite your speciesism, you're decent people who want to do the right thing. As such, we believe you'll be receptive to Égalitéan culture, which by 2376 has achieved much good that your culture failed to achieve."

"I don't understand. Are you planning to feed us Égalitéan propaganda, to brainwash us? Will you then return us to our time so that we may spread Égalitéan ideas? Are you hoping to replace my culture with your own? Are you trying to conquer the past—and to use me and others from my time to do it?"

"No, no! Nothing so sinister! We want only to give you information. What, if anything, you do with this information is entirely up to you."

"I see. But what if I don't want to visit your world? If I asked you to return me to my time, would you do so?"

"Of course. Égalitéans don't hold sentient beings against their will! But are you sure that's what you want? Don't you find it pleasant here? Aren't you curious about us?"

Safiya is right. It's pleasant, and I'm curious. But I have one more concern. "How long will it take you to show me Égalité? It was Sunday night when I fell asleep on my couch, and I have to be at work by 9:30 AM on Monday. If I'm late, I'll get into trouble."

"No need to worry! Whether you stay here a few hours, a few days, or even a few years, I have the ability to return you to the very moment that you left. You won't miss anything you don't want to miss."

I hesitate. For all I know, Égalité is dangerous. What if Égalitéans are devil-worshippers? What if they use people as slaves, snaring their victims from the past? I have no way of ruling out such possibilities. The prudent thing would be to insist on going back to my time immediately. I almost do the prudent thing. Almost. But then I look at Safiya. I see the warmth of her smile, the gentleness of her demeanor. I realize I'm beginning to like her. I decide to take a leap of faith.

"Very well," I say. "You may show me Égalité."

Chapter 3
What Is Equality?

With the same enthusiasm that Mrs. Shoemaker's poodle displays when she hears the word "walk," Safiya wraps her arms around me and kisses me on the cheek. "Excellent!" she says. "We're not far from my village. I'll introduce you to my friends. You can see firsthand how we educate our children, how we make our clothes, how we feed ourselves, and how we entertain ourselves. You can learn about our art, our politics, our science, and—most importantly—our philosophy. I'll give you the grand tour!"

I feel like one of the old explorers—Columbus or Magellan or de Soto—about to discover a brand new world. How does my century compare with the twenty-fourth? Have people of the future colonized other planets? Do they live in glass bubbles? Can they grow tomatoes the size of watermelons? Have they found cures for cancer and AIDS? Have things gotten better, as Safiya claims, or have they gotten worse?

"But perhaps," Safiya continues, "we should begin with a little historical background." Holding her pendant between thumb and forefinger, she says, to no one in particular, "Produce the Declaration of Equality."

As if by magic, a document appears two feet in front of us, hovering in midair. I nearly fall off the bench. When I recover my breath, I ask, "How did you do that?"

Safiya points to her pendant. "This is called a PAD, or Personal All-in-one Device. With my PAD, I can read documents, record my thoughts, play games, talk to people from any part of the world, or monitor my vital signs. I can even view the Martian landscape or locate the catfish in the river below us. PADs are similar to the computers of your era, but they can do much more, and, as you can see, they take up less space."

I'm intrigued. Safiya's PAD is no larger than a bumblebee. I'm also intrigued by the floating document. I ask Safiya what it is.

"It's a holographic image of the document that marks the founding of Égalité. It was written, by your calendar, on July 4, 2076. Go ahead. Read it."

I start reading. "When, in the course of interspecies events, it becomes necessary to reconfigure the relations that have connected human beings with other species, and to grant those other species the equal station to which the moral law entitles them, a decent respect to opinions around the globe requires a declaration of the causes that impel the reconfiguration."

The words are familiar. I've read them, or something like them, somewhere before. But I can't pinpoint where. I read further. "We hold these truths to be self-evident, that all animals are equal, that as sentient beings they are endowed with certain unalienable rights, that among these are life, liberty, and bodily integrity."

The words are becoming even more familiar. Weren't these the hallucinatory words I heard in my hallucinatory cave—if that was a hallucination? Uh-huh. I remember the pitch darkness, the reedy voice. Those were the words that the voice spoke. But don't I know the words, or something like them, from somewhere else, too? I'm pretty sure I do. But where?

Ah, yes! The Declaration of Independence! The Égalitéans have changed some of the words, but the document is clearly based on the Declaration of Independence. Both Declarations, I see as I continue reading, support individual rights, and both support the overthrow of oppressive governments. According to the Declaration of Equality, the major governments existing in 2076 egregiously violated the unalienable rights of nonhuman animals, and had done so for centuries. The document speaks of "a long train of abuses and usurpations" and "a design to reduce sentient beings under absolute despotism." It proves these charges by listing the forms of speciesism that were prevalent during the twenty-first century. The list is long: factory farming, animal testing, the wearing of furs and skins, hunting and fishing for sport, whaling, bullfighting, cockfighting, greyhound racing, the abuses of animals in zoos and circuses and rodeos, the widespread destruction of natural habitats, the dissection of live frogs in biology classes, the injection of carcinogens into lab rats, the flourishing of puppy mills, the branding of cattle, the trimming of chickens' beaks, the docking of pigs' tails, the clubbing of seals, the electrocution of foxes, the boiling alive of lobsters, the confinement and slaughter of billions of animals. The list goes on.

Eventually, I reach the closing paragraph of the document: "We, therefore, the representatives of Égalité, in General Congress, assembled, do solemnly publish and declare that the Égalitéan Republic is established, that all political connection between it and any speciesist or otherwise prejudiced government is and ought to be totally dissolved, and that as a free and independent republic, it has full power to do everything that independent states may of right do. And for the support of this declaration, with a firm reliance on the unerring guidance of love and wisdom, we mutually pledge to each other our lives, our fortunes, and our sacred honor."

o o o

When I finish reading, Safiya instructs her PAD to discontinue the holographic image. We get up from the bench and resume our walk along the footpath. As we walk, Safiya provides some historical context. The modern animal movement began in the 1970s with the publication of a book entitled *Animal Liberation*. Its author, Peter Singer, one of the most brilliant and controversial philosophers of his day, made a case in this book that all animals are equal, thus providing a philosophical basis for the liberation of animals, a version of which Égalitéans embrace even four centuries later.

Singer's book helped spawn a wide range of animal organizations in the late twentieth and early twenty-first centuries. Some of these focused their attention on one or a few forms of speciesism, such as animal testing or the fur industry, whereas others, more ambitious, tried to tackle speciesism in all its forms. Some of the organizations were more militant than others, some were more respectable than others, and some were more successful than others. Among the most notable successes in the first half of the twenty-first century was the abolition once and for all of the infamous Draize eye irritancy test.

I ask Safiya what the Draize eye irritancy test was. She answers that it used rabbits to test the hazardousness of household products—everything from inks and shampoos to paint thinners and oven cleaners. Rabbits were restrained inside boxes, with only their heads protruding, and the substance to be tested was placed in the rabbits' eyes and allowed to sit there for several hours or days. Then the rabbits' eyes were examined to see how much damage had been done. The more damage that had been done, the more hazardous was the substance. Often the rabbits received no anesthetic. As Safiya speaks, I remember the shampoo I used a few hours ago, just after I threw the chicken bones into the dumpster. Usually, when I buy shampoo or other household products, I grab whatever is on sale. Never—not even once—have I thought about whether these products have been tested on animals.

Safiya goes on with the history lesson. Despite the early successes, the animal movement, with its motley assortment of organizations, lacked unity. The result was, not a decrease, but an increase in the numbers of animals that suffered and died. This increase continued until the middle of the twenty-first century, when a new organization—People for Animal Liberation, or PAL—was founded. Its president, a savvy, charismatic activist who'd taken the name Koko, in honor of a gorilla that had learned sign language, was able to unify the many factions of the animal movement. Over the next quarter century, despite persistent opposition from governments around the world, the animal movement grew in popularity. Hundreds of millions of people voluntarily abandoned speciesist practices. The lives of billions of animals improved.

By 2076, the time was ripe for a worldwide revolution. Koko and the executive board of PAL drafted the Declaration of Equality and set up the capital of Égalité along the eastern coast of Canada. The Canadian government quickly ceded power, and within the next twenty years most other world powers joined the Égalitéan Republic. The last holdout was the United States, at one time the most powerful and most speciesist nation in the world. By the dawn of the twenty-second century, speciesism had been forever stamped out, as had all other prejudices—classism, racism, sexism, heterosexism, ageism, and the rest. It was a complete victory, all the more remarkable in that, since the founding of PAL, no animal advocate had shed a single drop of blood. There had been no wars, no assassinations, no terrorist bombings. Koko and her followers had relied solely on philosophical argumentation and the compassion native to the human heart.

o o o

The footpath veers away from the river. We're now trudging up a long, steady incline. Normally, when I travel from point A to point B, I hop in my car. I'm not used to walking. No doubt, Safiya's PAD can tell me the precise number of beats per minute that my heart is racing, or the exact rate at which the beads of sweat are dripping from my brow. I wonder if it can also transport us to Safiya's village in the blink of an eye. One would think that, by the twenty-fourth century, the human race would have devised a speedier, and less strenuous, means of locomotion than walking. Safiya, I observe, is completely free of perspiration.

Sucking the tropical Égalitéan air into my lungs, I reflect on the Declaration of Equality and the history of the animal movement. It all began with Peter Singer's contention that all animals are equal. This contention provided the impetus for the animal movement, which in turn led to the Declaration of Equality, which in its turn laid the foundation for Égalitéan society. Singer's contention, then, is the key. If it's self-evident, as the Declaration of Equality insists, Égalitéan society is, at least in its treatment of animals, an improvement over my own speciesist society. But is Singer's contention self-evident? Is it even true? It's certainly not what I've been taught.

There was, for example, my Sunday school teacher. To his face, his students respectfully addressed him by his proper name, Brother Bell; behind his back, with peals of laughter, they called him Phony Belloney. They were never able to take him seriously. It was partly the glasses he wore, much too large for his face and smudged with his fingerprints, and partly the exaggerated enthusiasm with which he spoke. But mostly it was the way he bobbed his head like a pigeon. Although, in contrast with the other kids, I avoided using denigrating nicknames, even I, when I saw that bobbing head, had to suppress a smirk.

Brother Bell had the habit, before every class, of carefully reproducing on a portable blackboard a verse from the Bible—each Sunday a different verse, though for the most part the verses he selected came from the Sermon on the Mount, for which he had an especial fondness. One Sunday, as I entered the classroom, I saw on the blackboard, written in his impeccable script, these words: "Look at the birds of the air; they neither sow nor reap nor gather into barns, and yet your heavenly Father feeds them. Are you not of more value than they?" Brother Bell, his bespectacled head bobbing, expounded on this verse for an hour. I was amazed that a person could find so much to say about two little sentences. He spoke at length about sowing and reaping and gathering into barns, about worrying about tomorrow, and about human beings and birds and other animals. Somewhere in the middle of the hour, he told his fidgeting young pupils that, yes, God loves birds and other animals, but he loves human beings most of all.

I say to Safiya, "I can understand that animals have value and that cruelty to animals is wrong. I can understand the animal movement's opposition to the Draize test and many other forms of speciesism. But is it really true that all animals are equal? Human beings can build cathedrals, palaces, and pyramids. We can clear forests, drain swamps, and convert deserts into farmland. We can study history, physics, and psychology. We can create paintings, music, and literature. We can explore outer space and use PADs. No other species has the abilities we have. Isn't it obvious that other species are not our equals, but our inferiors?"

The crest of the long hill we're climbing, though still a ways off, is now in view. It's a good thing, because I'm huffing and puffing like the wolf that blew pigs' houses in. Safiya says, "I appreciate your objection, Phil. It's good that you question Égalitéan beliefs, rather than accept them uncritically. I hope you continue to ask questions, as any serious philosopher would. However, I think the objection you've raised has a satisfactory answer."

I give Safiya a quizzical glance. What could be wrong with my objection? Safiya continues, "You see, the word 'equal,' like so many other words, is ambiguous. In several senses, it's false that all animals are equal. But in at least one sense—the most important sense—it's true."

There's more than one kind of equality? I say, "Okay. What are some of the senses of 'equal'?"

"The statement 'All animals are equal' could mean any of the following: that all animals have the same abilities, that all animals have the same interests, that all animals should be treated in the same ways, that all animals should have the same rights, or that the interests of one animal have the same value as the comparable interests of any other animal."

"I think that, a moment ago, I had the first sense in mind."

"I think so too. You were emphasizing abilities that human beings have but that nonhuman animals lack. Clearly, there are many such abilities. I, for example, can play my oboe here, but pigs and iguanas can't."

"So in a way I was right. Animals are *not* all equal—at least in the sense of having the same abilities."

"Correct. However, we should be careful to add that just as human beings have many abilities that nonhuman animals lack, so nonhuman animals have many abilities that human beings lack. For instance, can you hover in midair like a hummingbird, or sprint as fast as a cheetah, or smell as keenly as a dog?"

"Uh-uh."

"So whereas human beings are superior to nonhuman animals in some abilities, nonhuman animals are superior in others?"

This is a point I've never considered. Nonetheless, it's true. I nod in agreement.

"Furthermore, although human and nonhuman animals don't share all of the same abilities, isn't it true that they share some, such as the ability to reproduce and the ability to feel pain?"

"Uh-huh."

"Hence, on some abilities, nonhuman animals are our equals?"

"Uh-huh."

During the last half minute, our climb has become steeper. As the shortness of my breath increases, so does the shortness of my answers to Safiya's questions. To catch my breath, I pause to retie a shoelace that's already well tied. When I stand up again, I ask Safiya about the second sense of "equal." I say, "Do Égalitéans claim that all animals have the same interests?"

"No, we don't. To be sure, just as human and nonhuman animals share some of the same abilities, so they share some of the same interests—for instance, an interest in drinking when thirsty or eating when hungry. But many of their interests differ. Thus, I have an interest in philosophy, but I haven't been able to convince my cat to share in it. She prefers that I give her a cloth mouse to bat about, or that I stroke her under her chin. I'm guessing, though, that you'd rather I didn't stroke you under your chin."

The image of Safiya stroking me under my chin makes me laugh, in spite of my labored breathing. I say, "Right. I wouldn't be interested."

"Does this suggest anything about our third sense of 'equal'? Should we treat all animals in the same ways?"

"Obviously not. If I were to give gifts to you and your cat, the philosophy book should go to you and the cloth mouse should go to your cat. This would be differential treatment, but appropriate treatment, since you have an interest in philosophy books but not cloth mice, while your cat has an interest in cloth mice but not philosophy books."

"Indeed! To the extent that different animals have different abilities and interests, it's appropriate to treat them in different ways."

"Agreed. But what about equality in the sense of having the same rights? Aren't Égalitéans animal rights advocates, and don't animal rights advocates claim that animals should have the same rights as human beings? Mustn't Égaliténs accept that all animals are equal in the fourth of your five senses?"

"No, they don't. To be sure, Égaliténs believe that nonhuman animals should be accorded *some* rights. The Declaration of Equality lists three of these rights: the rights to life, liberty, and bodily integrity. But no Égalitéan believes that nonhuman animals should be accorded exactly the *same* rights as human beings. Consider, for example, the right to vote, or the right to get a college education. Do you think you should have these rights?"

"Of course."

"Do you think cows and raccoons should have them?"

"Uh-uh."

"Why not?"

"Because, unlike me, cows and raccoons can't vote or go to college, and because they have no interest in voting or going to college?"

"Exactly."

We're finally within a few yards of the summit of the hill, about to emerge from the cover of the trees onto a small grassy clearing that I expect will afford a fine view of the surrounding landscape. I say, "That leaves us with just one more sense of 'equal.' Do Égaliténs believe that the interests of one animal have the same value as the comparable interests of any other animal?"

"That's exactly what we believe."

And then we're on top of the hill. Safiya gestures to the broad valley that lies before us. She says, "Do you see the village below? That's where I live."

∘ ∘ ∘

Never in my life did I attempt to imagine what the twenty-fourth century would look like. Had I done so, I wouldn't have come up with much. The distant future is hard to forecast. Nonetheless, I'm certain I'd have made two predictions: more people and more technology. I know that in my time more than seven billion people inhabit the globe, and I know that these more than seven billion people are reproducing at an alarming rate—"like bacteria in a Petri dish," to borrow a favorite phrase of Mr. Bhayq, my high school biology teacher. I also know that technology is advancing at much the same exponential rate that people are reproducing. Only thirty years old, I've already witnessed the introduction of the Internet, DVD players, high-definition TV, and iPads, not to mention a host of other technological innovations. If these are the facts of the late twentieth and early twenty-first centuries, surely the twenty-fourth century will see people as crowded as bees in a hive and technology as abundant as sand in a desert.

Yet, if what I've seen so far is any indication, Égalité bears little resemblance to anything I might have predicted. I've encountered lots of wilderness and quite a few animals, but only two people—Safiya and the old woman who resembles Mrs. Shoemaker. Of the few human artifacts I've observed, only PADs are technologically impressive. Everything else—the footpath, the bridge, the bench, the oboe, the clothing—is unremarkable.

Safiya's village does nothing to contradict these impressions. From my distance of about a mile, it appears primitive, something that might have existed three centuries in the past but certainly not three centuries in the future. The village is heavily wooded, with a stream winding through it. Widely scattered on either side of the stream are a handful of long rectangular buildings, each two or three stories high, connected to each other by footpaths or sidewalks. Given the size and number of the buildings, I estimate the population of the village to be three or four hundred, about the same as the number of people who live in my apartment complex. Here and there, a few cleared areas, possibly farmland or playgrounds, interrupt the wooded landscape. I see no highways or parking lots, no cars or buses, no streetlights or utility poles, no billboards or neon signs, no skyscrapers or shopping malls—nothing that indicates an advanced civilization. Is all of Égalité as backward as Safiya's village? Are these primitive conditions somehow related to Égalitéan attitudes toward animals?

Like a bird alighting on the top branch of a tree, Safiya settles down on a rock at the highest point on the hill. Beckoning with one hand, she invites me to join her, suggesting that, while she catches her breath, I can examine the village at greater length. Safiya, however, doesn't appear to be out of breath. Perhaps she's offering a kind deception, merely pretending to be out of breath so I don't have to admit that I'm the one who needs a breather. It occurs to me that any deception from Safiya, even a kind one, would be inconsistent with her statement, made at the restaurant, that, as a student of philosophy who values truth above all else, she never tells lies, not even white lies. But instead of letting this thought worry me, I merely sink down with gratitude beside Safiya.

As I gaze down on the village, my thoughts return to the equality of animals. Safiya said that the interests of one animal have the same value as the comparable interests of any other animal. I'm not sure what to make of this contention. It's too abstract for me to evaluate. I ask Safiya if she can clarify it.

She begins with an illustration. "Suppose," she says, "that a mouse and a human being have an equal interest in avoiding pain of a certain intensity and duration. Suppose further that this pain, if the mouse and the human being were to experience it, would have no impact on any other interests. The mouse would still be able to satisfy her interest in foraging for food, the human being would still be able to satisfy his interest in playing the piano, and so on for other interests. According to the Égalitéan notion of equality, under these circumstances, inflicting the pain on the mouse would be just as bad as inflicting the pain on the human being."

"Your example helps," I say. "Thanks. But I'm still confused about interests. Can you say more about what an interest is?"

"Yes, I can," Safiya replies. "There are two types of interests. On the one hand, sometimes we say that *someone has an interest in something*—for example, I have an interest in reading philosophy, or my cat has an interest in batting about a cloth mouse. When we say such things, we mean that someone has a liking or preference for something: I like to read philosophy; my cat likes to bat about a cloth mouse. This type of interest is called a *preference-interest*.

"On the other hand, sometimes we say that *something is in someone's interest*: studying is in a student's interest, wearing a helmet is in a bicyclist's interest, seeing a vet is in a sick dog's interest. In such cases, we're not talking about what someone likes or prefers. Indeed, some students dislike studying, some cyclists dislike wearing a helmet, and I've known many a dog who has disliked seeing the vet. Instead, we're talking about what is good for someone, whether he or she likes it or not. This type of interest is called a *welfare-interest*."

"So when you say that the interests of one animal have the same value as the comparable interests of any other animal, which type of interest do you have in mind?"

"Both," Safiya says. "According to Égalitéans, the preference- and welfare-interests of one animal, human or nonhuman, have the same value as the comparable preference- and welfare-interests of any other animal."

I pause to think. Something's troubling me, and I need a moment to pin it down. Presently, I get it. "But how can we know when two preference-interests, or two welfare-interests, or one of each, are comparable? How can we know when they have the same value? Suppose, for instance, that a farmer is growing lettuce. The farmer has an interest in selling the lettuce, but a rabbit, let's say, has an interest in eating the lettuce. Are the two interests—in this case preference-interests—comparable, or is one weightier than the other? Whose is weightier, the farmer's or the rabbit's? How can we tell? Or what about a patient who needs a heart transplant? Would it be all right to give the patient a pig's heart? Let's assume that the procedure has been perfected and that no human hearts are available. Let's also assume that, at the time of the transplant, the pig is alive and healthy. Getting the heart would be in the patient's interest, but keeping its heart would be in the pig's interest. How are we to compare the two welfare-interests? How can we determine which has greater value?"

Safiya wraps an arm around my shoulder and gives it a friendly squeeze. "These are excellent questions," she says. "They're the sort of questions that the Regional Planning Committee, our local political body, takes up. With any luck, the Regional Planning Committee will meet during your visit, so that you can see Égalitéan politics in action. For now, though, let me say just this. Often, we don't know how to compare interests. I'm not sure, for example, whether my interest in reading philosophy is weightier than my cat's interest in batting about a cloth mouse, or whether studying is more in a student's interest than wearing a helmet is in a bicyclist's interest. If I had to choose between these interests, I don't know which I'd choose. However, at the same time, we should recognize that we're not completely ignorant. Often, we *can* compare interests. To take just one example, in your time, some women had an interest in wearing a mink coat. But it sometimes took sixty-five minks to make one coat, and each of those minks, raised on a fur farm, suffered significantly. Didn't the interests sixty-five minks had in avoiding significant suffering clearly outweigh the interest one woman had in looking stylish, especially given that the woman could have found other ways to look stylish?"

∘ ∘ ∘

As Safiya speaks, I survey the countryside surrounding the village. In front of me, past the village, lies a series of gently rolling hills, each of them covered with trees, extending all the way to the horizon. The hills are to the west; in a couple of hours, the afternoon sun will melt into them, like a pat of butter on a stack of pancakes fresh from the griddle. To the south, on my left, the stream that passes through the village joins a river, probably the same river that Safiya and I earlier walked beside. Farther south, the river empties into a lake that's narrow in the middle and broad at each end. In the opposite direction, to my right, four egg-shaped hills, two large and two smaller, huddle together. These hills too are covered with trees. Except for the village, the scene before me is a wilderness. Into this wilderness no human being, it seems, has ever set foot.

I stiffen. My eyes go wide; my heart skips a beat. Something is odd. What is it? In a flash, it hits me. The appearance that no human being has ever set foot here is deceptive. Lots of people have been here; *I* have been here. In fact, I know the place well. The four hills to the north are called the Dinosaur Eggs. The lake to the south is Hourglass Lake. During the summer months, I sometimes swim there with Chaz and Blake, two friends I've known since early childhood. Fancying themselves superb swimmers, Chaz and Blake like to showcase their talents in front of the pretty girls. For Chaz in particular, everything is about sex. Even the lake he thinks of as a voluptuous woman, mischievously nicknaming her 36-24-36. In a similar vein, he speaks of the Dinosaur Eggs as the D cups and the A cups.

Safiya may have brought me to a different time, but not, evidently, to a different location. I'm still in the place I was born and raised, the place I've lived my whole life. But the place I know is a thriving town. What has happened to its sixty thousand inhabitants? Where have all the streets and houses gone? The sporting goods store where I work, the public library where I met Safiya, the high school from which I graduated, the church I attend, the Wal-Mart, the two parking garages, the three golf courses, the four supermarkets, the five Dunkin' Donuts shops, the goodness knows how many pizza places—what has become of all of these? A wave of sorrow sweeps through me. I love my town. I can't imagine preferring the wilderness I see in front of me. If Safiya wants to convince me that the future is an improvement over the past, she has her work cut out.

Chapter 4
Are All Human Beings Equal?

"Phil? Phil! Are you with me?" Safiya's arm, still wrapped around my shoulder, shakes me gently.

I turn to Safiya, blinking. "Hmm? Oh. I'm sorry. I must have let my mind wander."

Laughing, Safiya says, "That's all right. You remind me of Socrates. Sometimes, in the middle of a conversation, Socrates would stop talking and wander off, consumed by some philosophical puzzle he'd just thought of. Once, he was found on someone's porch, where he'd been standing for hours. When he snapped out of it, he said he'd had a 'fit of abstraction.'"

As Safiya says this, she has a faraway look in her eyes and a nostalgic smile on her lips, as if she personally knew Socrates. Like Socrates, she abruptly snaps out of her reverie and, blushing, says that she too must be susceptible to fits of abstraction.

Then she resumes her explication of equality. She says that Égalitéans accept two principles of equality. One is the principle we've been talking about, that all animals are equal. The other is that all human beings are equal. Égalitéans have names for these principles: *the principle of animal equality* and *the principle of human equality*, respectively. The two principles are related. Specifically, the principle of animal equality implies the principle of human equality. Since human beings are a kind of animal, it follows that if all animals are equal, then all human beings must be equal in particular. Égalitéans take the principle of human equality every bit as seriously as they take the principle of animal equality.

I'm delighted that Égalitéan culture has something in common with my own. In my culture, too, human equality is widely touted. Almost everyone I know preaches it—even if some don't always practice it. For my part, the principle of human equality, as expressed by the words "all men are created equal," has been an article of faith since childhood. I've never questioned it. Nor have I thought much about what it means.

Clearly, though, it doesn't mean that all human beings have the same abilities or interests. Just as different animals have different abilities and interests, so do different human beings. Neither does the principle mean that all human beings should be treated in the same ways or granted the same rights, since different treatment and different rights are appropriate for those who have different abilities and interests. For instance, only some people should have a right to drive a car. Others—such as the blind, the inebriated, those who fail their driving test, and those who, like Blake, suffer from an incurable lead foot—should no more have a right to drive than should cows or raccoons. Presumably, Égalitéans maintain that all human beings are equal in the sense that the preference- and welfare-interests of one human being have the same value as the comparable preference- and welfare-interests of any other human being. When I ask Safiya about this, she confirms it.

The principle of human equality, thus interpreted, seems plausible enough. But I wonder whether, like me, Égalitéans accept it as an article of faith, without proof, or whether they think they have a compelling reason to accept it. If a skeptic insisted on a proof of the principle, would Égalitéans be able to supply one? I ask Safiya about this as well.

She answers, "I don't know that we have anything as rigorous as a proof. Ethics, after all, isn't like mathematics—we can't prove the correctness of moral principles the way we can prove the theorems of geometry. As Aristotle said many centuries ago, 'precision is not to be sought for alike in all discussions.' It doesn't follow from this, however, that we have no reason at all to accept the principle of human equality. On the contrary, several considerations weigh in its favor."

"What are these considerations?"

"There are at least three of them. First, the principle can nicely explain a great many of our commonsense convictions. Suppose, for instance, that a small child is playing near the edge of a swimming pool. You happen to be passing by, taking a leisurely stroll, in no particular hurry to be in any particular place. You see the child fall into the shallow end of the pool. She's in danger of drowning, and no one else is in the vicinity. To save her life, all you need to do is wade into the water, pick her up, and carry her out of the pool. Doing so would take no more than sixty seconds of your time, though your clothes would get wet. If you were in this situation, what would you do? Would you save the child's life? Or would you keep walking past?"

"I'd save the child's life, of course."

"You seem to have a strong conviction about this. Would you call it a commonsense conviction?"

"Sure. Saving the child's life seems common sense to me."

"Okay. So far, so good. Now what does the principle of human equality say about this situation? Do you have an interest in keeping your clothes dry?"

I glance down at my shirt. It's still slightly damp with sweat, from my earlier climb up the long hill. At least, though, it has stopped clinging to my skin like a baby monkey to its mother. I hate that. I say, "I prefer that they be dry, absolutely."

"What about the child's interest in staying alive? How does it compare with your interest in wearing dry clothes?"

"It must be greater. Much greater. By comparison, my interest is insignificant."

"So, according to the principle of human equality, what should you do?"

"I should save the child's life."

"In other words, the principle of human equality agrees with your commonsense conviction?"

"That's right."

"Is that all it does, or does it do more? Might it not also provide a reasonable explanation for your commonsense conviction? Might we not plausibly say that you should save the child's life *because* the child's interest in staying alive is greater than your interest in keeping your clothes dry?"

"I suppose we could say that."

"I think you'll find, if you run through your other commonsense convictions, that the principle of human equality can explain a lot of them too."

I'm about to test this claim, but Safiya doesn't give me an opportunity, for she turns abruptly to the second consideration in support of the principle of human equality. The principle, she says, "is incompatible with all prejudices against human beings: racism, sexism, heterosexism, and the rest. According to the principle of human equality, the interests of one human being—light-skinned or dark-skinned, male or female, heterosexual or homosexual—have the same value as the comparable interests of any other human being. In contrast, white racists discount the interests of people of color; male chauvinists discount the interests of women; homophobes discount the interests of homosexuals. Prejudice, in short, presupposes human inequality. Thus, if you're opposed to racism, sexism, and other such prejudices, you might find the principle of human equality attractive."

A couple of months ago, a gay couple expressed an interest in renting an apartment in my complex. The manager, however, turned their application down. When the news leaked to the residents in the complex, all hell broke loose. On one side were those residents who congratulated the manager. They held that if even one gay couple were allowed in the complex, soon more would move in, until eventually the whole complex would be swarming with homosexuals. This, they were convinced, would ruin the neighborhood. On the other side were those residents who accused the manager of discrimination. These residents circulated a petition. When they asked me to sign, I declined, since I hadn't heard the manager's side of the story. For all I knew, the manager had rejected the couple not because they were gay but because they wouldn't have been able to pay the rent. If, though, I'd had clear evidence of discrimination, I would have signed. To my mind, prejudice against any human being is deplorable. If the principle of human equality affirms this, it has something in its favor.

"Finally," Safiya continues, "suppose it turns out that human beings aren't all equal. Suppose it turns out, for example, that your interests have greater value than my comparable interests."

"*My* interests? Why would my interests have greater value than your comparable interests?"

"Exactly! Doesn't a claim of inequality invite the question 'Why?' Wouldn't something have to account for the inequality between us? Wouldn't we have to differ in some way? Moreover, wouldn't this difference, whatever it is, have to give your interests greater value than my comparable interests? If no such difference exists, there could be no basis for the inequality between us."

"I guess that's true."

"But what could this difference be? Could it be the difference in our skin color, or our gender, or our sexual orientation? These are the sorts of things prejudiced people appeal to. But these differences are irrelevant. They couldn't possibly give your interests greater value than my comparable interests. Could some other difference fare better? But what could it possibly be?"

I think for a moment. Then an idea springs to mind. "What about intelligence? Could we defend human inequality on the grounds that some people are more intelligent than others?"

"All right. Let's consider intelligence. Sometimes, when defending racism and sexism, racist and sexist people don't appeal directly to skin color and gender. Instead, they appeal to intelligence. Thus, many centuries ago, during the time of American slavery, white slaveholders commonly argued that black people should be slaves because black people aren't as intelligent as white people. Similarly, at one time, sexist people often argued that a woman's place is in the home because women aren't as intelligent as men. What do you think of these arguments, Phil? Are they convincing?"

"I don't think so."

"Why not?"

"Because black people are every bit as intelligent as white people, and women are every bit as intelligent as men."

"Are you sure? How do you know this?"

I swallow awkwardly. In fact, I don't know. I don't know whether black people and women score as well on intelligence tests as do white people and men, and, even if they do, I don't know how accurately intelligence tests measure intelligence. In addition, I've heard that women often perform better than men on tasks that require verbal skills, while men often perform better than women on tasks that require spatial skills. Maybe intelligence isn't one thing, but many things. Maybe on average white people and men have more of some kinds of intelligence, and maybe on average black people and women have more of other kinds of intelligence. To know one way or the other would require extensive scientific investigation. I admit as much to Safiya.

"Since we're not scientists," Safiya says, "perhaps we should look for a different reply to the racist and sexist arguments."

"Do you know of a different reply?"

"I do. The reply was given by a black feminist who lived more than five hundred years ago. Her name was Sojourner Truth. At a feminist convention held, by your calendar, in 1851, she made an insightful remark about intelligence."

"What did she say?"

"She said, 'What's that got to do with women's rights or Negroes' rights? If my cup won't hold but a pint and yours holds a quart, wouldn't you be mean not to let me have my little half-measure full?' Notice that Sojourner Truth didn't try to show that black people and women are as intelligent as white people and men. Instead, she argued that intelligence is irrelevant. No matter how intelligent or unintelligent black people may be, slavery is wrong; no matter how intelligent or unintelligent women may be, confinement to the home is wrong."

"I like Sojourner Truth's reply. It's better than mine."

"I like it too. But what makes slavery and confinement to the home wrong? Might they not be wrong because they discount the interests of black people and women, respectively?"

"That seems reasonable."

"What shall we say then? Does intelligence give the interests of one individual greater value than the comparable interests of another individual?"

"It doesn't appear to, at least when we're talking about race and sex. But when I asked about intelligence a moment ago, I wasn't thinking about race or sex. I had something else in mind."

"What did you have in mind?"

I ask Safiya for a moment to gather my thoughts. When I'm ready, I say, "I was imagining something like this. Two people—let's call them Ms. X and Mr. Y—are dying. Ms. X is a genius, an eminent scientist, perhaps, or a surgeon or inventor. Mr. Y, by contrast, has an IQ of 75 and is capable of unskilled labor only. Each, let's assume, has an equal interest in prolonging her or his life. If we can save only one of these people, which should we save?"

"Wow! What a terrible dilemma! I hope I never have to make a decision like that in real life."

"I hope I don't either. I'm sure I'd lose a lot of sleep if I did. Nonetheless, my gut's telling me we should save Ms. X. Because she's more intelligent, her life seems more important than Mr. Y's. If this is right, wouldn't Ms. X's interest in prolonging her life have greater value than Mr. Y's comparable interest in prolonging his life?"

"I'm not so certain, Phil. In the first place, it occurs to me that genius can be used for either good or ill. Thus, while one genius cures a disease, another might create and unleash one. Do you think a person with an IQ of 75 could do either of these things?"

"I doubt it."

"Because she's more intelligent, then, Ms. X can do more good than Mr. Y, but can also do more evil?"

"It seems likely."

"Do you think we should save Ms. X if she uses her intelligence to harm people?"

"Uh-uh. In this circumstance, it might be better to save Mr. Y."

"What if Ms. X doesn't harm anyone, but also doesn't benefit anyone? Then whom should we save?"

"Hmm. I'm not sure. I don't have a clear intuition in this case."

"So, when your gut tells you that we should save Ms. X, it does so on the assumption that Ms. X uses her intelligence to benefit people?"

"I guess that's what I have in mind. Right."

"Then it's not intelligence by itself that adds value to Ms. X's life? It's a combination of intelligence and benevolence?"

"That's how it looks."

"But what now does the principle of human equality say about whom we should save? Might it not agree with you that we should save Ms. X?"

"I'm sorry. I don't follow."

"Don't people have an interest in being benefited?"

"Sure."

"Is this interest a preference-interest or a welfare-interest?"

"I would think both. Most people like to receive benefits, and receiving benefits is good for people."

"So, by using her intelligence to benefit people, Ms. X satisfies people's preference- and welfare-interests?"

"Uh-huh."

"Ms. X can satisfy a larger set of preference- and welfare-interests than Mr. Y can?"

"Probably."

"By saving Ms. X, we wouldn't just help Ms. X satisfy her interest in prolonging her life? We'd also help other people satisfy their interests—both their preference- and welfare-interests? Moreover, we'd probably help satisfy a larger set of interests than we would if we were to save Mr. Y?"

"Apparently so."

"According to the principle of human equality, when one set of interests is greater than a second set of interests, we should give preference to the first set of interests?"

"Right."

"Thus, according to the principle of human equality, we should probably save Ms. X—even if Ms. X's interest in prolonging her life is comparable to Mr. Y's interest in prolonging his life?"

"I guess that's correct."

"Your scenario featuring Ms. X and Mr. Y doesn't challenge the principle of human equality, as you thought? If anything, it confirms it?"

"I guess that's also correct."

"It appears, then, that intelligence doesn't give the interests of one individual greater value than the comparable interests of another individual. Can you think of any characteristic other than intelligence that we should look into?"

I try to think of one, but nothing comes to mind. "Not off the top of my head," I say.

Safiya is the first animal advocate I've spoken to at length. Before last night, virtually all the information about animal advocates that came my way was second- or third-hand—from the TV, from my speciesist friends, and the like. These sources left me with the impression that animal advocates are flaky, sentimental, misguided fools who care so much about animals that they neglect human beings. After all, don't they advocate vegetarianism when millions of people are starving? Don't they lobby against animal experiments when millions more are dying of cancer and other diseases? Don't they picket stores that sell leather and fur clothing, despite the multitudes of people who go naked?

Safiya, however, doesn't fit this impression. No doubt she cares about animals, but she obviously has concern for people too—not only me but people of either sex and any race, class, sexual orientation, and so forth. Nor can her warmth and compassion be confused with sentimentality, for they're informed by her keen intellect. I'm not sure whether I agree with everything Safiya has told me, and I'm not sure exactly how she and other Égalitéans balance human interests against the interests of animals. For example, do Égalitéans oppose all animal experiments, or do they think that some—such as those designed to find cures for lethal diseases—are justified? Do they abstain from all meat, or only meat that comes from animals that are raised and slaughtered with especial cruelty? What about other animal products— eggs, milk, cheese, and the like? Do they eat any of these? These are questions I hope will be answered as my tour of Égalité continues. But one thing, at least, I know already: Safiya is no fool, and if other Égalitéans at all resemble her, neither are they.

Chapter 5
Are All Animals Equal?

Safiya's PAD bleeps three times, and then a voice that could be either male or female announces, "Three black bears. East-northeast. One kilometer away."

"Bears?" I say with alarm. I've never heard of animals in the area that are capable of eating a human being. But that, I remind myself, is in my time, centuries ago, in a less forested environment.

Touching her PAD, Safiya says, "Show the three black bears."

An image appears two feet in front of us. The view is from the sky looking down on trees. Appearing and disappearing under the foliage, three dark figures, one large and the others smaller, shuffle slowly along.

"Zoom in. Five meters." Obediently, Safiya's PAD zooms in. The large figure stops shuffling and stands on its hind legs, peering about. Taking advantage of the pause, the two smaller figures start wrestling with each other.

"A mother and her cubs," Safiya says. "We should head in to the village. I'd rather not disturb them."

Commanding her PAD to discontinue the image, Safiya stands up and starts down the hill toward her village. I follow close behind.

"Safiya," I say, "does your PAD warn you every time an animal approaches?"

"No. My PAD warns me only about potentially dangerous animals, and only when I'm outside the borders of a village. In the case of a black bear, my PAD warns me when the animal is a kilometer away, and it warns me again should it come within half a kilometer. If, despite these warnings, the bear still manages to reach striking distance, my PAD will produce a holographic image of an even larger animal—say, a brown bear—who will charge the black bear. Most villages have instituted this defensive system. Since doing so, no one from these villages has been hurt or killed in an attack."

"Most villages? What about places that don't use your defensive system? What do they do?"

"In some villages, instead of relying on PADs, people carry defensive weapons when they travel. These weapons can stun an attacking animal for a few minutes without harming him or her. In other villages, people use neither PADs nor weapons. They avoid attacks by learning where dangerous animals are likely to be and what provokes them."

"Do attacks ever occur? Are people ever hurt or killed?"

"Attacks are extremely rare, and injuries and fatalities even rarer. People in your time were far more likely to be hurt or killed in an automobile accident than people in my time are to be hurt or killed by an attacking animal."

"You said your PAD warns you only when you're outside the borders of a village. What happens when you're in a village? Suppose a hungry black bear wanders into a village, attracted by the smell of garbage. How do the villagers avoid an attack?"

"Animals are never attracted by the smell of garbage, because our villages produce no garbage. Some animals might be attracted by the crops we grow, but most villages have dogs, who effectively keep unwanted guests at a distance. We can also create holographic images of predators at the perimeters of our villages. I can assure you that any village you may visit, including mine, is absolutely safe."

Safiya's words reassure me. Nonetheless, from time to time, I can't help but glance to the east-northeast.

o o o

Safiya has now made a case for the principle of human equality. After walking in silence for a couple of minutes, I ask her if she can likewise make a case for the principle of animal equality.

"Yes," she says. "A moment ago, we imagined how things would be if human beings weren't all equal, if, for example, your interests had greater value than my comparable interests. Under these circumstances, the two of us would in some way have to differ, and the difference would have to give your interests greater value than my comparable interests. However, we weren't able to find such a difference. If no such difference exists, it follows that all human beings are equal."

"I remember," I say. "But what of it?"

"We may use the same argument to show that all animals are equal."

"The same argument?"

"Yes. Suppose that animals weren't all equal. In particular, imagine that the interests of human beings had greater value than the comparable interests of nonhuman animals."

"In other words, you want me to imagine how things would be if speciesism were justified?"

"That's right. If speciesism were justified, human beings would in some way have to differ from nonhuman animals, and this difference would have to give the interests of human beings greater value than the comparable interests of nonhuman animals. The challenge is to find such a difference. Égalitéans haven't been able to."

I consider Safiya's challenge. At first, I think it will be easy to meet. Human beings differ from animals in so many ways. We're more intelligent, for one. It isn't for nothing that we define ourselves as the rational animal, and it isn't for nothing that we designate our species *Homo sapiens*—wise man. What other species could invent telescopes, design golf courses, or compose symphonies? Surely our intelligence ennobles us. Surely it gives us a value that other species don't have.

But then I recall that, only a few minutes ago, I admitted that a lesser intelligence in no way diminishes the value of a human being's interests. If it doesn't diminish the value of a human being's interests, why should it diminish the value of an animal's interests? I can't think of a good reason.

Moreover, some human beings, such as newborn infants and the most severely brain-damaged people, are arguably less intelligent than some animals, such as chimpanzees. If greater intelligence implied greater value of interests, then the interests of chimpanzees would have greater value than the comparable interests of newborn infants and the most severely brain-damaged people. This implication, however, seems to me unacceptable. Evidently, greater intelligence doesn't imply greater value of interests.

But maybe something else does. Human beings differ from animals in other ways too. For instance, unlike mice and pelicans and black bears—once again I glance to the east-northeast—human beings use language, and human beings understand moral concepts such as "good," "wrong," "ought," and "duty." Can these differences justify speciesism? Uh-uh. Immediately, I realize that they can't, for the same reasons that differences in intelligence can't. Newborn infants and the most severely brain-damaged people are in the same boat as mice and pelicans and black bears: they also don't use language, and they also don't understand moral concepts. Yet their interests count as much as anyone else's.

To justify speciesism, I need to find something that separates *all* human beings, including infants and brain-damaged people, from *all* animals, including chimpanzees and the like. Is there any such thing? Uh-huh. The most obvious difference between human beings and animals is that human beings are *human*—that is, all and only human beings have the genetic makeup of human beings. However, this still isn't enough to meet Safiya's challenge. I have to do more than point out the genetic differences between human beings and animals. In addition, I need to show that these genetic differences give the interests of human beings greater value than the comparable interests of animals. Can I show this? Offhand, I don't see how. Genetic makeup seems to have no more bearing on the value of interests than does skin color, gender, or sexual orientation.

At this point in my reflections, I'm disturbed by a raucous cawing. A crow, sitting on a branch of a nearby tree, the leaves of which partially hide the bird, gazes down on Safiya and me with suspicion. Do the interests of this crow have the same value as my comparable interests? Maybe they do. I'm beginning to see how difficult it is to justify speciesism. Still, I'm not ready to give up. My thoughts turn to Brother Bell, my Sunday school teacher. He taught that all human beings are created in God's image, but no animals are. Perhaps being in God's image is the characteristic I'm looking for, the characteristic that gives human interests special value. I ask Safiya what she thinks. As I do so, the crow flies down to the footpath, several yards in front of us. It cocks its head, continuing to gaze at us suspiciously.

Safiya halts, smiling at the crow; I halt with her. She says, "I'm not sure how to answer your question, Phil, because I don't know what it means. The expression 'God's image' puzzles me. It suggests having something in common with the divine, but it's not clear to me what. Can you tell me the sense in which all human beings, but no nonhuman animals, are created in God's image?"

"Well," I say, stumbling over my words, "religion is not my area of expertise. However, according to my Sunday school teacher, all human beings, but no animals, have an immortal soul. Just as God is immortal, so a part of each human being is immortal. This is what we have in common with the divine. It's the sense in which we, and only we, are created in God's image."

"I see. I'm afraid, though, that I'm still puzzled. In fact, several things are puzzling me. First, what is a soul? Second, how do you know that human beings have souls? Third, how do you know that nonhuman animals don't have souls? Fourth, how do you know that human souls are immortal?"

Safiya pauses to give me a chance to respond. I, however, remain silent, because Safiya's questions are beyond my ability to answer. According to Brother Bell, a soul is a nonphysical substance, but he never explained just what this nonphysical substance is. As for Safiya's last three questions, Brother Bell would have claimed that he knew these things because they're in the Bible, either explicitly or implicitly. But whether they're really in the Bible, and where in the Bible they are, I can't say. I look into the eyes of the crow, which still holds its ground several yards in front of me. Does a soul reside somewhere on the other side of those eyes? I honestly don't know.

Just as the silence is becoming awkward, Safiya breaks it. "But perhaps we don't need to answer my four questions. Let's assume for the sake of argument that we know sufficiently well what a soul is, and let's assume for the sake of argument that all and only human beings have immortal souls."

"All right." I exhale with relief.

"Even so, I don't see a justification for speciesism. If anything, I see a reason to reject speciesism."

"How do you mean?"

"Let me explain. Suppose I discount your interests, making you suffer terribly so that I may satisfy my lesser, possibly even trivial, interests. Would it be wrong of me to do this?"

"I think so, clearly."

"But according to our assumption, you have an immortal soul. Isn't that so?"

"Uh-huh."

"So even though I make you suffer in this life, it's possible that you'll be compensated with an eternity of happiness in the afterlife?"

"I suppose so."

"Does this possibility justify the discounting of your interests, or do you think the discounting of your interests is still wrong?"

"It seems to me that it's still wrong."

"Very well. Now what about speciesists? They discount the interests of nonhuman animals. Correct?"

"Right."

"For instance, they test household products on mice, and they confine laying hens in battery cages?"

"Uh-huh."

"Do such speciesist activities cause nonhuman animals to suffer?"

"A great deal, it seems." For no apparent reason, the crow starts flapping its wings, stamping its feet, and cawing loudly. Safiya waits for the bird to settle down.

"We're now assuming, aren't we, that nonhuman animals lack immortal souls?"

"Uh-huh."

"The only life nonhuman animals have is their life in the here-and-now? They have no life in the hereafter?"

"So our assumption implies."

"Speciesists, then, cause nonhuman animals to suffer during the only life they have?"

"Given our assumption, this would have to be true."

"The suffering that nonhuman animals endure in this life won't be compensated with an eternity of happiness in the afterlife?"

"This, too, would have to be true."

"Then, if anything, isn't speciesism more seriously wrong than the discounting of your interests? You, at least, have a chance of finding happiness in the afterlife; nonhuman animals, we're assuming, don't. Isn't it nothing short of cruel to rob others of their only shot at happiness?"

Brother Bell's defense of speciesism isn't working. When I admit as much to Safiya, the crow flies off, cawing several times in succession. The cawing sounds vaguely like gloating laughter.

I've now run out of ideas. Although I've been a speciesist all my life, I'm not able to justify speciesism. I feel humbled. I consider making some remark about eating crow, but then think better of it. From an Égalitéan point of view, the attempted humor would be in poor taste.

∘ ∘ ∘

Safiya and I arrive at the outskirts of the village. Although the climb down the hill didn't take long, it was at times arduous. Once again, I'm sweating like a pig. My leg muscles are beginning to cramp, and I'm thirsty, incredibly thirsty. I can no longer think about the principle of animal equality; I'm too tired to think about anything. Safiya must sense my condition, because she tells me that she'll take me directly to the dining hall, where I can eat and drink as much as I need.

Along the way there, the footpath, now a broad cobblestone walkway, bisects one of the cleared areas I saw from the hilltop. On one side of the walkway, crops are growing—not a vast, undifferentiated sea of wheat or row upon endless row of corn, but a little of this and a little of that. I recognize many of the crops, thanks to the time I spend helping my mom in her vegetable garden. Among others, there are carrots and peas, zucchini and yellow squash, beets and Swiss chard, several varieties of lettuce, including romaine and oak leaf—and, yes, some wheat and corn as well. Each crop is assigned its own square plot of ground, so that the entire field resembles an oversized checkerboard. The squares are well-groomed, and the soil is a rich, dark brown.

On the other side of the walkway lies a field lushly carpeted with grass. The purpose of the field is unclear. No cows, horses, or other animals are grazing on it, so it doesn't appear to be a pasture. Nor does it appear to be a playground: there are no swing sets, merry-go-rounds, or teeter-totters, and there are no baseball diamonds, basketball hoops, or volleyball nets. A man wearing red and black is mowing the grass. The lawnmower is quieter than any I've ever known; it may run on electricity rather than gasoline. When the man spots Safiya and me, he leaves his lawnmower, walks over to us, and embraces us. He's young and tall, his dark hair parted on the right side, much like the first officer from the science fiction program that I watched the night before. The man says to us, "Go with love and wisdom." Safiya replies with the same words. The man then returns to his lawnmower.

Soon, Safiya and I reach the outermost building of the village. It's three stories high, with ivy climbing its walls, solar panels covering its roof, and, like a lei, sweet-smelling flowers and herbs encircling its base. Along the second and third stories, at regular intervals, decks poke out. Some of the decks are empty, whereas others hold lawn chairs or potted plants. All of the decks are clean, none a cluttered mess of personal possessions, like my apartment. On one deck, a plump girl, blowing bubbles with her bubble gum, sits on a lawn chair with a cat curled on her lap. She's reading a holographic document produced by her PAD.

Safiya steers me around this building and on toward the next. Rats! I was hoping the dining hall would be in the first building we encountered. I could kill for a tall milkshake—or in case Égalitéans disapprove of robbing cows of their milk, a cold Mountain Dew. It's too bad that a spigot isn't attached to Safiya's PAD.

When we reach the next building, we appear to be at the center of town. This building is identical to the first, except that it has no decks. Just behind it, the stream that threads its way through the village gurgles like a happy baby. All around, the grounds are immaculate: not so much as a cigarette butt, bubblegum wrapper, or shard of glass to be found anywhere. Safiya may have spoken truthfully when she said her village produces no garbage.

I have to admit that the village is attractive, in a rustic way. It wouldn't be a bad spot to vacation, if I wanted to get away from it all. But the village is hardly opulent. The cobblestone walkway is no Yellow Brick Road, and the ivy-clad buildings are no Emerald City. I like opulence. I wouldn't want to live in a town bereft of luxury. In my hometown, with its wide variety of shops, I can have anything. I feel a pang of longing for my hometown. There's no place like home.

Safiya and I enter the building. At last, we're in the dining hall. It's spacious, larger than I expect, taking up the entire ground floor. Soft, soothing music filters through unseen speakers; paintings adorn the walls; sculptures and tropical foliage plants fill empty spaces. In the back of the room, people are picking up trays and, buffet-style, filling their plates with food and their glasses with drink. From what I can see, a wide selection of food and drink is available. In the front of the room, scores of diners occupy dozens of tables. Light conversation and the tinkle of glasses waft through the air, blending with the soft music. A gentle light emanates from elegant chandeliers. Perhaps Safiya's village is more opulent than I surmised.

Safiya glances about the room, as if in search of something, and then, apparently finding it, she leads me to a table at which four people are seated. After greeting the four people, embracing each in turn, she grasps my hand and says, "Phil, I'd like to introduce you to some of my friends. These are Franz Bach-Kuhn, Édouard Bel-Ami, Charlie Perkins-Goodman, and I think you already know Blake."

My eyes bulge. The blood rushes from my head. I of course recognize Blake, one of my friends since childhood. But I also recognize the other three. Franz bears an uncanny resemblance to Mr. Bhayq, my high school biology teacher. Édouard looks almost exactly like Brother Bell. Charlie is the spitting image of Chaz, another of my friends since childhood. The coincidence is impossible, too much for me to handle—especially as it follows the exhausting walk to Safiya's village and, before that, the disturbing images of factory-farmed animals and the shock of finding myself in the twenty-fourth century. I try to return the greetings that the four people offer me, but my lips and tongue won't work. A loud thud reverberates around the dining hall. My body has met the floor.

Chapter 6
What Is Good Health Care?

When I come to, I'm no longer in the dining hall. Instead, I find myself in a room about twice the size of my living room. Aside from the queen-size bed I'm lying in, the room contains a plush chair, a large mahogany—faux mahogany?—desk, a lamp on top of the desk, a ceiling fan, and, set in one wall, a cupboard and microwave oven. Three of the room's four doors are open. One leads into a bathroom and a second into a closet. The closet is empty, except for a pair of paint-spattered tennis shoes—my tennis shoes—sitting on its floor. The third open door is a patio door, on the other side of which is a deck. Since the dining hall is in a building that has no decks, I know I've been moved to a different building. I look out onto the deck. Late afternoon has turned to twilight. Unless it's another day, I wasn't unconscious for long.

An ancient woman, wrinkles crisscrossing her ebony face like cracks in a sidewalk, is sitting on the edge of the bed. Through the bottom lens of her trifocals, she gazes intently at a holographic maze of numbers, letters, and unfamiliar symbols produced by her PAD. I remember seeing her before. She's the woman Safiya and I encountered on our way to the village, the woman who looks similar to Mrs. Shoemaker. She's wearing the same T-shirt that she wore earlier, the one that displays the words "I ♥ BRUSSELS SPROUTS." Turning to me, she grins, revealing a remarkably well-preserved set of teeth. Then she opens a black medical bag.

"Safiya," she announces in a reedy voice, "he's coming around."

"Thank wisdom!" Safiya says. Safiya has been pacing the length of the room, back and forth between the patio door and the closed door. Upon hearing the old woman's voice, she stops pacing and rushes to the bed. Her oboe, sticking out of the pocket on her creamy yellow robe, bobs up and down as she runs. Kneeling by my side, she says, "Phil, are you all right?"

"I'll be the judge of that," the old woman says before I can reply. She rummages through her medical bag, bringing out a teabag. Glancing at Safiya, she says, "Get me a bowl of boiling water."

"Yes, Peacemaker." Safiya opens the cupboard and picks out a bowl with a handle attached to one side. She runs to the bathroom to fill the bowl with water.

"Peacemaker?" I say.

"That's what people call me, son." The old woman turns back to the numbers, letters, and unfamiliar symbols. Frowning, she says, "Hmm."

"Why do people call you Peacemaker?" I say. Safiya returns from the bathroom and places the bowl of water in the microwave oven.

"Partly because I'm a physician. Physicians keep the body in a state of health, harmony, or peace. But mainly because of my involvement in politics. I'm chair of the Regional Planning Committee. It's my job to prevent minor disagreements from flaring into all-out brawls."

"Peacemaker is highly adept at achieving consensus," Safiya says. She's peering inside the microwave oven, as if keeping an eye on the bowl will make the water boil sooner.

"You're a doctor *and* a politician? You have two jobs?" I ask Peacemaker.

"I have many jobs. I also grow herbs in the herb gardens and help clean the dining hall on weekends. My favorite job is playing with my great-granddaughters." Peacemaker frowns again, and then says, "You must be god-awful thirsty, son. And your legs must be as stiff as a gale-force wind."

"Right, doctor."

"You don't have to call me 'doctor.' 'Peacemaker' will do just fine."

"Right, Peacemaker."

"You'll find, Phil," Safiya interjects, still keeping an eye on the bowl, "that most Égalitéans dislike titles. Titles are too formal for our taste, and they're inegalitarian. For example...."

"You can skip the speech, daughter. It's interfering with my concentration."

"Yes, Peacemaker. I apologize." Safiya's face flushes.

"How far did you two walk?" Peacemaker asks. "Wasn't it just from the cave to the village?"

"Yes," Safiya says. "And we rested twice: once on the bench, where you saw us, and once at the top of the hill."

"Hmm. I know we had a warm day today, warmer than folks from the twenty-first century are used to. But it wasn't *that* much warmer. Son, your legs shouldn't be so stiff. How often do you exercise?"

"Not as much as I should," I admit.

"Well, that's one thing that's going to change."

A pinging sound emanates from the microwave oven. Safiya grabs the bowl and runs to the bed. In her haste, she spills a few drops of the boiling water. One drop lands near Peacemaker's sneaker-clad feet. Snatching the bowl, Peacemaker glares at her. "What's wrong with you, daughter? Are you trying to scald a hundred-four-year-old woman?"

"No, Peacemaker! I'm sorry!"

Peacemaker's glare softens, and then disappears. "Oh, don't worry about it. You know I love you to pieces. But if you want to know the truth, you're not helping me. Why don't you go play your oboe somewhere?"

"Yes, Peacemaker."

"And don't fret over Phil. He's going to be fine. I promise."

Safiya's face brightens. She embraces the old woman. "Yes, Peacemaker."

"Go with love and wisdom," says Peacemaker, returning the embrace. Safiya walks to the closed door, opens it, steps into the hallway on the other side, and shuts the door behind her. The sound of oboe music begins to drift into the room, loud and clear at first but growing steadily fainter as Safiya works her way down the hall.

"So, son, what do you think of Safiya? Beautiful, isn't she? She cares about you too. And she's honest, the most honest person I know. You two would make a cute couple." Peacemaker winks at me as she drops the teabag into the bowl.

"Uh-huh." My face flushes, just as Safiya's did.

Peacemaker scowls. "'Uh-huh'? What's this 'uh-huh'? Can't you say 'yes' like a regular person? You sound like you're grunting."

"Yes, Peacemaker." For as long as I can remember, I've been saying "uh-huh" for yes and "uh-uh" for no. Peacemaker, however, is right: my uh-huhs and uh-uhs sound more like grunts than yeses and nos. This is one habit I'll have to change.

"That's better!" Peacemaker says. "Now, I'm going to let this tea steep for a bit, and then I'm going to ask you to drink it. It should ease your thirst, and it'll help calm your nerves. It's not caffeinated, so it won't keep you awake tonight."

"Yes, Peacemaker. Thanks." The smell of the tea, evidently an herbal blend, reaches my nostrils. The effect is relaxing. I take a deep, satisfying breath.

o o o

Over the next hour, as I enjoy two bowls of tea, Peacemaker plies me with questions. Some of the questions are clearly medically motivated.

"What happened just before you lost consciousness?"

"I was in the dining hall. Safiya was introducing me to some of her friends."

"Did you experience any stress or shock at that moment?"

"Yes. Safiya's friends looked almost exactly like people I know from my century. I don't understand how that could have happened."

"Have you experienced any other stress or shock recently?"

"Yes. The biggest shock was finding myself in the twenty-fourth century. Before that, I saw depictions on my TV of the mistreatment of food animals. In addition, the walk from the cave to the dining hall took a lot out of me."

"Have you ever fainted before?"

"No."

"Are you susceptible to dizziness?"

"No."

"Are any members of your family susceptible to fainting or dizziness?"

"Not that I know."

"Is your mother still alive?"

"Yes."

"How old is she?"

"She's fifty-eight."

"Is she in good health?"

"Not exactly. She has type-2 diabetes."

"What about your father? Is he still alive?"

"No. He died of a heart attack when he was forty-five."

"Are any of your grandparents still alive?"

"No. My paternal grandparents both had heart disease. My maternal grandfather died of lung cancer. He smoked a lot. My maternal grandmother, like my mom, was diabetic."

"Do you have any siblings?"

"Uh-uh." When Peacemaker scowls at me, I correct myself. "No," I say.

"How old are you?"

"Thirty."

"Have you ever had any health problems?"

"Nothing serious. Except that a year ago, I started to experience occasional abdominal pain. It would usually hit about an hour after eating. A couple of times, though, the pain came during the small hours of the night, long after I'd eaten my dinner."

"Did you see a doctor about this?"

"Of course. He prescribed some pills—in case I was developing an ulcer, he said. Then he ordered a battery of tests, including an endoscopy. The pills didn't help, and all the tests came up negative."

"So what did you do?"

"I stopped seeing the doctor."

"Did you see another doctor?"

"No. That would've been too expensive. Although I have health insurance, it doesn't cover everything."

"How's your stomach now?"

"It's about the same."

"Twenty-first century medicine! Thank wisdom I live in the twenty-fourth century!"

Most of Peacemaker's questions, however, seem motivated by nothing more than curiosity. She asks me about my past and present friends and girlfriends, my job and hobbies, my favorite music and foods, my talents and educational background, my political leanings and philosophical beliefs. She's also interested in my personality—for example, whether I'm shy, loyal, generous, loving, responsible, aggressive, or intellectually curious. She especially wants to know how satisfied or dissatisfied I am with my life. How different she is from the gastroenterologist I saw a year ago! He never asked questions like these. In fact, he asked hardly any questions at all. For the most part, I dealt with his assistant, not him.

After she asks all her questions, Peacemaker applies a soothingly aromatic ointment to my sore legs and massages them, her gnarled fingers kneading my flesh with surprising deftness. Then she asks me if I have any questions for her. I tell her I'm too tired to think of questions; I just want to go to sleep. "Good idea," she says. "As the adage goes, 'Early to bed and early to rise makes people healthy, loving, and wise.' I'll check in on you first thing in the morning." With that, she embraces me and leaves the room.

"Go with love and wisdom," I say.

o o o

That night I have a nightmare. I'm in a laboratory, immobilized, my head protruding from a box as if I were a rabbit about to undergo a Draize eye irritancy test. But I'm not a rabbit, and I don't undergo an eye irritancy test. A man wearing a white lab coat and a white surgical mask enters the room. I can't tell who the man is; the mask hides his identity. The man pries open my mouth. He says he's sorry he has to do this to me, but he needs to conduct a very important experiment. He assures me that my suffering won't be in vain, that the experiment will benefit all of humankind. He inserts a device into my mouth and down my throat. The device resembles an endoscope, but it isn't an endoscope. He deposits pills into the device, one pill after another. The pills resemble the ulcer pills my gastroenterologist prescribed for me, but they're not ulcer pills. I feel the pills enter my stomach. The man picks up a clipboard and records my reactions. He's calm and detached, the very model of a scientist. Soon, I feel pain. Initially, the pain is similar to the pain that a year ago led me to see my gastroenterologist. But then the pain intensifies. It turns into a searing, unbearable pain. I want to vomit, but I can't. Sweat streams down my face; veins bulge in my forehead. The pain continues to increase. It becomes so intense that I'm on the verge of passing out. The man puts down his clipboard and removes his mask. I see his face clearly. He's Blake!

I awake with a start, sweat streaming from my face exactly as in my dream. For a moment, I sit in bed, orienting myself. Then I stand up to test my legs for stiffness. They're hardly sore at all. I walk out onto the deck. Although it's early morning, the sun just having risen, the air is already warm. A few people are sauntering toward what I recognize is the dining hall; a couple more are working in the flower garden directly below my deck. Four decks from mine, the plump girl I saw yesterday is watering her plants. Her cat sits at the edge of the deck, eyeing a bird's nest propped in a tree that's just out of reach. Two children, each six or seven years old, run along the cobblestone walkway, squealing with delight. A dog, unfettered by any leash, bounds after them.

I hear water running. In the quarters next to mine, someone is taking a shower. I need a shower myself, so I leave the deck and step into the bathroom. The bathroom is much like the one in my apartment, only larger and cleaner. The toilet flushes like any toilet from the twenty-first century, and the showerhead sprays water like any showerhead I've encountered. I feel let down. I keep expecting technological innovation, and, except for PADs, Égalité keeps failing to provide it. At least, though, my hosts have stocked the bathroom with a generous supply of necessities: everything from toothpaste and towels and toilet paper to shampoo and deodorant and razor blades. I'm especially delighted to find a bathrobe hanging from a hook, because the clothes I'm wearing reek of sweat.

When I finish my shower, I put on the bathrobe and sink into the plush chair beside the desk. I start to think about Blake. Why did the Égalitéans bring him to the twenty-fourth century? Safiya has already told me that I'm not the only visitor from the past. Others have also been invited because, although they're speciesists, they're nonetheless—how did Safiya put it?—decent people who want to do the right thing. Does this description apply to Blake?

Blake is certainly a speciesist, and has been for as long as I've known him. Once, when we were in the second grade, our teacher—what was her name? Ms. Harmon?—took the class to a zoo. Upon our arrival, she announced with great excitement that the zoo had a real live tiger and that, if we were good boys and girls, she'd let us see it. Blake very badly wanted to see the tiger. He especially wanted to hear it roar. He tried to be patient, but patience has never been one of his virtues. The other animals on display—the alligators, the hippos, the ostriches, the zebras—were too lethargic to hold Blake's interest. Finally, Blake was unable to wait anymore. He had to see the tiger right then. But how to slip away undetected? How to evade Ms. Harmon's watchful eye? Whispering, Blake dared Chaz, who was also in our class, to punch Gus Sherwood, a beefy, unpopular kid who was always picking his nose. As faithful to Blake as Voltaire's Cacambo was to Candide, Chaz complied. When Gus' howl distracted Ms. Harmon, Blake and I quietly stole off to the tiger's cage. The floor of the cage was littered with feces; a foul odor filled the air. The tiger paced back and forth, back and forth, half a dozen paces to one end of the cage, half a dozen paces to the other end of the cage. The two of us stood there, holding our breaths as best we could, waiting for the tiger to roar. A minute went by, then two. Nothing. No roar; just the pacing. Disappointed, I suggested that maybe tigers didn't roar. Maybe they didn't make any sound at all. Blake insisted that tigers did so roar and he was going to prove it. He threw a stone at the tiger, and then two more. The first stone struck the back of the tiger's head; the second landed on its back; the third bounced off its shoulder. Even at age six or seven, Blake had a good arm. The tiger, though, didn't roar, or make any other sound. It merely retreated to the back of the cage. For a time, Blake continued to throw stones, but with no effect. Eventually, he gave up.

Later, in high school, Blake, Chaz, and I took biology together. One day, Mr. Bhayq, our teacher, gave the class sheep's brains to dissect. Stinking of formaldehyde, the brains bore an unsettling resemblance to cauliflower. One of the girls in the class, who when speaking had the slightly irritating habit of emphasizing excessively many words, made a face and flatly refused to participate. With a defiant shake of her head, like a horse shaking its mane, she flung back a renegade lock of hair that had a tendency to flop across her face. Mr. Bhayq, twirling a finger through his massive beard, said that, if she was squeamish, she could let her lab partner do the dissecting while she took notes. The girl, however, declined the offer. She said that Mr. Bhayq didn't *understand*. She wasn't *squeamish*; she just didn't see why sheep had to be *killed* for the sake of a *biology* lesson. Weren't there *other* ways to learn about the brains of sheep? At this point, Mr. Bhayq had enough. He gave the girl an ultimatum: either she would carry out the assignment or he would give her a zero. When the girl complained that that wasn't *fair* and accused Mr. Bhayq of being an accessory to the *murder* of sheep, Mr. Bhayq sent her to the principal's office. As she stormed out of the classroom, Blake surreptitiously flicked a fragment of sheep's brain into her renegade lock of hair. Imitating her, he whispered to Chaz and me, "For *God's* sake, they're just *sheep*! Get *over* it!" Then Chaz chimed in, "Could we dissect *her* brain instead?"

Blake's speciesism was never held against him. When he was a senior, Blake was voted both Prom King and Most Likely to Succeed. He also pitched the baseball team to a state championship. After graduating as salutatorian, he was awarded a full scholarship at a nearby university. He completed his degree in biology there in three years, maintaining a near-perfect grade point average of 3.97. Four years later, after earning a D.Pharm., he accepted a six-figure salary at the largest pharmaceutical company in the region. With his newfound wealth, he bought a Jaguar and a ten-room house in the northern, wealthier part of town, near the Dinosaur Eggs. He installed a pool table in the basement and a swimming pool in the backyard. For the floor in front of the fireplace, he bought a bearskin rug. Once, I asked him what kind of work he did at the pharmaceutical company. Smiling faintly, he replied, "Philsbury, I kill more rats than an exterminator!" Philsbury is a nickname Blake gave me. It's short for Philsbury Doughboy.

Crowning all of his achievements, like a maraschino cherry topping a sundae, is Blake's reputation. People admire—and sometimes envy— his good looks, his athleticism, his intelligence, and especially his character. They say he's a cut above other folks, unusually loyal, courageous, and principled. Other folks are ordinary, like hamburger; he's more like prime rib. I'm lucky, people say, to have a friend like Blake. And they're right. One episode in particular stands out in my mind. When I was in the ninth grade, five older, and more heavily muscled, boys cornered me by my locker. They wanted my lunch money. Seeing the bullies, Blake interposed himself between me and them. He said that if any of them wanted my lunch money, they'd have to get by him first. The bullies took his words to be a bluff, but his words weren't a bluff. He punched one of them in the Adam's apple and kicked another in the kneecap. The five boys fled without laying so much as a finger on either Blake or me.

Chaz, who witnessed the whole thing, told and retold the story, with increasing embellishment. Soon, word spread to the prettiest, most desired girl in my high school, Mr. Bhayq's daughter Frances. Blake called her Shakin' Bhayq, because of the way her ample rear end jiggled as she walked. She was two grades ahead of Blake, and ordinarily would never have considered dating a younger boy. But Blake was different. The two of them dated on and off for the next two years, until Shakin' Bhayq went off to college in a different state.

o o o

I hear a knock at my door. Peacemaker is checking in on me as promised. With her are Safiya and Blake. Safiya holds a bundle of clothes in one hand and a PAD in the other. Like yesterday, she wears sandals and a creamy yellow robe. Poking out of the robe's pocket is Safiya's oboe. Blake, by contrast, wears a white shirt and white pants, as bright and pure as the white lab coat he had on in my nightmare.

"How are you feeling, son?" says Peacemaker. The T-shirt she has on this morning displays the words "I ♥ CAULIFLOWER."

"Much better, thanks."

"It's good to see you upright, buddy!" says Blake with a grin. "I wish I could have been here when you came to, but the good doctor kicked everyone out of the room—even Safiya, I hear."

"Blake's a good friend to you," says Safiya. "When you passed out yesterday, he insisted on carrying you to your quarters all by himself."

"It wasn't easy, you know, Doughboy. You need to lose a little weight!" Blake pokes a finger in my flabby stomach.

Safiya hands me the PAD she's holding. She explains how it works and tells me that if I ever need anything, I can use it to contact her. Then she hands me the clothes. They're identical to the clothes I wore yesterday, except they're brand new and presumably all non-leather. She says if I want to pick up more clothes later, she'll be happy to take me shopping. When I go into the bathroom to put the clothes on, I find they're precisely my size, even a better fit than my other clothes. Returning, I ask Safiya how she knows my size. She blushes. She replies that she doesn't know my size, that she must have made a lucky guess.

"Lucky guess, my foot!" says Blake, teasingly. "I'll bet you used your PAD to get his measurements."

"I did not!" Safiya protests. "That would be a violation of Phil's privacy. No Égalitéan would do such a thing."

"The lady doth protest too much, methinks! Are you sure you're not telling a little fib?" Blake winks mischievously.

"I don't lie," Safiya says firmly. "As a student of philosophy, I value the truth above all else."

Ignoring Safiya and turning to me, Blake points to his own PAD. "These PADs are great," he says. "Maybe we can take some back to the twenty-first century. We could use them to get Shakin' Bhayq's measurements!" Even though Blake was once Frances Bhayq's boyfriend, he was never able to extract her measurements from her. He and Chaz had a prolonged and earnest dispute over the size of her rear end.

"Enough horsing around!" Peacemaker scolds. "I need to tend to my patient." Blake grows immediately quiet.

Peacemaker's PAD brings up a maze of numbers, letters, and unfamiliar symbols. After quickly scanning them, Peacemaker seems satisfied. She assures me that I'm in reasonably good health, except that for the past year my stomach has rebelled against all the junk I keep feeding it. She also has to agree with Blake: I'm at least twenty kilograms too heavy. Her gnarled hand digs into her medical bag and comes out with a cloth wallet. Inside the wallet are three cards, each of which can unfold like the maps I keep in the glove compartment of my car. I pick out one of the cards. Labeled DIET, it indicates the number of calories I should consume each day and lists foods that would be good for me to eat. None of the listed foods appears to contain meat, or, for that matter, any animal product. I glance at the other two cards. They're labeled EXERCISE and STRESS REDUCTION.

As I pocket the wallet, Peacemaker asks if I have any questions. I tell her that I'd like to know more about the Égalitéan health care system. It seems so different from the health care system of my day. What principles underlie Égalitéan medical practice? Peacemaker says I can find these principles in a document entitled "The Six Precepts." "The Six Precepts" was drafted and ratified in 2076, the year Égalité was founded, at the inaugural meeting of the EMA—the Égalitéan Medical Association. Ever since then, the document has lain at the heart of Égalitéan medical practice. With her PAD, Peacemaker produces "The Six Precepts." Blake and I read the document together:

"*1) Égalitéan health care shall be universal.* Good health is a basic human interest. Without it, our other interests are more difficult or impossible to satisfy. Therefore, to deny quality health care to any portion of the population is to discount some people's interests, a clear violation of the principle of human equality. Under the Égalitéan health care system, everyone shall have access to quality health care.

"*2) Égalitéan health care shall be patient-centered.* A good health care system serves the health-related interests of the patient. It does not require patients to sacrifice their health-related interests for the sake of the convenience or profit of medical personnel. For example, if, as sometimes happens, a patient will recover most effectively in the comfort and familiarity of his or her home, medical personnel shall make house calls to treat the patient rather than require the patient to come to them.

"*3) Égalitéan health care shall emphasize preventive care.* If a patient suffers from an injury or illness, medical personnel shall do everything in their power to restore the patient to health. However, the primary concern of medical personnel shall be to prevent the injury or illness in the first place. As the adage goes, 'A milligram of prevention is worth a kilogram of cure.'

"*4) Égalitéan health care shall emphasize herbal remedies.* Unlike herbalists, pharmacologists extract what they take to be the active ingredients in herbs and then deliver these ingredients in concentrated form. The pharmaceuticals they create, however, tend to be less beneficial, and more harmful, to patients than herbal remedies tend to be. They tend to be less beneficial because an active ingredient tends to cure most effectively when it interacts with, not when it is extracted from, the other ingredients in herbs. They tend to be more harmful because, being more potent than herbal remedies, they tend to produce more, and harsher, side effects.

"5) *Égalitéan health care shall be holistic.* A person is an integrated whole, not a collection of unrelated parts. Therefore, to restore a patient to health, medical personnel shall adopt a holistic approach, treating not just the ailing part but the entire patient.

"6) *Égalitéan health care shall be consistent with the principles of human and animal equality.* Medical personnel shall, as the ancient principle states, 'do no harm.' They shall take every precaution not to harm human beings, and they shall take every precaution not to harm nonhuman animals. The ancient principle, thus interpreted, has implications for physicians and researchers alike. Physicians shall provide quality health care not only for their human patients but for their nonhuman patients as well. Researchers shall do everything within their power to avoid harming not only the human participants in their studies but the nonhuman participants as well."

When I finish reading, I look over at Blake. The expression on his face is hard to read, but his earlier joviality has clearly disappeared. For a brief moment, his upper lip quivers. Then, his white shirt and pants flashing, he abruptly strides out of the room, slamming the door behind him.

Chapter 7
Are Animal Experiments Justified?

Peacemaker shakes her head, the loose skin on her neck waggling like a turkey's wattle. "He reminds me of an untrained puppy," she mutters, "running off goodness knows where for goodness knows what reason!"

Safiya starts after Blake, but I hold her back. I've seen Blake like this before. He's angry, and he needs time to cool off. If we confront him now, he'll only lash out like a trapped animal.

I have a pretty good idea why Blake is angry. He doesn't simply disagree with "The Six Precepts." In addition, he perceives the document—especially its fourth and sixth precepts—as a personal threat. Blake makes his living testing pharmaceuticals on animals. But Égalitéans seem to reject the use of pharmaceuticals, or at least most of them, and they disapprove of testing that harms animals. Thus, if my society were to adopt the Égalitéan health care system, Blake would find himself out of a job. If he were to lose his job, he'd no longer be able to make payments on his Jaguar and his house. He'd lose everything he's worked so hard to achieve. Blake could never accept anything that threatens his livelihood.

Like Blake, I have reservations about Égalitéan health care. How can I be sure that herbal remedies really tend to be better than pharmaceuticals or that universal health care really is the best health care? The EMA document, which doesn't thoroughly defend the six precepts but merely outlines them, is far from convincing. On the other hand, for all I know, the Égalitéans have devised a better health care system than the one I'm familiar with. Certainly my gastroenterologist did nothing for my stomach. Moreover, if my society, like Égalité, more heavily emphasized prevention, maybe my dad wouldn't have gotten his heart attack and I'd still be going to ballgames with him. Sometimes I miss my dad.

Peacemaker suggests that she, Safiya, and I get some breakfast. I second the suggestion. I haven't eaten anything, except two bowls of tea, since my arrival in Égalité. I'm so hungry I could eat ... well, anything the Égalitéans are serving. As we walk to the dining hall, I express one of my reservations about Égalitéan health care.

"If herbal remedies tend to be better than pharmaceuticals, why did my society go out of its way to develop pharmaceuticals?"

The question is directed at Peacemaker, but Safiya's the one who answers. "Because there was money to be made. In your day, people were obsessed with money. The poor wanted to become rich, and the rich wanted to become richer. The desire for money was built into your capitalist economic system. All business owners sought to make a profit. But there was little profit in herbal remedies. Since people could grow their own herbs, they didn't need to purchase them. So medical companies invested in pharmaceuticals instead. Unlike herbs, pharmaceuticals can be produced only by people who have a very specialized knowledge, and, unlike herbs, pharmaceuticals can be patented. When pharmaceutical companies persuaded the masses, and medical personnel, that pharmaceuticals were superior to herbal remedies, people began to purchase pharmaceuticals in vast quantities. In your day, the pharmaceutical industry, worldwide, was more than a trillion dollar a year industry. Nearly half of that more than a trillion dollars came from the United States."

Peacemaker breaks in to clarify the fourth precept, pointing out that Égalitéan medical personnel don't claim that herbal remedies are *always* preferable to pharmaceuticals. Indeed, on occasion, Égalitéans prefer a pharmaceutical over an herbal remedy. Peacemaker also explains the scientific basis for the generally superior medicinal value of herbal remedies. Her explanation includes details of the chemical composition of various herbs as well as nuances of the theory of evolution by natural selection, but it's all too technical for me to grasp adequately. She's still speaking when we enter the dining hall. A mélange of aromas starts my mouth watering. More interested in food than anything else, I stop listening to Peacemaker. I also let Safiya's claims pass by unchallenged, even though I suspect they're exaggerated at best. The three of us load our trays and find an unoccupied table. Peacemaker has taken three bowls, containing tea, mixed fruit, and oatmeal, respectively. In front of Safiya are a glass of water, muesli with almond milk, and something half-liquid and half-solid that I don't recognize. After reaching for the wallet that Peacemaker gave me and consulting the card labeled DIET, I have only a glass of orange juice and a dish consisting of scrambled tofu, mixed vegetables, and herbs, with a hint of garlic and lemon. Normally, I'd eat scrambled eggs instead of scrambled tofu, but there aren't any eggs. I have to admit that the tofu dish is tastier than any eggs I've ever eaten.

∘ ∘ ∘

Rejuvenated by my breakfast, I'm ready for further discussion of "The Six Precepts." I'm particularly interested in the last precept—that Égalitéan health care is to be consistent with the principles of human and animal equality. According to the EMA document, medical researchers are to do everything within their power to avoid harming the participants in their studies, even if the participants are animals. I know that in my time legislation was enacted to protect lab animals from unnecessary harm. But I don't know which harms the legislation holds to be necessary and which unnecessary, and so I don't know how far the protections extend. I suppose, though, that the protections afforded animals are much less extensive than those afforded human beings. This must be the case if medical research is anything like the testing of household products, as when rabbits are blinded in the Draize test. But exactly how does Égalitéan medical research differ from medical research conducted in my time? I'm not sure. As we continue to sit at our breakfast table, our plates and bowls and glasses now empty, I ply Peacemaker with questions about medical research, much as the night before she plied me with questions relating to my health. While the two of us speak, Safiya strolls to a dais at the far end of the dining hall, settles down in a chair there, and asks the breakfast crowd if they have any requests. One man—the man who looks like the first officer from the science fiction program—calls out, "'Lonely Among Us.'" Bringing her oboe to her lips, Safiya plays a jazzy tune.

"According to 'The Six Precepts,'" I say to Peacemaker, "medical researchers should avoid harming the participants in their studies. But what counts as harm? Does the EMA define harm? If so, how?"

"The EMA defines harm in terms of the interests individuals have," Peacemaker replies. "To harm individuals is to prevent them from satisfying one or more of their interests, without at the same time helping them satisfy any of their equally weighty or weightier interests. Suppose, for instance, that you have a headache. You come to me for help. I give you an experimental drug. The drug relieves your headache, but it also produces side effects that are worse than the headache you suffer from. In this case, I harm you. How? First, I prevent you from satisfying one of your interests—namely, your interest in avoiding the side effects of the drug. Second, I don't at the same time help you satisfy any of your equally weighty or weightier interests. To be sure, I help you satisfy your interest in relieving your headache. But since the side effects of the drug are worse than your headache, your interest in relieving your headache isn't weightier than, or even as weighty as, your interest in avoiding the side effects of the drug."

"Your example is clear. But can you tell me more about how the EMA uses its definition of harm to determine which medical research is permissible and which isn't?"

"I'll be happy to tell you. The EMA distinguishes two kinds of medical research: therapeutic and nontherapeutic. Therapeutic research aims to benefit the participants in the research. Thus obese people, hoping to lose weight, might try an experimental diet; people with heart disease, hoping to improve the functioning of their hearts, might undergo experimental surgery. This kind of research is the less controversial kind. Instead of harming participants, it aims to help them satisfy their health-related interests. As long as any risks that the procedures involve are reasonably low and as long as the participants give their free and informed consent, no ethical problems arise."

"What's nontherapeutic medical research?"

"Nontherapeutic research aims to benefit individuals other than the participants in the research. Sometimes such research harms the participants; sometimes it doesn't. Consider an example of the former, a kind of research that was sometimes conducted in your era. Researchers have a new therapy that they hope will heal severe burns, thereby benefiting millions of people. The participants in the research, however, aren't any of the millions of people who might benefit. Instead, they're dogs—perfectly healthy dogs. The researchers first give the dogs severe burns, and then they administer the therapy, carefully observing how well the burns heal. Clearly, the dogs are harmed. First, the researchers prevent the dogs from satisfying an important interest—their interest in avoiding severe burns. Second, the researchers don't at the same time help the dogs satisfy any of their equally weighty or weightier interests. The sixth precept forbids research of this sort."

"I see. Can you give an example of nontherapeutic research that doesn't harm the participants?"

"Of course. About a century ago, an Égalitéan researcher developed a hypothesis: the more time people spend using PADs, the more likely they are to develop cancer. To test this hypothesis, the researcher secured the free and informed consent of ten thousand people and then recorded the number of minutes these people used their PADs each day. After thirty years of recording, she noted which participants had developed cancer and which participants hadn't. The hypothesis was disconfirmed. There was no correlation between using PADs and developing cancer. But even if the hypothesis had been confirmed, the study would have caused no harm to the participants, since they would have used their PADs and gotten cancer regardless. In a case like this, the sixth precept isn't violated. The research is permissible."

"So sometimes we can be reasonably sure that nontherapeutic research will harm the participants, and sometimes we can be reasonably sure that nontherapeutic research won't harm the participants. But isn't there also a third category: sometimes we can't be reasonably sure one way or the other? How do Égalitéans proceed when they simply don't know whether their research will or won't harm the participants? Do Égalitéans ever conduct research like this?"

"Sometimes, if the potential harms aren't too great, and the researchers first secure the free and informed consent of the participants. If participants are aware of the potential harms and still freely consent to participate in the research, they presumably have an interest in participating. Thus to deny them the opportunity to participate would be to prevent them from satisfying one of their interests. To prevent them from satisfying one of their interests would be, other things being equal, to harm them, as Égalitéans define harm."

"You keep emphasizing the importance of securing the free and informed consent of the participants. With human participants, this is often possible. Animals, however, can't give free and informed consent. Does this mean that, from an Égalitéan standpoint, research that uses animal participants—whether the research is therapeutic or nontherapeutic—is more morally problematic than research that uses human participants?"

"It can be. Research that uses human infants or severely brain-damaged human beings can likewise be problematic, since they too can't give free and informed consent. Most Égalitéan researchers, though, believe that, if the research is therapeutic, it's often justified. The risks must be minimal, and the researchers must secure the free and informed consent of the relevant proxy: an infant's parents, a brain-damaged person's guardian, a companion animal's caretaker. In the case of a wild animal, researchers can ask whether the animal would consent if she or he could, or they can ask whether they would consent if they were in the animal's place. The important thing is to do whatever is in the participant's best interest."

"What if the research is nontherapeutic?"

"There's currently a fierce debate within the Égalitéan medical community about nontherapeutic research that uses participants incapable of giving free and informed consent. Most of us think that, as long as the participants face some risk, however minimal, the research isn't justified. A vocal minority, however, argues that the research is justified under the same conditions that therapeutic research is justified. First, the risks can't be too great. Second, the researchers must secure the free and informed consent of the relevant proxy."

∘ ∘ ∘

Safiya finishes her performance of "Lonely Among Us." The audience claps. The man who looks like the first officer from the science fiction program whistles as well as claps. Three more musicians—a flutist, a clarinetist, and a bassoonist—join Safiya on the dais. A child, aged six or seven, makes a request. The child reminds me of Gus Sherwood, except that he's less beefy than the second-grader whom Chaz punched at the zoo so that Blake and I could slip away to the tiger's cage. The four musicians play a piece called "The Friendly Pig." The bassoon, representing the pig, grunts contentedly. As I listen to the piece, I recall a question I asked Safiya yesterday.

"Yesterday," I say to Peacemaker, "I asked Safiya whether it would be permissible to transplant a pig's heart into a human patient. We were imagining that the procedure had been perfected and that no human hearts were available. We were also imagining that, at the time of the transplant, the pig was alive and healthy. The sixth precept seems to imply that the transplant would not be permissible. Am I correct?"

"That's right, since the transplant would harm the pig. The EMA also disapproves of research that would make the transplant possible. This too would harm pigs."

"But what about the potential benefit to human beings? The EMA seems to assume that the interests of pigs outweigh the interests of human beings. Isn't this assumption inconsistent with the principle of animal equality?"

"It is, but the EMA doesn't make the assumption. For one thing, the EMA disapproves of a transplant whether it's a pig's heart that goes

64

into a human being or a human being's heart that goes into a pig. By disapproving of both, the EMA gives preference to neither pigs nor human beings. This contrasts with many researchers of your time, who, approving of the first transplant but not the second, gave preference to human beings over pigs. For...."

"I see your point. Nonetheless...."

"Please don't interrupt me, son. I wasn't finished. At my age, I don't have time for interruptions." Peacemaker shakes her head, the loose skin on her neck once again imitating the waggle of a turkey's wattle. Then she continues, "Now, as I was about to say, you raise an interesting ethical puzzle. Which is of greater value: the life of a pig or the life of a human being? On what basis might we give preference to the human being? On the basis that human beings are more intelligent than pigs? That with our greater intelligence we can benefit the world in ways that pigs can't? That we're better equipped to satisfy interests, our own as well as those of others, than pigs are? But notice that if we adopt this position, we'd similarly have to maintain that our lives have greater value than the lives of human beings who suffer from severe brain damage. And if our greater intelligence implies that we may justifiably receive the heart of a pig, it would likewise imply that we may justifiably receive the heart of a severely brain-damaged human being. I don't know about you, but I'm not prepared to embrace this conclusion."

After a brief silence, I say timidly, "Are you finished now?"

"Yes, I'm finished."

"I also don't approve of using severely brain-damaged people for their organs. I'm less certain about using pigs. But wouldn't I have to approve of using both if I were to accept the principles of animal and human equality? You yourself made the point: we're better equipped to satisfy interests than are either pigs or severely brain-damaged people."

"If this were the only point to make, I might agree with you. But there are other considerations. For example, just because we *can* satisfy more interests than a pig or severely brain-damaged person can, it doesn't follow that we *will* satisfy more interests. Furthermore, there's the possibility of a slippery slope."

"Slippery slope?"

"That's right. Imagine a slope made of ice. If you take so much as one step down the slope, you'll lose your footing and slide all the way to the bottom. You can't stop partway down the slope. Using pigs and severely brain-damaged human beings for their organs is like taking the first step down the slope. The worry is that we may not be able to stop there. Our sense of empathy could weaken, our callousness increase. We might start treating pigs and severely brain-damaged human beings with cruelty, or we might start harvesting the organs of less severely brain-damaged human beings. We might start discounting interests. In short, we might slide all the way to the bottom of the slope. The EMA judges that the risk is too great. It prefers to play it safe, to remain at the top of the slope."

"I'm not sure I agree with your slippery slope argument. Why couldn't the government pass and enforce legislation that allows the use of animals and severely brain-damaged human beings for their organs, but allows nothing further? Wouldn't this ensure that we stop partway down the slope?"

"In theory, it could. But in practice? In the real world, appropriate legislation sometimes isn't passed, and sometimes it isn't adequately enforced. In your time, for instance, laws against cruelty to nonhuman animals were passed, but these laws didn't prevent factory farming, the Draize test, and other cruel practices. In light of the human propensity to take a kilometer when given a millimeter, Égalitéans see good reason for caution."

○ ○ ○

Safiya and the other three musicians are now playing a piece called "Empty Cages." The music starts with a triumphant flourish but soon turns serenely peaceful.

"I take it," I say to Peacemaker, "that the EMA condemns much more than the use of pigs for their organs? It must condemn many of the ways my society treated laboratory animals?"

"I'm afraid so, son. Your society bred nonhuman animals specifically for use in medical research. The EMA condemns this. Your society confined these animals in cages. The EMA condemns this. Your society inflicted illnesses and injuries on nonhuman animals for the purpose of testing new drugs, surgical procedures, and the like. The EMA condemns this. Your society often knew little about the effects these drugs, surgical procedures, and the like would have, yet tested them on nonhuman animals anyway. The EMA condemns this. Your society had an Animal Welfare Act designed to prevent the abuse of nonhuman animals used in medical research, but the legislation didn't go far and was poorly enforced. The EMA condemns this. Your society estimated that between one and a half and two million nonhuman animals were used annually in medical and pharmaceutical research, but it didn't count rats, mice, and birds, which together made up about ninety percent of so-called laboratory animals. The EMA condemns the use of such a vast number of nonhuman animals, and it condemns the refusal to count rats, mice, and birds. In Égalité, such things never happen. Thank wisdom!"

"I'm sure my society could have treated lab animals better. But didn't its use of animals in medical research work? Wasn't it thereby able to cure many diseases?"

"It's true that your society made a number of advances in the treatment of illnesses and injuries. It's also true that some of these advances came about only after carrying out medical research that used nonhuman animals. Examples include the development of insulin for diabetics and the development of the vaccine that wiped out polio. But to say the use of nonhuman animals in medical research worked is misleading. It would be more accurate to say it sometimes worked and sometimes didn't work. Consider thalidomide, a drug that reduces nausea. In the overwhelming majority of species of nonhuman animals, pregnant females who are given the drug give birth to normal offspring. But when thalidomide was given to pregnant women, many babies were born without arms or legs. Why did medical research that used nonhuman animals sometimes work? Because in some respects nonhuman animals are physiologically similar to human beings. Why did medical research that used nonhuman animals sometimes not work? Because in some respects nonhuman animals are physiologically dissimilar to human beings. Did such research work more often than it didn't work? It's hard to say. According to one study conducted in your time, about half of drugs approved by the Food and Drug Administration, drugs that had been tested on nonhuman animals, had to be relabeled or taken off the market because they posed a danger to human beings. According to another study, about two million Americans had to be hospitalized each year because of adverse reactions to prescription drugs, and more than a hundred thousand died. This made fatalities from prescription drugs the fourth leading cause of death in your time. All of these prescription drugs had first been tested on nonhuman animals."

"Let's assume that the conclusions these studies reached are correct. How should my society have proceeded? What's the alternative to animal testing?"

"There are many alternatives. Rather than cure a disease with a drug, we might cure it with an herbal remedy, or we might prevent it rather than cure it. If we need to test an herbal remedy or preventive technique, or even a drug, we don't need to use nonhuman animals. Instead, we might use computer models, stem cells, or—in less risky cases—human volunteers. These are just a few of the alternatives. Which alternative works best depends on the circumstances."

"If there are so many alternatives to animal testing," I say, "why didn't my society adopt them?"

"On occasion it did, but for the most part it didn't. As Safiya might say, there was money to be made. The breeding of so-called laboratory animals and the manufacture of cages and other such equipment were big businesses. Once the use of nonhuman animals had become entrenched, medical researchers had a hard time even imagining alternatives. Sometimes animal activists suggested alternatives, but most medical researchers were contemptuously dismissive, accusing the activists of being ignorant of medical science."

"Is it really fair to say that my society cared more about money than about quality health care? Weren't researchers trying to cure diseases, and didn't they often succeed? Didn't people in my time live longer, healthier lives than did people who lived at any previous time? Doesn't my society deserve credit for the advances it made?"

"Not to worry. The EMA acknowledges every medical advance your society made. A moment ago, I mentioned two such advances: insulin and the vaccine that wiped out polio. These two alone—and there were hundreds of others—prevented untold amounts of human suffering. However, the fact that your society made advances in health care, even numerous advances, doesn't entail that all was well. Even in your day, public health officials were aware that the bulk of the decline in deaths from diseases that your society achieved—at least ninety-five percent of it—resulted not from animal experiments or the development of drugs but from changes in the environment and improvements in personal hygiene. Nonetheless, your society continued to invest heavily in animal experiments and the development of drugs. Why? Clearly, the reasons had little to do with the health benefits such investment brought. No. The chief motive was the desire to make money. Thankfully, all this changed in 2076, when Égalité abolished capitalism and moved away from animal experiments and the development of drugs. Today, people live on average to the age of ninety-two, and they are ill only a third as many days per year as were people from the early twenty-first century."

"Maybe my society went too far in its reliance on animal experiments. But it seems that Égalité doesn't go far enough. Should we really reject all experiments that harm animals? Don't some of them benefit human beings? Don't some of them add to our stock of scientific knowledge? Égalité's reluctance to conduct animal experiments seems anti-science."

"Anti-science?" Peacemaker peers at me through the bottom lens of her trifocals. "Not at all. Égalitéan medical researchers adhere to the strictest scientific protocols. But they also abide by the ethical constraints under which all good scientists do their work. Even your society acknowledged that scientists must abide by ethical constraints. Would your society have condoned giving human beings cancer, or AIDS, or heart disease, or muscular dystrophy, or third-degree burns, or any other such condition, all for the purpose of testing a new therapy or adding to our stock of scientific knowledge? Of course not! The difference between your society and mine is not that yours was pro-science while mine is anti-science. The difference is that mine abides by a more extensive set of ethical constraints than yours did. Being speciesist, your society conducted experiments that harmed nonhuman animals; being nonspeciesist, my society doesn't."

"So if the only way to cure a deadly disease is to conduct an experiment that harms a handful of animals, Égalitéan medical researchers wouldn't conduct the experiment? They'd rather let thousands, even millions, of people suffer and die?"

"Hmm. I honestly don't know. Perhaps many of them would—just as medical researchers from your time would have refused to cure a deadly disease by conducting an experiment that harmed a handful of human beings. Égalitéan medical researchers, however, don't waste their time pondering your question, because the question is purely hypothetical. The situation you describe will certainly never arise. In the first place, curing a disease takes years of painstaking research. It can't be done by conducting a single experiment that harms a mere handful of nonhuman animals. Second, there's the problem of the slippery slope that I mentioned a moment ago. If we permit one experiment that harms a handful of nonhuman animals, will we stop there? Might we not permit another, and then another, and then another? Might we not end up harming millions of nonhuman animals, as your society did? Finally, as I also mentioned a moment ago, there are alternatives to experiments that harm nonhuman animals—computer models, stem cells, and the rest. It simply isn't true that the only way to cure a deadly disease is to conduct an experiment that harms nonhuman animals."

"I have one more question. Suppose someone discovers a cure for a fatal illness, but only after conducting a number of experiments that harm animals. Suppose I then contract the fatal illness. What should I do? If I refuse the cure, I'll be giving myself a death sentence. But if I go for the cure, won't I be supporting experiments that harm animals?"

"Very few Égalitéans would condemn you if you availed yourself of the cure. We'd disapprove of the experimenter, yes, but not you. In such a circumstance, it's far from clear that you'd be supporting…."

Chapter 8
Can a Vegetarian Utopia Exist?

Peacemaker's PAD bleeps three times. A voice that could be either male or female announces, "Urgent message." Trailing a bony finger through her wispy hair, Peacemaker listens to the message. A girl from a nearby village needs medical attention. She has taken a tumble, hitting the back of her head hard against a rock. Her parents are worried sick. Quickly embracing me, Peacemaker says, "Go with love and wisdom." Then, with the surefootedness of a mountain goat, the old woman strides to a corner of the dining hall and disappears down a gently descending ramp.

I turn my attention to the dais at the far end of the dining hall. Safiya and the other three musicians are about to play a piece called "The True City." Safiya explains to the audience that she composed the piece herself, after rereading Book Two of Plato's *Republic*. The composition is for a woodwind quartet, each instrument representing a different inhabitant of Plato's true city. Safiya is going to play the part of the farmer. The other three musicians—the flutist, the clarinetist, and the bassoonist—are going to play the parts of the weaver, the shoemaker, and the builder, respectively. When Safiya finishes her prefatory explanation, the four musicians begin to play. Although each musician plays a different melody, the four melodic strands intertwine harmoniously, just as the inhabitants of a city, though playing different roles, work harmoniously together. Given that the word "city" appears in the title, I find the music strangely bucolic.

When the music ends, the audience applauds warmly. Some stand up, whistle, and shout, "Bravo!" The four musicians bow graciously and embrace each other. Then, threading her way through the audience, pausing to shake one or two hands, Safiya rejoins me at my table. I inform her that Peacemaker had to leave on a medical errand; Safiya asks me how I liked the performance. I reply that I liked it just fine, but that I probably would have appreciated it more if I was familiar with Book Two of Plato's *Republic*. Safiya thinks for a moment and then says, "I have an idea. Follow me."

Grasping my hand, Safiya leads me to a corner of the dining hall and up a gently ascending ramp. The second floor of the building, she tells me, is devoted to works of art. Two of the works there, a watercolor painting and a one-act play, should, she says, give me a better understanding of Book Two of Plato's *Republic*.

Safiya shows me the painting first. It's in an intimate little room, part of an exhibit entitled "Ideal Meals." The painting depicts four people eating a simple vegetarian dinner. They're squatting on the ground in front of a fire; there are no chairs or table or other furniture. Next to one diner is a plow, and beside a second is a loom. The third holds a pair of shoes in one hand, while the last carries a hammer. Below the painting, in impeccable handwriting, are the words, "The True City." To the right, also in impeccable handwriting, is a quotation attributed to Plato: "For food, they'll knead and cook the flour and meal they've made from wheat and barley…. [T]hey'll obviously need salt, olives, cheese, boiled roots, and vegetables of the sort they cook in the country. We'll give them desserts, too, of course, consisting of figs, chickpeas, and beans, and they'll roast myrtle and acorns before the fire, drinking moderately. And so they'll live in peace and good health, and when they die at a ripe old age, they'll bequeath a similar life to their children."

As I study the painting, Safiya supplies some context. In the *Republic*, Plato describes two societies, which he labels "the true city" and "the luxurious city." Each society, in its own way, represents an ideal. In the true city, people live simple lives. They meet their basic needs but produce no luxuries. Basic needs include food, clothing, shoes, and shelter. Thus, among the inhabitants of the true city are a farmer, a weaver, a shoemaker, and a builder, all of whom are shown in the painting. Luxuries, by contrast, include such things as furniture, perfumed oils, incense, pastries, painting, embroidery, gold, and ivory—and meat. None of these is found in the true city. The inhabitants of the true city, then, are vegetarians, though, as the quotation to the right of the painting makes clear, they're not vegans, since they eat cheese.

Plato has mixed feelings about the true city. On the one hand, he believes that it promotes "peace and good health," both of which are laudable ideals. On the other hand, he doubts that the true city is attainable. People love luxuries. Who would want to live their lives without furniture, painting, and gold? The problem with the true city is that it seems incompatible with human nature. Human nature, according to Plato, consists of a rational as well as an appetitive part. To some degree, our reason is able to control our appetites, but our appetites are powerful. They can never be denied all luxuries. Consequently, Plato abandons the true city in favor of the luxurious city.

The inhabitants of the luxurious city are divided into three classes: craftspeople, guardians, and rulers. The craftspeople not only meet people's basic needs but in addition provide luxuries, including meat. In an ideal luxurious city, the craftspeople provide luxuries in moderation. But even if people consume luxuries in moderation, the luxurious city needs many more craftspeople than does the true city— not just farmers, weavers, shoemakers, and builders, but also furniture makers, painters, embroiderers, swineherds, and so on. As a result, the population of the luxurious city is much larger than that of the true city. To feed its larger population, the luxurious city has to have a larger amount of pasture and plow-land. To get this pasture and plow-land, it has to invade neighboring cities. Hence, inevitably, the luxurious, meat-eating city goes to war. For this reason, it needs guardians, who serve partly as soldiers and partly as police officers. Finally, the rulers ensure that the inhabitants of the city work together in harmony, each performing his or her role to the best of his or her ability. The best ruler, according to Plato, is a philosopher-king.

∘ ∘ ∘

A tangle of tropical foliage luxuriates in a pot that stands in the center of the room. Encircling the pot is a well-cushioned bench. Safiya and I are sitting on the bench.

Although Égalitéans enjoy some luxuries, such as the bench Safiya and I are sitting on and the paintings we're viewing, Safiya's village seems to have more in common with the true city than with the luxurious city. Like the true city, Safiya's village is small, its people presumably vegetarians, possibly even vegans, who apparently prefer a simple lifestyle, at least a simpler lifestyle than is generally preferred in my time. In light of these similarities, I want to ask Safiya what she thinks of Plato's criticism of the true city. If the simple, vegetarian lifestyle of the true city is incompatible with human nature, shouldn't the simple, vegetarian lifestyle of Safiya's village likewise be incompatible with human nature? How can people, with their powerful appetites, be persuaded to give up cars and highways, leather and fur, chicken and steak?

I have, however, no opportunity to pose my questions. At that moment, Édouard Bel-Ami enters the room, followed by half a dozen nine- or ten-year-old children. Édouard embraces Safiya and me, and asks how I'm feeling. The children wave and say, "Bonjour! Bon matin!" Blushing, Édouard explains that he's been teaching the children French. Then he and the children move to one of the paintings, where Édouard delivers a lecture on the artistic techniques the painter used to convey the painting's message. Édouard, it seems, is an art teacher as well as a French teacher.

As I observe Édouard, I shiver. He's a dead ringer for Brother Bell. Everything is the same: the receding black hair, slicked back; the oversized, smudged glasses, which he readjusts every several seconds; the repeated blushing; the bobbing head; the toes pointing sharply outward; the exaggerated enthusiasm with which he speaks. Even the impeccable handwriting beside and beneath each painting is the same, I now notice, as the handwriting Brother Bell used in Sunday school when he wrote biblical verses on the portable chalkboard.

Well, no. Not *everything* is the same. As Édouard continues speaking to the children, I can discern a difference. The difference concerns the one thing that Brother Bell cherished above all else—the Bible. Édouard is lecturing on a painting that's biblically inspired. The painting shows three people wandering about in a lush garden. One of the three people, taller than the others and standing fully erect, wears a long, white, flowing beard and a long, white, flowing robe. The other two people, a man and a woman, each stark naked, are bending forward reaching for fruit. Underneath the painting is the impeccably handwritten word, "Eden." To the right is an impeccably handwritten verse from the Bible: "God said, 'See, I have given you every plant yielding seed that is upon the face of all the earth, and every tree with seed in its fruit; you shall have them for food.'"

"Notice this figure," says Édouard to the children. Bobbing his head, he points to the tall man wearing the robe. "How would you describe him?"

"Old!" says one child.

"Noble!" says a second.

"Wise!" calls out a third.

"Good!" says Édouard. Then, blushing, he points to the two naked people. "What about these two people? Do they also look old, noble, and wise?"

"No!" shout the children in unison.

"Why not? What did the painter do to make the one, but not the other two, appear noble and wise?" Édouard waits for an answer, but, when none is forthcoming, he readjusts his glasses and gives the children a hint: "Think about the colors and the kinds of lines the painter used."

Suddenly beaming, one child says, "The old man is painted in light colors, but the two naked people are surrounded by dark colors!"

Another child adds, "The painter used up-and-down lines to paint the old man, but slanting lines to paint the two naked people!"

"Exactly! Light colors and vertical lines indicate qualities such as nobility, wisdom, and superiority."

The children look at each other in puzzlement. One of them says, "But why would the artist want one person to look superior to others? Aren't all human beings equal?"

"Yes! All human beings are equal. But the figure wearing the robe isn't a human being. He's God!"

"God?" the same child asks. "Who's God?"

"According to a very, very old book called the Bible, God was the creator of the universe. He made everything in just six days—the earth, the heavens, plants, animals—everything! The last thing he made was human beings. Human beings were special. We, and only we, were made in God's image. The first two human beings that God made, shown here in this painting, lived in a place called the Garden of Eden. All other human beings came from them. At one time, long before you were born, millions and millions of people believed that everything the Bible said was true. Do you think these people were right?"

"No!" shout the children.

"Neither do I. Thank wisdom!"

The children giggle. They're laughing at those millions and millions of people. "Suckers," says the laughter, "millions and millions of suckers." Brother Bell was one of those suckers.

o o o

For the next hour, Édouard guides his pupils from painting to painting. All of the paintings are watercolors; none is an oil painting.

Édouard explains why. Oil-based paint, he says, has a tangible quality. To say that something is tangible means that it feels real. Oil-based paint, then, is good for making realistic paintings. Using his PAD, Édouard shows the children a series of Dutch oil paintings from the seventeenth century. The realism is incredible; the paintings look almost like photographs. They contrast sharply with the watercolors hanging on the walls of the little room. The watercolors, Édouard tells the children, are based on passages taken from pieces of utopian literature. Utopian literature describes ideal societies; it doesn't describe real societies. The watercolors reflect this fact, because the water-based paint with which they were made has a much less tangible feel than oil-based paint.

Whispering in my ear, so as not to disturb Édouard and his students, Safiya gives me an overview of utopian literature. It had its roots in Plato's *Republic* and the opening chapters of Genesis, but the word "utopia" wasn't coined until the sixteenth century, when the English philosopher and statesperson Thomas More wrote *Utopia*. From the sixteenth to the twenty-first centuries, a good deal of utopian literature was produced, recommending a wide range of ideals—communism, feminism, environmentalism, and a whole host of other isms. A few advocated vegetarianism. These last were the utopian works that inspired the exhibit Safiya brought me to see. Insofar as they advocated vegetarianism, they were ahead of their time. But none of them provided an adequate philosophical basis for vegetarianism; some provided no basis at all. Despite its flaws, though, utopian literature flourished through much of the twenty-first century. It was popular because many people sensed something seriously wrong with their society, and they yearned to find a better alternative. After the founding of the Égalitéan Republic, however, utopian literature, like the state in Karl Marx's communist utopia, withered away. Égalitéans lost the need to imagine utopian societies. They created a *real* utopian society.

Édouard finishes talking about the paintings. Like a mother duck leading her ducklings, he leads the children out of the room and up a gently ascending ramp to the third floor of the building. As they leave, the children call out to Safiya and me, "Au revoir! Allez avec l'amour et la sagesse!"

Safiya and I remain on the second floor but move down the hall into an intimate little theater. A short aisle, bisecting three rows of well-cushioned benches, descends to the stage. Safiya and I settle down in the second row, where Safiya commands her PAD to run a play entitled *The Vegetarian Republic*. No one else is in the theater.

Plato's criticism of the true city is still on my mind. Is it just the true city that's incompatible with human nature? Aren't *all* utopias, including Égalité, incompatible with human nature? Isn't a utopia by definition an ideal, and aren't human beings inevitably less than ideal? How, then, can a utopian society be real? How is Égalité possible? I want to ask Safiya these questions, but I hold off because the play has already started.

The play takes the form of a Platonic dialogue. The scene, a holographic image appearing on the stage, is the agora in ancient Athens; the speakers, also holographic images, are Plato and Philozoon. Unlike Plato, Philozoon is a fictional rather than a historical character. He represents the Égalitéan point of view.

The play is about Plato's true city. After describing the true and luxurious cities, Plato tells Philozoon that the former has two great advantages over the latter. The inhabitants of the true city are first of all healthier, and they're second of all more peaceful, than the inhabitants of the luxurious city. Plato, however, confesses that ultimately he prefers the luxurious city, because he finds it more compatible with human nature.

Philozoon objects. Although he's a vegetarian, he doesn't think that a simple, vegetarian lifestyle, such as that found in the true city, is the only one that promotes health. Some omnivorous diets, and in particular those in which meats are consumed in modest quantities, are perfectly healthy. Philozoon also doubts that a simple, vegetarian lifestyle is the only one that promotes peace. A luxurious, meat-eating lifestyle can also be peaceful. Even if the luxurious city has a larger population than does the true city, it doesn't follow, as Plato imagines, that the luxurious city has to invade neighboring cities to feed its people. Instead of invading neighboring cities, why can't the luxurious city find ways to grow more food on the land it has? Why can't it, for example, develop better pesticides, fertilizers, or breeding techniques? Alternatively, why can't land be distributed in such a way that every city, whether luxurious or true, has enough land to feed its people? Or why can't food be distributed from cities that have more than enough to feed their people to those that have less than enough?

Plato defends his position valiantly, but in the end he's unable to answer Philozoon's questions. The play concludes as follows:

PLATO: *It seems, Philozoon, that, no matter what argument for a vegetable diet I put forward, you find an objection. This perplexes me, because I know you consume no meat. If none of my arguments satisfies you, then what argument will?*

PHILOZOON: *All of your arguments for a vegetable diet appeal to the interests of human beings, not the interests of the nonhuman animals whom human beings consume. If you could demonstrate that a meatless diet is the best way to promote health or peace or any other human interest, no one would be more delighted than I. What worries me is not that you proffer such arguments, but that you rest your entire case on them. It seems to me that these arguments are peripheral, that at the heart of the matter lies a different argument, one that appeals to right or wrong done to nonhuman animals.*

PLATO: *Exactly what form do you envision this argument taking?*

PHILOZOON: *As I see it, the argument needs to establish two propositions: first, that the interests of a nonhuman animal have the same value as the comparable interests of a human being; second, that the first proposition implies that we should abstain from meat.*

PLATO: *How can these two propositions be established?*

PHILOZOON: *I'm afraid that here our road grows muddy. Luckily, I have with me the most celebrated philosopher in Greece and beyond. I'm sure that, with you leading the way, we can successfully navigate the mire of arguments and counterarguments that we're bound to encounter.*

PLATO: *Your confidence in me is flattering. But I see from the position of the sun in the sky that noon is upon us. I promised to meet my students at the Academy—we're going to discuss my story about the prisoners in the cave. You remember the story, I told it at last night's symposium.*

PHILOZOON: *I remember it vividly. But can't you stay a little longer? I crave to know whether we have a moral obligation to abstain from meat, and to this end I could use your expert guidance.*

PLATO: *I wish I could stay, but even the most celebrated philosopher in Greece and beyond can't be in two places at the same time.*

PHILOZOON: *Then I fear that, like the prisoners in your story, I'm condemned to remain ignorant. Just as their bonds prevent them from knowing the world outside the cave, so your departure keeps me from the knowledge I seek. Do the interests of a nonhuman animal have the same value as the comparable interests of a human being? If so, do we have a moral obligation to give up meat? How far should we restrict our diet? May we indulge in cheese, as the inhabitants of the true city did? What about seafood? How about honey, the product of bees? Even if we have a moral obligation to give up meat or other animal products, will some people inevitably eat such foods anyway, because they can't control their appetites? Is the power of our appetites a good reason to permit meat-eating? These are a few of the questions we haven't yet addressed. Until we do, until we have a full discussion, as all good philosophers do, how can I be sure that my meatless diet is the wisest choice?*

The holographic characters and the holographic agora vanish. "What!" I exclaim. "That's it? The play's over? We're not going to hear answers to Philozoon's questions?"

"That's right," says Safiya. "The play ends in the same way that many of Plato's dialogues end, without answers."

"But I want to know whether a vegetarian, nonspeciesist society is possible. I want to know whether any utopian society is possible. Could the true city ever exist? Could Égalité ever exist? How?"

Safiya pauses. For a split second—a time so short I might be imagining it—she averts her eyes, as if she has something to hide. Then she looks back up, smiling warmly. "Don't you trust your senses? Can't you see Égalité all about you? Do you really doubt that Égalité exists? As for *how* it could exist, please be patient. Once you've seen more of my world, all of your questions will be answered. I promise!"

This is the second time I've seen Safiya avert her eyes. The first time was shortly after my arrival in Égalité, when I asked her if Égalité is real.

It doesn't make sense. Earlier, when I was in my quarters, Safiya claimed she doesn't lie, and Peacemaker described Safiya as the most honest person she knows. Now, however, Safiya appears to be hiding something. What's going on?

Chapter 9
Should People Be Vegetarians?

From hidden outposts, cicadas thrum an insistent melody. High in a maple tree, baby birds, vying for mama's attention, cheep-cheep. Daylilies whisper in a hot, breathy breeze, while the stream that meanders through the village gurgles languidly. Where the stream widens into a sandy wading pool, children—no less a part of nature than the baby birds and daylilies—splash and squeal with laughter. Thrum, cheep-cheep, whisper, gurgle, splash, squeal. Nature is performing a summer symphony.

Safiya and I sit at a picnic table, taking refuge from the midday sun under the merciful boughs of the maple tree. We're drinking ice cold water and eating grilled vegetable wraps and strawberries. The strawberries, though small, burst with flavor, so different from the strawberries sold in my supermarket. The picnic table, grayed and bowed from years of exposure to the elements, is one of half a dozen scattered outside the dining hall.

At one of the other tables, two teenage girls appear to be playing a game. Their PADs announce words—... *comestible* ... *gustatory* ... *masticate* ... *victual* ...—and the girls try to define the words. The girls work as a team; the game, if it is a game, isn't a competition. With a deft shake of her head, like a horse shaking its mane, one of the girls flings back a renegade lock of hair that the breeze has blown into her face. She reminds me of the girl in my high school biology class, the one who refused to dissect the sheep's brains—except that, when she speaks, she doesn't have the slightly irritating habit of emphasizing excessively many words. Her teammate, chewing furiously on her bubble gum, is the plump girl who, earlier in the day, watered her plants four decks from mine. The two girls have just correctly defined ten words in a row. Each time they correctly define a word, they clap their right hands together in a high five. Thrum, cheep-cheep, whisper, gurgle, splash, squeal, clap.

For a time, I sit silently, savoring the sounds around me. Eventually, my thoughts return to the vegetarian art Safiya showed me. Should I become a vegetarian? What kind of vegetarian should I become? What are the different kinds of vegetarians? I ask Safiya what foods Égalitéans eat and what foods they refrain from eating.

Safiya answers that Égalitéans eat a wide variety of foods but generally avoid animal products. At one time, when Égalité was newly founded, some people were *conscientious omnivores*, eating meat and other animal products, usually in modest quantities, while striving to treat food animals as humanely as possible. These days, however, nobody's an omnivore, though a small minority, almost five percent of Égalitéans, practices a limited *pescetarian* diet—they eat a certain class of seafood, namely bivalves, which include clams, scallops, oysters, and mussels. They argue that such a diet is consistent with the principle of animal equality because, in their view, bivalves, unlike other animals, are incapable of feeling pain. A smaller minority, less than one in a hundred Égalitéans, eats eggs and dairy. Called *lacto-ovo vegetarians*, these Égalitéans make sure that the eggs and dairy products they eat are free-range—that is, that the animals from which they get their eggs and dairy are treated with kindness and allowed to roam freely outdoors.

All other Égalitéans are *vegans*, refusing to eat any animal products—no meat, not even bivalves, and no eggs or dairy. Many Égalitéans avoid even honey, and some abstain from mushrooms. Some Égalitéans are *macrobiotic vegans*, enjoying sea and land vegetables, beans and miso, and whole grains. A few are *noninterventionist vegans*. This group consumes fruits, nuts, and those vegetables that can be eaten without killing the plant. Thus, peas and corn are acceptable, but carrots and beets are off limits. Noninterventionist vegans maintain that the principle of equality of interests should extend not only to all animals but to plants as well.

Safiya adds that, as far as is practicable, Égalitéans are *locavores*, which is to say they prefer locally grown food. For example, the ingredients of the meal Safiya and I are eating—the strawberries, the grilled vegetables, the whole wheat used in the wraps—were all produced either in Safiya's village or in one of the neighboring villages. Only a few foods, such as rice, which doesn't grow well in the local climate, have to be imported. In all, more than ninety-five percent of the food that the inhabitants of Safiya's village consume is grown locally. Most other villages achieve a comparable percentage. The exceptions are villages located in less hospitable environments. Some of them have to import nearly half their food.

I ask Safiya how her village imports rice and other foods. I see no highways or trucks, nor any other system of transportation, such as airplanes and airports. How does the rice get from there to here? Safiya replies that Égalité has an efficient electric rail system. Trains periodically arrive and depart—Safiya's village exports too—carrying food and other necessities, as well as occasional passengers. I look about, confused. Where are the trains? Where is the train station? Smiling slyly and pointing a finger downward, Safiya says that we're sitting on the train station—it's directly underneath the dining hall. The Regional Planning Committee chose an underground site so that residents wouldn't be disturbed by the hustle and bustle of arriving and departing trains and the loading and unloading of cargo. Once outside the village, however, the train tracks rise to the surface.

But if Égalité has an efficient rail system, why do Égalitéans prefer locally grown food? Why be locavores as well as vegans? Isn't a vegan diet already restrictive enough? What's wrong with relishing the exotic delicacies of distant lands? The problem, Safiya explains, is that extensive exporting, requiring vast quantities of energy, is environmentally unsound. Three centuries ago, the profligate use of fossil fuels and other unsustainable practices caused so much environmental damage that nature even now hasn't fully recovered. Égalitéans are staunch environmentalists, because damage to the environment prevents human and nonhuman animals from satisfying many of their most vital interests.

o o o

As Safiya and I chat, Blake, his white clothes glinting in the sun, steps out of the dining hall and, spotting us, joins us. He too has a grilled vegetable wrap, strawberries, and water. At first, he seems recovered from the pique he vented this morning. He even tries to be jocular. Winking mischievously in my direction, he says to Safiya that the trouble with Égalitéan food is that it isn't manly. Real men eat meat. It's in their blood, dating as far back as the days of hunters and gatherers. Without meat, a man would wither away. Blake, for example, hasn't been in Égalité for so much as a week, and he's already lost five pounds. If he and I stay in Égalité long enough, we'll eventually become as skinny as pea vines, and then he'll need to find a new nickname for me. He pokes me in the stomach and adds, "Right, Doughboy?"

But as Safiya expatiates on the virtues of an Égalitéan diet, Blake grows increasingly agitated. His eyebrows knit; a vein on his temple bulges. Finally, unable to restrain himself any longer, he truculently declares that he isn't about to let Safiya get away with slander against meat eaters. With passion, he defends an omnivorous diet, shooting out one argument after another, like bullets from a machine gun, hoping to pierce Safiya's vegetarian armor. To no avail. Calmly, patiently, Safiya disposes of Blake's arguments, fifteen in all.

1. Blake: *But meat tastes good.*

Safiya: This was probably the chief reason that people from your era ate meat. They didn't care so much about the well-being of the nonhuman animals they consumed. Nor did they care so much about the impact that meat-eating had on their health and on the health of the environment. No doubt people have an interest in eating delicious food. The power of this preference-interest shouldn't be underestimated; it's far from trivial. After all, imagine how dreary our lives would be if we could eat nothing but insipid food! However, a vegetarian diet need not be insipid. Consider the strawberries that we're all enjoying—so sweet and refreshing. And what about the grilled vegetable wraps? Are they any less tasty than hamburgers or ham sandwiches? If grilled vegetables weren't to our liking, we could have taken any number of other foods from the dining hall. Often people from your time, accustomed to eating meat every day, had a hard time imagining the variety of delicious foods that vegetarians—even vegans and locavores—can choose from. As far as taste goes, switching to a vegetarian diet requires little sacrifice.

2. Blake: *But many cultures value meat.*

Safiya: Throughout much of human history, this was true. In hunting and gathering cultures, for instance, hunters shared with the whole band the game they'd killed. These cultures valued meat as a symbol of communal sharing. In your own culture, on a holiday called Thanksgiving, people traditionally ate turkey. Turkey was valued as a symbol of giving thanks. Other cultures valued meat in other ways. Certainly, communal sharing, giving thanks, and other such practices are laudable. We should respect, and even encourage, them. But respect for other cultures should have limits. Should we respect a culture insofar as it permits slavery, or female genital mutilation, or honor killings, or witch burnings, or ethnic cleansing—even if the culture values these things as symbols of communal sharing, giving thanks, or other laudable ideals? Of course not, because the culture violates the principle of human equality. Similarly, insofar as a culture values meat, we shouldn't respect that culture either, because it violates the principle of animal equality. If a culture wishes to promote communal sharing or giving thanks, then by all means let it do so. But surely it can do so without sacrificing the vital interests of nonhuman animals.

3. Blake: *But some people need meat to survive.*

Safiya: Not as many as you might think. Perhaps at one time the Eskimos needed meat to survive. Maybe also a starving person who, lost in the wilderness, has the good fortune to run across a deer and a loaded rifle in working condition. In extreme cases like these, eating meat may well be justified. But you and I aren't Eskimos, and we're not starving and lost in the wilderness. We can't reasonably claim that *we* need meat to survive. Nor can we reasonably claim that the fact that *some* people need meat to survive justifies *our* eating meat.

4. Blake: *But the healthiest diet includes meat.*

Safiya: Some omnivorous diets are healthier than some vegetarian diets; some vegetarian diets are healthier than some omnivorous diets. An omnivorous diet heavy on fatty meats is decidedly unhealthy. So is a vegetarian diet heavy on chips and soda. When you say, then, that the healthiest diet includes meat, which omnivorous diet do you think is healthier than which vegetarian diet? The healthiest of each? In that case, we find little or no health difference. What about the most common of each? But in your society, the most common vegetarian diet was hands down the healthier. The scientific evidence is clear: vegetarians can be perfectly healthy. Even vegans can be perfectly healthy. One potential problem for vegans is getting enough vitamin B_{12}, given that vitamin B_{12} is found naturally only in animal products. But this problem is surmountable, because vegans can eat foods that are fortified with vitamin B_{12} or take vitamin supplements. The vitamin B_{12} found in these sources is produced by bacteria cultures.

5. Blake: *But a vegetarian society would discriminate against several groups of people.*

Safiya: In your time, some people argued that a vegetarian society would discriminate against men. Since men tend to have more muscle than women, they're more likely than women to crave foods, such as meat, that are high in protein. Thus, for men, a vegetarian diet seems to be an undue hardship. Ironically, others argued that a vegetarian society would discriminate against women—as well as other groups, such as children, the elderly, and the poor. Women have nutritional needs that men don't have. More susceptible to osteoporosis, they need more calcium. During menstruation, they need to replace the iron they lose with their blood. During pregnancy, they have an increased need for a wide range of nutrients, among them protein, iron, calcium, zinc, vitamin D, and vitamin B$_{12}$. To deny women meat or other animal products would seem to make it unnecessarily difficult for them to get all the nutrients they need. Children, the elderly, and the poor also have nutritional needs that meat or other animal products conveniently supply.

Discrimination against any of these groups would be morally problematic, a clear violation of the principle of human equality. Luckily, though, a vegetarian society need not discriminate against any of these groups. Vegetarian, even vegan, foods are capable of satisfying everyone's nutritional requirements—men's and women's, children's and the elderly's. Thus, to avoid discrimination against men or women, children or the elderly, a vegetarian society has only to do two things. First, it must produce enough vegetarian foods containing the right nutrients for the right people. Second, it must properly distribute these foods. Égalité does both of these things. In Égalité, everyone receives proper nourishment.

But what about the poor? How can Égalité ensure that its poor are properly nourished? Égalité has no poor. It eliminated poverty when, at its founding, it replaced capitalism with egalitarianism. Egalitarianism is an economic system grounded in the principles of human and animal equality. Unlike capitalism, it doesn't permit some people to be billionaires while others wander the streets homeless. But even a capitalist society could ensure that its poor receive a well-balanced vegetarian diet. Your capitalist society, for example, was willing to make numerous provisions for the poor. It provided homeless shelters, unemployment benefits, and Medicaid. It also provided food stamps. If your capitalist society was able to provide its poor with food stamps, surely it could have taken the further step of providing them with nutritious vegetarian foods.

6. Blake: *But athletes need meat.*

Safiya: Nonsense! Athletes can get muscle without eating muscle. In the late twentieth and early twenty-first centuries, vegetarians were far less common than omnivores. Nevertheless, a significant number of world class athletes were vegetarians—some for their whole lives, some for much or all of their athletic careers. Among others were Scott Jurek, a record-holding ultramarathoner; Dave Scott, six-time winner of the Ironman Triathlon; Desmond Howard, a professional football player and winner of the Heisman trophy; Keith Holmes, a world champion middleweight boxer; Stan Price, a weightlifter who held the world record for the bench press in his weight class; Chris Evert, a number one ranked tennis player; Surya Bonaly, an Olympic ice skating champion; Edwin Moses, an Olympic champion hurdler; Bill Walton, a champion basketball player; and Ridgely Abele, winner of multiple U.S. national championships in karate. The day after tomorrow you'll meet several Égalitéan athletes. They don't participate in the same sports as the athletes I've just listed—Égalitéans prefer cooperative sports to competitive ones. But they'll show you what vegetarian athletes are capable of!

7. Blake: *But eating meat is natural.*

Safiya: I'm not certain what you mean by this statement. Do you mean to say that human beings evolved as omnivores? That we're not like horses or cows or our frugivorous, tree-dwelling ancestors? That our teeth and digestive system are different, allowing us to extract nutritional value from meat? Very well. But so what? What follows? Does it follow that eating meat is good? Does it follow that a vegetarian diet is unnatural and bad? If this is what you think, then I must disagree.

Long ago, people often argued that something was good because it was natural, or that something was bad because it was unnatural. Some people, for example, believed that male dominance was natural and therefore good, and that homosexuality and genetic engineering were unnatural and therefore bad. Such arguments are known as *arguments from nature*, and they commit a fallacy known as the *naturalistic fallacy*. Just because something is natural doesn't mean that it's good; just because something is unnatural doesn't mean that it's bad. Human beings evolved as bipeds, but in the process of becoming bipedal, we developed a propensity to suffer from lower back pain. Lower back pain, we may say, is natural. But no one would say that it's good! Similarly, human beings evolved with arms instead of wings. Consequently, for birds flying is natural, while for human beings it's unnatural. Yet we wouldn't condemn someone for flying in an airplane!

Exactly the same points apply to meat-eating and vegetarianism. Like lower back pain, meat-eating may be natural, but it doesn't follow that meat-eating is good. Like flying, vegetarianism may be unnatural, but it doesn't follow that vegetarianism is bad.

Perhaps you'll object. You're committing no fallacy, you may say. Although what is natural isn't always good, often it is, and eating meat is one of the things that are both natural and good. In particular, over billions of years of evolution, nature has produced meat eaters, and it's a good thing it has done so. It's a good thing because, without meat eaters, the species that meat eaters prey upon would become overpopulated. Human meat eaters, then, serve an invaluable function. They help to preserve the balance of nature. But if this is your argument, your argument is disingenuous. Your meat-eating society hardly preserved the balance of nature. On the contrary, with its practice of factory farming, it upset the balance of nature. To make room for the billions of nonhuman animals whom people consumed, it razed entire forests. The feces and urine these nonhuman animals produced polluted the air, land, and water. Transportation of nonhuman animals to slaughterhouses and supermarkets required vast quantities of fossil fuels. Seas and lakes were overfished, and fishing methods damaged sea floors. About a quarter of all fish caught were bycatch—unwanted species, thrown back into the water, usually dead or dying. Was any of this natural? Was any of it good? Égalitéans don't think so.

8. Blake: *But animals eat each other.*

Safiya: Benjamin Franklin advanced this argument six centuries ago. When he was a teenager, he committed himself to a vegetarian diet. He reasoned that killing nonhuman animals for food was "unprovoked murder, since none of them had, or ever could do us any injury that might justify the slaughter." But when he took his first trip from Boston to Philadelphia, the sailors aboard the ship he was on caught and fried some cod. The cod, he noticed, "smelt admirably well." Franklin wavered. Then he recalled that, when the sailors had cut open the cod, the cod had had smaller fish in their bellies. Joining his shipmates at the dinner table, Franklin feasted on cod, thinking to himself, "If you eat one another, I don't see why we mayn't eat you."

Franklin's argument is ambiguous. Possibly, Franklin meant to argue that because members of species A eat members of species B, we may eat members of species *A*. Alternatively, he might have meant to argue that because members of species A eat members of species B, we may eat members of species *B*. Do you see the difference? According to the first version of the argument, we may eat *predators*; according to the second version, we may eat *prey*. Maybe Franklin meant to advance both versions: we may eat predators as well as prey. Whatever he meant, he seems to have found his argument less than fully convincing. In his autobiography, immediately after presenting the argument, he commented, "So convenient a thing it is to be a *reasonable creature*, since it enables one to find or make a reason for every thing one has a mind to do."

Consider the case for eating predators. On this line of reasoning, eating cod is all right, because they're predators. But why should the fact that cod are predators imply that we may eat them? Are we supposed to believe that, when Franklin dined on cod, he was applying a sort of *lex talionis*—an eye for an eye, a tooth for a tooth, a life for a life? Was he arguing that just as we may execute a human being who kills other human beings, so we may eat a nonhuman animal who eats other nonhuman animals? Was he giving the cod their just comeuppance? But *lex talionis* is dubious even when applied to human criminals. When applied to nonhuman animals, who hardly qualify as criminals, it makes no sense at all.

Cod, however, aren't just predators. They can also be prey—as can cows, pigs, sheep, chickens, turkeys, and other nonhuman animals whom people used to eat. Does the case for eating prey fare any better than the case for eating predators? I'm afraid not. Why should the fact that predators eat cod and other nonhuman animals imply that we likewise may eat cod and other nonhuman animals? Why should we model our dietary practices after those of predators? Aren't we importantly different from nonhuman predators? Unlike many of them, we can survive without eating meat. And unlike them, we can understand moral considerations. I can share with you my concerns about eating fish, and, although you may disagree with me, you can at least understand me. But imagine how ridiculous I'd be if I wagged an accusing finger in front of a brown bear and said, "Shame on you for eating that poor, defenseless salmon!"

9. Blake: *But plants feel pain too.*

Safiya: I think I know where you're going with this. You're objecting to the argument that eating nonhuman animals is wrong because nonhuman animals feel pain. You're objecting that if this argument were correct, then eating plants would similarly be wrong, because plants too feel pain. But if we may eat neither plants nor nonhuman animals, there's precious little left—salt comes to mind—that we *may* eat. Since we have to eat something, we may as well eat whatever we want. That includes nonhuman animals.

But how can we be sure that plants feel pain? Consider a particular plant. Suppose, as I'm mowing my lawn, the blade of my lawnmower slices through the stalk of a dandelion. The yellow flower lies lifelessly on the ground. How does the plant respond? It not only grows a new flower but grows it lower to the ground, so that the next time I mow my lawn, the blade of my lawnmower slices through nothing but air. A clever plant, the dandelion! Could it be that the dandelion grows its second flower lower to the ground in response to the pain it felt when it lost its first flower?

I object to this argument in two ways. First, I doubt that dandelions, or other plants, can feel pain. For one thing, plants lack a brain or nervous system, or anything that appears to serve the same function as a brain or nervous system. For another, it makes little sense that plants would evolve with the ability to feel pain, given that they're rooted to the ground and have little opportunity to avoid painful stimuli. Imagine a fire sweeping across my lawn. The flames lick at my skin; I feel pain; I run away. But what about the dandelion? The flames lick at its leaves; it feels pain … and then what? The plant can't run away. How cruel nature would be to endow plants with the ability to feel pain when this ability does nothing to benefit them! But didn't the ability to feel pain benefit the dandelion when I mowed my lawn? Not necessarily. Growing a second flower lower to the ground could be genetically hardwired, without the dandelion responding to pain. Some of our own behavior—such as when we develop a fever that bakes a virus to death—is much the same.

Second, and more decisively, even if plants feel pain, and even if they feel pain as intensely as nonhuman animals, it doesn't follow that we may as well eat nonhuman animals. Suppose we're given a choice: we can share a kilogram of chicken or a kilogram of grain. If we eat the chicken, the chicken (let's assume) will suffer; if we eat the grain, the grain (let's assume) will suffer. However, before we can eat the chicken, we must feed the chicken. To get one kilogram of chicken, we must feed the chicken two kilograms of grain. Consequently, eating a kilogram of chicken will involve more suffering—that of the chicken as well as that of two kilograms of grain—than will eating a kilogram of grain. Nor will eating other kinds of meat, such as pork or beef, be any better. On the contrary, it takes even more grain or other vegetation to get a kilogram of pork or beef than to get a kilogram of chicken. Thus, if we wish to minimize suffering, we'd do better to be vegetarians— even on the assumption that plants feel pain.

10. Blake: *But food animals can be reared and slaughtered humanely.*

Safiya: Of all the arguments for eating meat, this one is the strongest. Eating humanely reared and slaughtered animals would seem to make everyone happy. People would be happy because they'd get to eat tasty meat, and food animals would be happy because they'd be treated well. They wouldn't live their whole lives in cages; they wouldn't be crammed in sheds and crates; they wouldn't eat foods laced with growth-promoting substances; they wouldn't wallow in their own excrement; they wouldn't be castrated, dehorned, or debeaked. On the contrary, provided with an environment suitable for their species, they'd be able to pursue their interests—until the day they're slaughtered, that is. But even that day wouldn't be so bad because they'd be slaughtered painlessly. On the face of it, such an arrangement would seem to be a win-win situation.

Three points, however, are worth emphasizing. First, suppose we accept your argument. Suppose that vegetarianism isn't a moral obligation, but that meat-eating is justified on the condition that food animals are reared and slaughtered humanely. Even so, people from your time would have been obligated to make massive changes in their eating habits. They'd have had to give up Big Macs, Whoppers, and KFC chicken, and they'd have had to stop eating the vast majority of meat, eggs, and dairy sold in supermarkets. In the United States of your day, all of these products came from factory farms, where animals suffered greatly.

Second, I question the humaneness of even the most humane rearing and slaughtering of food animals. Take, for example, the farmers working on an early twenty-first century farm in Virginia called Polyface Farm. If ever farmers treated their animals humanely, it was the farmers at Polyface. But consider how these farmers treated their chickens. Although they allowed their chickens outdoors, they kept them in crowded mobile wire pens. Before they slaughtered them, they put them in crates for twelve hours, eight birds crammed into each crate. At the time of slaughter, they cut their throats without first stunning them or rendering them unconscious. If this is the most humane that farmers can be, I prefer to be a vegetarian.

But why didn't farmers, even the most humane ones, treat their animals more humanely? The answer is simple: because food animals were commodities. The *raison d'être* of food animals—their reason for being—was to satisfy human interests. If human beings hadn't wanted meat, eggs, or dairy, food animals would never have been reared and slaughtered. Thus, farmers necessarily treated food animals as means to human ends. This being so, they had a hard time seeing food animals as ends in themselves.

Third, even if farmers could rear and slaughter food animals with perfect humaneness, they would still in the end have to slaughter them. Furthermore, the end would have to come sooner rather than later. Food animals live only weeks or months rather than several years. But this means that most food animals never get to experience the things that members of their species have the deepest interest in experiencing. They don't, for instance, get to experience courtship, copulation, pregnancy, and parenthood. Consequently, the rearing and slaughtering of food animals, no matter how humanely done, seems to violate the principle of animal equality.

11. Blake: *But food animals wouldn't exist unless we ate them.*

Safiya: This argument was most famously stated by Leslie Stephen, the father of Virginia Woolf: "Of all the arguments for Vegetarianism none is so weak as the argument from humanity. The pig has a stronger interest than anyone in the demand for bacon. If all the world were Jewish, there would be no pigs at all."

Stephen's argument lacks force if the demand for bacon is met through factory farming. For then the choice is between a life of suffering and no life at all, and, if this is the choice, no life at all seems preferable. But what if pigs were reared and slaughtered humanely? Or more precisely, what if they were reared and slaughtered as humanely as were the animals on Polyface Farm—which is probably the best we could hope for? Would such a life, as short as it may be, be better than no life at all?

My hunch, insofar as I have one, is that neither alternative is hands down better than the other. But suppose for the sake of argument that my hunch is wrong, and that Stephen is right: breeding pigs is good for the pigs. Nonetheless, if farmers are going to breed pigs, they're going to need land. And if they're going to give the pigs a pleasant life, they're going to need lots of land, so that the pigs have room to roam. Giving the land to pigs will alter the ecosystem. Wild animals who once lived on the land may no longer be able to. Thus, even if breeding pigs is good for the pigs, it may not be good for other animals. According to the principle of animal equality, we should consider not only the interests of human beings, and not only the interests of the pigs human beings consume, but also the interests of all other animals.

12. Blake: *But my becoming a vegetarian won't change the meat industry.*

Safiya: Becoming a vegetarian is like walking across a lawn. If you're the only one who does it, the impact is negligible. The lawn remains lush; the meat industry carries on business as usual. But if you're one among a multitude, you and the others you join will make a difference. Just as grass will die off and bare patches emerge, so the demand for meat will drop measurably. Fewer food animals will be reared and slaughtered. Farms and slaughterhouses will either downsize or shut their doors.

Even in your time, millions of people were vegetarians. So, if you become a vegetarian, you won't be going it alone. You'll be part of a large and growing movement. Think of the movement as a boycott. When an industry exploits consumers or tramples on the rights of workers, we shouldn't stand idly by. We should refuse to buy the products the industry produces. We should boycott the industry. Since the meat industry tramples on the rights of nonhuman animals, you should refuse to buy and eat meat.

But why must you boycott the meat industry? Aren't there other things you could do instead? Why not donate money to an animal rights organization, or picket outside a slaughterhouse, or rescue abused animals from factory farms, or write letters to your political representatives, or do any number of other things? By all means! Do as many of these things as you wish. But do them in addition to, not instead of, becoming a vegetarian. As long as people eat meat, the meat industry will continue to make profits. As long as the meat industry continues to make profits, it will have little reason to change.

13. Blake: *But widespread vegetarianism would be economically disastrous.*

Safiya: It probably would have been, if everyone the world over had become a vegetarian overnight. Then the meat industry would immediately have collapsed, devastating the millions of people who depended on it: farmers, slaughterhouse workers, butchers, truck drivers, employees in fast food restaurants, and on and on. A global economic recession, if not depression, would have been a virtual certainty. There would also have been the problem of what to do with the millions upon millions of food animals people no longer wanted to consume.

People, however, didn't all become vegetarians overnight. The transition from your meat-eating society to my vegetarian society was gradual, spanning decades. This gave the economy time to adjust. Some businesses, such as McDonald's, not only survived, but thrived. McDonald's prospered by gradually reducing the number of Big Macs and Egg McMuffins it made, and replacing them with healthier alternatives. By the middle of the twenty-first century, McDonald's had become the most profitable vegetarian restaurant in the world, employing even more people than it had half a century earlier.

To be sure, not all businesses survived. Perdue, for example, repeatedly had to downsize, and by 2037 went out of business. But all in all there was no more economic upheaval than in any other period of your capitalistic society. Some businesses thrived, some downsized, and some failed. People adjusted, as they always have.

One more point: sometimes economic upheaval is justified. The abolition of slavery is a case in point. The years following the U.S. Civil War were in many respects economically painful. The southern parts of your country had to adjust to radical changes. Yet the economic upheaval was justified, because slavery was an intolerable injustice. Similarly, the treatment of food animals was an intolerable injustice. Even if ending the injustice had caused economic upheaval, the economic upheaval would have been justified.

14. Blake: *But widespread vegetarianism would still result in the deaths of animals.*

Safiya: Sadly, this can be true. Any vegetarian society will need to grow and harvest crops. Plows, however, can inadvertently crush field mice or destroy the burrows moles inhabit. Pesticides can kill birds. The harvesting of crops can expose animals to predators. Does this mean that a vegetarian society is no better than a meat-eating society?

Here's one way we might frame the issue. Suppose we have an acre of land. We want to use the acre to feed as many people as possible while killing as few nonhuman animals as possible. Should we use the acre to grow crops? Or should we use it to raise food animals?

We might think that a lot depends on what kind of food animals we raise. Cattle, for example, are much larger than chickens. One cow can feed many more people than one chicken can. So if we want to kill as few nonhuman animals as possible, we'd do better to use our acre to raise cattle than to raise chickens. But what should we feed our cattle? If we feed them grain, as your society commonly did, we'd first have to grow the grain. But if we grow grain, our plows might crush field mice, our pesticides might kill birds, and so on. This wouldn't kill as few nonhuman animals as possible. It would be better if we ate the grain ourselves, rather than feed it to cattle and then eat the cattle.

Perhaps, though, we could feed our cattle grass instead of grain. If our cattle graze on grass, we wouldn't need to use plows or pesticides, and so we'd kill fewer nonhuman animals. Which, then, kills fewer nonhuman animals: using our acre to grow crops, or using it to raise grass-fed cattle? One animal scientist from your era attempted to answer this question. After carrying out a complex calculation, he concluded that growing crops kills twice as many nonhuman animals as raising grass-fed cattle. His calculation, however, rested on an erroneous assumption. The assumption was that an acre used for crops feeds exactly as many people as an acre used for grass-fed cattle. In fact, an acre used for crops feeds ten times as many people. From this, it follows that growing crops kills fewer, not more, nonhuman animals—five times fewer.

To be more precise, I should say *at least* five times fewer. When we grow crops, we can do without pesticides, and we can relocate field mice and other animals before we plow. Égalitéans do both these things, with significant results.

15. Blake: *But God tells us we may eat meat.*

Safiya: This argument rests on three assumptions: that God exists, that we may do what he tells us we may do, and that he tells us we may eat meat. These assumptions are controversial, to say the least. Consider the last assumption. How can we be sure that God tells us we may eat meat? Because the Bible says so? But how can we be sure that the Bible conveys God's words accurately? Why prefer the Bible over other scriptures? What's wrong, for example, with Hindu or Jain scriptures that emphasize a vegetarian diet?

Furthermore, does the Bible unequivocally say that God tells us we may eat meat? In Genesis 9:3, shortly after the Great Flood, God says to Noah and his sons, "Every moving thing that lives shall be food for you." Here God gives people nonhuman animals to eat. But how are we to weigh this against Genesis 1:29, where, just after creating human beings, God says, "I have given you every plant yielding seed that is upon the face of all the earth, and every tree with seed in its fruit; you shall have them for food"? And what about Isaiah 11:6-9, which looks forward to a vegetarian future: "The wolf shall live with the lamb, the leopard shall lie down with the kid, the calf and the lion and the fatling together, and a little child shall lead them. The cow and the bear shall graze, their young shall lie down together; and the lion shall eat straw like the ox. The nursing child shall play over the hole of the asp, and the weaned child shall put its hand on the adder's den. They will not hurt or destroy on all my holy mountain; for the earth will be full of the knowledge of the LORD as the waters cover the sea."

Finally, even if we could be certain that God tells us we may eat meat, a very important question would remain. *Why* does God tell us we may eat meat? God has either a convincing reason to tell us this, or an unconvincing reason, or no reason at all. If God has an unconvincing reason, or no reason at all, I don't see why I should pay the slightest attention to what he tells me. But if God has a convincing reason, I would no longer need to appeal to the authority of God, as you have done, to know that I may eat meat. I could instead appeal to the reason God has for the permissibility of eating meat. But what could this reason be? You've already offered fifteen defenses of meat-eating, none of which has held up after a critical examination. Can you think of a sixteenth reason we may eat meat, a reason that is stronger than any of your first fifteen? If so, what is it?

○ ○ ○

For a brief moment, Blake's upper lip quivers. I expect him to leave in anger, as he did this morning. Instead, he smiles affably. He says, "Looks like I just got my butt kicked. Bet I'd have been sharper, though, if I'd had a steak for lunch! Right, Philsbury?"

Behind Blake, the two teenage girls are still playing their word game—if it is a game. Their PADs announce in androgynous voices, "… *dissemble* … *duplicitous* … *mendacity* … *prevarication*…." The girls correctly define the words. Thrum, cheep-cheep, whisper, gurgle, splash, squeal, clap. The summer symphony plays on.

Chapter 10
How Should People Treat Companion Animals?

At last! I'm in my quarters, alone, the door shut. I peer anxiously out the window. In the distance, partially hidden behind a screen of foliage, Safiya and Blake continue to converse at the picnic table.

I told them that the afternoon heat was making me drowsy and that I wanted to take a nap. They offered to accompany me to my quarters, but I insisted that it wasn't necessary, that I knew how to get there. Safiya asked if she could drop by around dinnertime. She said she wanted to give me a gift. I said that would be fine. Blake poked me in the stomach. "You lucky dog!" he exclaimed. "Safiya's sweet on you!" Safiya blushed but said nothing.

I lied to Safiya and Blake: I'm not sleepy. I don't like lying, but something's fishy. Égalité is too perfect, for one thing—too goody-goody. How could Égalité produce no garbage, for instance, and how could it have eliminated poverty? I don't believe in utopias; they don't seem possible. Furthermore, why do so many Égalitéans bear an uncanny resemblance to people from my time? I can think of no reasonable explanation. Finally, there's Safiya. She seems to mean well, but she hasn't been entirely candid with me. She's holding something back, and what she's holding back might be important. I want to find out what's really going on. I need to be alone to do that.

Since I'm pretty good at snooping around with my computer and since PADs seem to be similar to computers, I'm hoping I'll be pretty good at snooping around with the PAD Safiya gave me. Holding the device between thumb and forefinger, I begin my investigation. Today, it announces in its androgynous voice, is the three hundred sixty-fifth day of a leap year, the year 300—or, by my calendar, July 2, 2376. In another two days, Égalité will celebrate its tricentennial.

Safiya's village is planning a big day, with music and dancing, games and athletic events. At 9:30 in the morning, a parade will pass through, having started an hour earlier in a village to the north. At 9:30 in the evening, after a celebratory feast, the entire village will meet on the community field to enjoy a display of fireworks. The community field, I learn, is the grassy area I passed by when I first entered Safiya's village, where the man who resembles the first officer from the science fiction program was mowing. Aside from some early morning fog and high humidity, the weather is expected to cooperate.

So far, so good: nothing odd, nothing to keep secret. But I've only just begun. I must be patient. I have perhaps three hours before Safiya knocks on my door, gift in hand.

I ask my PAD several questions about Égalitéan demographics. It informs me that, when Égalité was founded three centuries ago, more than ten billion people inhabited the globe. Over the next two hundred years, the population declined sharply. Since then, it has remained steady, at about half a billion people. What happened to all the people? Was there a plague? No. The early Égalitéans believed that a population of ten billion violated the principle of animal equality. So many people put too much of a strain on the planet, diminishing the quality of life of virtually every species. Thus the early Égalitéans made a conscious decision to slow human reproduction. To achieve this goal, they enacted a number of policies. First, they promoted the use of birth control. Second, noting that more highly educated and economically independent women tended to have fewer children, they promoted sex equality. Third, since the poorest parts of the world had the highest reproduction rates, they promoted a more egalitarian distribution of wealth. Fourth, they promoted extended families, so that those who didn't have children of their own could still enjoy the experience of raising children. Public support for these measures was so broad that no government enforcement was necessary.

The early Égalitéans not only slowed reproduction, but also dismantled all cities. New York and London, Beijing and Tokyo, Jakarta and Sydney—all disappeared. These were replaced with a network of villages. Some villages are larger than others, but no village has more than a thousand inhabitants. Safiya's village, typical in size, currently has a population of three hundred eighty-three. The advantage of villages, according to Égalitéans, is that everybody knows everybody else. Cities, by contrast, create a sense of anonymity. Lost in a crowd, people feel less connected, and less accountable, to others. They throw trash on the sidewalks; they cut each other off in traffic; they commit crimes. In 2376, crime is virtually nonexistent.

Égalitéans, I discover, embrace some technologies, but shun others. PADs, for instance, are acceptable, because they help people satisfy their interests without at the same time sacrificing anyone else's interests. Automobiles, on the other hand, are unacceptable, especially those that run on gasoline. The extensive use of automobiles in my time contributed to global warming, and vast numbers of human beings and nonhuman animals were killed or injured in accidents. When Égalitéans need to go someplace, they usually walk, since walking is good exercise and since walking gives them time to enjoy the scenery. If they're in a hurry, or they need to travel a long distance, they take an energy-efficient train—or, if they're crossing a sea, an energy-efficient boat. Only rarely, though, do Égalitéans travel a long distance. For the most part, they use their PADs to reach remote parts of the globe.

By the middle of the twenty-first century, partly as a result of the extensive use of automobiles, global warming became the most urgent problem the world faced. Parts of the world, once fertile, became arid, while other parts, such as much of the Florida Everglades, disappeared under rising sea levels. The United States had to build a wall around Manhattan to protect it from the encroaching waters. The Indian peninsula was less fortunate. Unable to afford walls, the people of India could only stand by as coastal cities were flooded. Millions of people were displaced; tens of thousands died. Toward the end of the century, when Égalité became the major world power, people finally stopped using fossil fuels, and finally stopped doing other things that contributed to global warming. But by then the damage was done. Even three centuries later, Égalitéans continue to suffer the effects of twenty-first-century stupidity.

How did Égalitéans overcome twenty-first-century stupidity? Did they find wisdom in religion? No. On the contrary, they abandoned religion. All of the major religions that existed in the twenty-first century were too speciesist and too inegalitarian to suit Égalitéan tastes. Some early Égalitéans attempted to devise a religion that was consistent with Égalitéan principles, but such attempts met with little success. Most Égalitéans saw no good reason to believe in either a deity or an afterlife. They were inclined to think that, if this is the only life they have, they might as well make the most of it. This attitude sufficiently motivated them to combat the mistakes of the twenty-first century.

The information my PAD provides only deepens my concerns. Are human beings really capable of reducing their population by nine and a half billion? Can they really dismantle all cities, abolish crime, and give up cars and religion? If anything, Égalité seems even less probable than it did before.

I continue my investigation, asking about Safiya and her friends. Safiya is twenty-eight years old and a philosopher as well as a musician. Charlie Perkins-Goodman is a mechanical engineer and an ecofeminist. An ecofeminist, as far as I can determine, is someone who is both a feminist and an environmentalist, and sees environmental and gender issues to be systematically interrelated. Édouard Bel-Ami, an economist, teaches French and art in his spare time. Franz Bach-Kuhn is a scientist and essayist. Édouard and Franz are a couple; they've been married for thirty-three years and have a thirty-two-year-old daughter named Frances. Safiya and Charlie are single and have no children. I also learn why everyone has a hyphenated last name. Égalitéans get half of their last name from one parent and the other half from their other parent. Charlie's parents, for instance, are Charlotte Perkins-Gilder and Ernest Goodman-Callenbach. According to Égalitéans, getting one's last name solely from one's father is sexist.

Beyond these few facts, however, my PAD tells me little about Safiya and her friends. Again and again, the androgynous voice says only that that information isn't available. Why do Safiya's friends look like people from my time? That information isn't available. Is Charlie a descendant of Chaz? That information isn't available. Is Édouard a descendant of Brother Bell? That information isn't available. Is Franz a descendant of Mr. Bhayq? That information isn't available. Why did the Égalitéans bring me here? That information isn't available. Why did they bring Blake here? That information isn't available. Has Safiya ever told a lie? That information isn't available.

I grow increasingly frustrated. I glance out the window. Safiya and Blake are no longer sitting at the picnic table. I don't see them anywhere. Safiya could knock on my door at any moment, and I still haven't found what I'm looking for. My mind races. At first I draw a blank, and then I get an idea. July 4, the Égalitéan tricentennial, is an important day. Perhaps I can find a clue in the celebration Safiya's village is planning. I ask my PAD about the parade, the games and sporting events, the music and dancing, the feast, and the fireworks. Nothing. Everything seems normal.

I probe more deeply. My PAD tells me the precise number and types of fireworks that the villagers are planning to set off during the fireworks display. Have the villagers already acquired all of the fireworks? Yes. Where are they being stored? Near the train station underneath the dining hall. Are all of them being stored there? Yes. I ask my PAD to show them to me. It shows them to me. I ask for the precise number and types of fireworks that are there. Taking great care, I compare the number and types of fireworks in storage with the number and types of fireworks the villagers are planning to use. There seems to be a match. Yes … wait. I check again, and then once more. Aha! A discrepancy! The villagers are planning to use more fireworks than they have in storage. Some fireworks—in particular, the most powerful ones—are missing!

"Where are the missing fireworks?" I ask.

My PAD says, "That information isn't available."

∘ ∘ ∘

Safiya's gift—a white dog with a black button nose, much like Mrs. Shoemaker's toy poodle—hops onto my lap and, standing on her hind legs, licks my face. With me are Safiya, Blake, Charlie, Édouard, and Franz. The six of us are sitting in a lounge down the hall from my quarters. In front of us, scattered about on a coffee table, are plates and forks and napkins—all that remains of our dinner, a lentil dish called dhal. Safiya, as usual, has her oboe with her, tucked away in the pocket on her robe.

"You have to admit," Blake says, as I stroke the dog behind her ears, "that people from my time lavish affection on their pets. They feed them, house them, pet them, play with them—spend billions of dollars on them every year. I don't know how many times I've heard people say they think of little Fifi or Fluffy as a member of the family. Maybe cows and chickens aren't treated so well in my time, but dogs and cats are in heaven." Waggling her stub of a tail, the dog leans forward on my lap to give Blake a snuffle.

"Heaven?" Charlie says quietly, arching one eyebrow. "Hardly."

Charlie's sitting next to Blake, on a plush sofa, one thick leg primly crossing the other. Like Chaz, Charlie has short-cropped hair, a square head, a ruddy complexion, and a thick neck, thick chest, thick arms, and thick legs—the build of a football player or a bodyguard or a person who breaks thumbs for a living. But though he and Chaz look alike, they don't act alike. Unlike Charlie, Chaz doesn't speak quietly, doesn't primly cross his legs, and doesn't contradict Blake. In addition, Chaz is no ecofeminist. He describes himself as a "simple grease monkey"—he works at a Jiffy Lube—who cherishes "traditional values." By "traditional values," he means that men have intrinsic value, whereas all other things have value only insofar as they're useful

100

to men. Trees have value insofar as they can be turned into planks and firewood; animals have value insofar as they provide men with food and leather jackets; women have value insofar as they wash men's laundry and give birth to sons. Chaz fancies that all women, especially the beautiful ones, find him irresistible. Chaz is sometimes delusional.

"Hardly?" Blake echoes, taken aback. "Would you care to elaborate?"

"People from your time," Safiya interjects, "often loved their companion animals. But there were problems. One problem concerned breeding. Dogs and cats were bred because people valued certain aesthetic standards, not because people wanted what was best for the animals. Thus bulldogs suffered from respiratory problems and Shar-Pei from skin problems. Many breeds suffered from many genetic disorders."

"Other problems," Édouard adds, speaking with exaggerated enthusiasm, as if he were talking to young children, "were declawing and devocalizing. People didn't want their furniture scratched, so they declawed their cats; they didn't like to hear barking, so they devocalized their dogs. Convenient for the people, but not nice to the cats and dogs. Some people from your time, for example, let their declawed cats outdoors. Without their claws, the cats were less able to defend themselves or to escape from danger. Other people, aware of this problem, kept their declawed cats indoors. But to keep them indoors was, in effect, to imprison them."

"Then there was the population problem," Franz says. He and Édouard are sitting on a love seat, holding hands. In many respects, the two men are opposites. Whereas Édouard is short and slim, Franz is tall and stout; whereas Édouard is clean-shaven, Franz wears a beard that reaches to his stomach; whereas Édouard's toes point outward, nearly in opposite directions, Franz is pigeon-toed. "People from your time," Franz explains, "let cats and dogs multiply like bacteria in a Petri dish. The result was that large numbers of animals became feral, unable to find a loving home. Feral cats and dogs left their droppings on sidewalks and lawns, and they spread diseases. Some of them couldn't survive."

Safiya says, "Many people sought to reduce the overpopulation of cats and dogs by spaying and neutering. To an extent, this helped. But sometimes no analgesia was used, and sometimes, for cat spays, only ketamine—which immobilized the animals but didn't effectively anesthetize them—was used. Besides, spaying and neutering prevented cats and dogs from satisfying some of their most vital interests—specifically, those related to copulating and to bearing and rearing offspring."

"Despite the overpopulation of companion animals," Édouard says, "puppy mills kept cranking out more puppies."

Interrupting, I ask, "What exactly is a puppy mill?"

"Puppy mills," Franz answers, twirling a finger through his massive beard, "bred puppies on a large scale, 'large scale' meaning the use of more than three breeding females. Some operations also bred cats."

"I've heard that animal activists are opposed to puppy mills," I say. "But I don't know why they're opposed. What's so bad about puppy mills, other than that they contribute to the overpopulation of pets?"

Safiya says, "Puppy mills were in business to make a profit. All too often what was profitable wasn't in the dogs' best interests. Thus breeders kept females constantly pregnant, and when the dogs could no longer produce profitable litters the breeders killed them. The mothers and their puppies were kept in overcrowded outdoor pens. The floors of the pens were made of wire, which allowed the dogs' urine and feces to pass through to the ground below, but the wire wasn't good for the dogs' paws. When the puppies were old enough—they were separated from their mothers at seven weeks of age—they were crammed into small crates and sent off to pet stores or laboratories. During transportation, the puppies often lacked adequate food, water, and ventilation. Some of them didn't survive the trip. Others developed respiratory or other disorders."

"Are there a lot of puppy mills in my time?" I ask.

"Oh, yes," says Édouard, bobbing his head and adjusting his oversized smudged glasses. "Although pet shop employees routinely denied it, the vast majority of puppies sold in pet shops came from puppy mills. If you ever want to get a puppy, you'd do better to get it from an animal shelter than from a pet store."

"Many animal shelters," Franz says, "didn't exactly shelter animals. People frequently bought puppies and kittens on a whim, and then, unable or unwilling to care for them, dumped them on animal shelters. Shelters received far more animals than they could place in loving homes. Unable to house so many animals, many shelters euthanized them. Of the six and a half million cats and dogs taken to U.S. shelters each year, more than one and a half million were euthanized: about 670,000 dogs and 860,000 cats."

"Not all shelters euthanized unwanted animals," Safiya says. "Some, called no-kill shelters, kept animals for as long as it took to find an adoptive family. Such shelters would seem to be ethically better than shelters that practiced euthanasia, but this appearance was sometimes deceptive. Many no-kill shelters turned away animals who were deemed unadoptable, and many of these animals wound up abandoned, abused, or killed."

"Some no-kill shelters," says Édouard, "kept their animals in cages, sometimes for their whole lives, and neglected to provide them with veterinary care. Other abuses occurred as well."

"Some shelters were genuinely caring," says Franz. "At these shelters, if no adoptive family could be found, the animals were allowed to live the remainder of their lives at the shelters, where they could roam freely over several acres of land. To pay for food, veterinary care, and other expenses, the operators of the shelters relied on donations from caring citizens. These citizens, as well as the operators of the shelters, were among the great heroes of your time."

"Of course," says Safiya, "not everyone who was unable or unwilling to care for their companion animals handed them over to shelters. Some simply abused or neglected them. This was another big problem in your time."

"I understand why some people get their pets from animal shelters," I say. "Doing so saves the animals' lives. But I've also been told that getting pets from animal shelters is a bad idea. Too many animals in animal shelters, having been abused or neglected by their owners, suffer from severe psychological problems. These animals would be difficult to care for, and might not be good for children to play with. Wouldn't it be better to get a dog or cat from a pet store?"

"But, as I just pointed out," Édouard retorts, "most pet stores got their animals from puppy mills, which likewise abused and neglected animals."

Franz adds, "Only some of the animals in shelters were in poor psychological health. Many were perfectly adoptable, and some shelters took great pains to place the right animals with the right people. Adopting an animal from a shelter is your best option. Second best would be to visit a small breeder, observe how the animals are treated, and then select an animal there. One reason this option is second best is that breeders, even small ones, contributed to the overpopulation of companion animals."

An ominous cloud slides in front of the sun, darkening the lounge. Thunder rumbles in the distance. A gust of wind shakes the window. The dog, which was snoozing on my lap, peers out the window, cocking her head to one side.

Charlie likewise peers out the window. Still primly crossing his legs, he says quietly, "Looks like we might get a whopper."

"Yes," Franz says. "Those clouds are spreading across the sky like bacteria in a Petri dish."

For a moment, we all watch the clouds roll in. Then Blake returns the conversation to the proper treatment of pets. "All right," he says. "So you've pointed out a few problems. But you're a little vague on solutions. How are people from my time supposed to treat their pets?"

"First of all," Safiya answers, "don't treat them as pets. Treat them as companions. When you take your dog for a walk, don't drag the poor thing by her leash wherever you want to go. This isn't what companions do. Instead, let the dog occasionally go where she wants to go. Who knows? You may find that the dog leads you to more interesting places than you'd go.

"A companion is very different from a pet," Safiya continues. "The word 'companion' suggests an egalitarian relationship—the interests of my companions have the same value as my comparable interests. The word 'pet,' by contrast, suggests property. My property is something I may use, or dispose of, as I see fit. If, for example, I no longer want my oboe, I may give it away, break it, or toss it in the recycling bin. It's my property. Dogs and cats and other companion animals, however, should never be treated as property. The cruelty our history books describe! People from your time sometimes drowned unwanted kittens, or left them at the dump to die. Sometimes they beat their dog, simply because, unable to control her bladder after having been left in the house all day, she peed on the carpet. At other times, on a hot summer day, they left their dog to bake in the car, its windows barely cracked open, as they leisurely shopped in a pleasantly air-conditioned supermarket. Such things happened as long as companion animals were treated as property. Thank wisdom this is no longer the case!"

"In the second place," says Édouard, "learn how to take care of companion animals before you acquire them. Familiarize yourself with their needs and preferences. Know, for example, that you shouldn't feed chocolate to dogs. It's poison for them. Know that you shouldn't give cats balls of yarn to play with. If they try to swallow the string, they could choke. Find out whether you're allergic to certain breeds of dog or cat. If you are, don't get them. In Égalité, all children know these basics by the time they're five years old. Our educational system requires such knowledge."

"Third," says Franz, "follow Phil's example. Be affectionate." Franz points to the dog on my lap as I gently stroke her blond curls. Blake hesitates, but then reaches out a hand to pat the dog on her head. He does it awkwardly, mechanically. When he tugs on a lock of the dog's hair that he manages to snag between his fingers, the dog lets out a yip. Blake withdraws his hand and places it in the pocket of his white pants. "Well," says Franz, "it's a start."

"Yes, yes, yes," says Blake. "This is all well and good. But what about the overpopulation problem that you mention? You don't seem thrilled with spaying and neutering. How do Égalitéans keep their dog and cat populations under control?"

Safiya says, "We allow most dogs and cats to have one litter, so they can at least partially satisfy their reproductive interests. But no more than that. Once they reproduce, we mix a birth control with their food. The birth control effectively prevents further pregnancies, with no significant side effects."

Édouard says, "Admittedly, this solution is less than perfect. It would be nice if all dogs and cats could have a litter. But if we allowed that, the population would quickly grow, since even a single litter tends to be large. There is no perfect solution. We have to keep the population steady, and the only way to do that is to limit reproductive opportunities. Sometimes we must sacrifice the interests of some in order to satisfy a larger set of interests."

"The same," says Franz, "is true of the human population. We can't allow people to reproduce as indiscriminately as they did in your time. The result would be another environmental crisis. So we limit our reproductive opportunities. It has to be done."

"Perhaps," I say, "your solution is as good as any. But my society doesn't put birth control in dog and cat food. Suppose, when I get back to my time, I want to get a cute little dog like the one I have on my lap. What should I do to make sure the dog doesn't reproduce?"

Safiya says, "Your simplest alternative is to use a leash. Égalitéans aren't fond of leashes, because they restrict a dog's mobility. They're also not needed, because we don't rear vicious dogs. In this village, for instance, no one has been the victim of a dog attack since I was born.

Your society, though, was different. It had laws requiring leashes. You might as well make the best of those laws."

"You could also consider higher tech solutions—including spaying or neutering," says Édouard, blushing for no apparent reason. "Spaying or neutering may not be an ideal solution, but it's better than doing nothing. If you take this route, consult a qualified veterinarian, to make sure the procedure causes as little discomfort as possible."

"And if you feel comfortable doing so," Franz says, "get the dog from an animal shelter. Other things being equal, it's better to adopt a dog who already exists than to ask a breeder to bring a new dog into existence."

"I have another concern," Blake says. "I know that Égalitéans are a bunch of vegetarians. Maybe—just maybe—human beings can get away with that kind of diet. But dogs and cats are carnivores. Don't you have to feed them meat? By doing so, aren't you sacrificing the interests of the animals you turn into dog and cat food? Aren't you violating your precious principle of animal equality? Doesn't this bother you?"

"Cats," Safiya replies, "are carnivores, yes. Dogs, though, like human beings, are omnivores. For both species, however, Égalitéans have devised healthy vegan diets. The trick is to synthesize all the nutrients cats and dogs need. Cats have special needs for taurine, arachidonic acid, and vitamins A and B_{12}; dogs have special needs for calcium and vitamin D, and some dogs have special needs for taurine and L-carnitine. All Égalitéan dog and cat food contains these and other nutrients in sufficient quantities."

"Is vegan dog and cat food available in my time?" I ask.

"Yes," says Édouard. "Some health food stores and online vendors offered such foods. However, the foods had only fairly recently been developed and hadn't yet undergone rigorous scientific testing. If you ever decide to try them, use caution. Monitor your dog or cat carefully. If your companion's health declines, you should contact a qualified veterinarian immediately."

Franz says, "If you prefer to feed your companion meat, make sure the meat comes from animals who were reared and slaughtered as humanely as possible. Such meat was also available at health food stores."

"Whatever you do," says Safiya, "don't buy factory-farmed dog or cat food—that is, the dog or cat food typically sold in supermarkets. This food often used meat deemed unfit for human consumption, and it contained the same growth hormones found in the meat human beings ate. Such food was cruel to the factory-farmed animals, and it was unhealthy for dogs and cats."

"What do you think," I say, changing the subject, "about assistance animals, such as seeing-eye dogs and capuchin monkeys trained to help the disabled? Do Égalitéans have any objections to these?"

"Not at all," says Safiya. "At least as long as the welfare- and preference-interests of the assistance animals are taken into account. In your day, this wasn't always the case. Sometimes trainers used training methods that were cruel. Sometimes disabled people didn't adequately understand what welfare- and preference-interests their assistance animals had.

"The services that assistance animals provide, however, illustrate something of great importance—namely, the deep and special bond that members of different species can develop for each other. Égalitéans seek out this bond wherever possible. In fact, Phil, this is why I brought you the dog. I understand that your abrupt arrival and experiences in Égalité have caused you stress. Your stress pains me. I'm hoping the dog will help you relieve your stress. Think of the dog as an assistance animal, whom you may interact with as long as you're with us."

"Thanks, Safiya," I say. I hadn't noticed it before, but my stress level plummeted from the moment the dog hopped on my lap. I tenderly stroke the dog's belly with my fingers. The dog lifts a hind leg to give me easier access.

At this moment, a flash of lightning brightens the lounge. The flash is accompanied by a deafening crackle of thunder. Rain starts to pummel the lounge window, so hard I'm afraid the window will shatter. A powerful wind whips helpless tree branches about. I've seen many thunderstorms in my life, but this one is unusually violent. Is it a result of the global warming brought on by twentieth- and twenty-first-century policies? Has the past intruded into the future? Will the choices that Blake and I and other people from my time make create a better future, or a worse one? The dog on my lap whimpers, and her teeth chatter.

Charlie says quietly, "It's raining cats and dogs."

Chapter 11
What Should People Wear?

Pitch black. Torrential rain … tornadic wind … tormenting heat.

I'm soaking wet, my hair and clothes clinging to my skin like a baby monkey to its mother. I need to take cover from the storm. Where should I go? Straining my eyes, I peer into the darkness. I see nothing; the darkness is impenetrable. Then a blinding flash, accompanied by a cacophonous bellow, rends the air. The flash leaves a momentary image on my retina: three doors—seemingly ordinary, seemingly identical—stand side by side in front of me.

Perhaps I should try one of the doors. Which one? Does it make any difference? I hesitate. I step toward the door to my left. I step back, indecisive.

A sound, barely discernible, rises above the pounding rain, roaring wind, and booming thunder. The sound is reedy. Is it Safiya's oboe? No. A voice. It's a voice. The voice calls my name.

"Who's there?" I shout. "Where are we?"

Another blinding flash. Again, the three doors. And Peacemaker. Peacemaker is standing at my side. She too is soaking wet. Her T-shirt, plastered against her bony frame, displays the words "I ♥ LENTILS."

"What's the matter, son? Don't you know what today is?"

"Today?" I don't know what today is; I've lost track. Could it be the Égalitéan tricentennial? Or is that tomorrow? Or the day after tomorrow? "July 4? Is it July 4?"

"That's right. Today is Judgment Day."

"Judgment Day! Are you here to judge me?" I picture Peacemaker listing my sins, all of the speciesist things I've done, all of the murders of innocent animals I've been accessory to. I picture her consigning me to Hell for all eternity. Despite the oppressive heat, a shiver runs up my spine.

Peacemaker laughs a cackling laugh. "Of course not! Do I look like the God you believe in? No, no, no. You're the one who's going to judge."

"Me? What am I supposed to judge?"

"The future of your society. Do you see the three doors in front of us?" Another flash lights up the three doors. "Behind each door lies a future that you may or may not support for your society. You're going to open one of the doors. By opening a door, you indicate which future you support."

"What future lies behind each door?"

"Behind the door to our left is Hell. Behind the middle door is Purgatory. Behind the door to our right is Heaven. Look at the etching on each door."

I have to wait for the next flash of lightning before I can see anything. When it comes, I notice the etchings. Etched into the left-hand door is an animal in a tiny cage. Etched into the middle door is an animal in a larger cage. The right-hand door depicts an empty cage.

Peacemaker continues, "The tiny cage on the door to our left represents business as usual. If you open that door, you support a future that resembles the past. Such a future is deeply speciesist. In it, billions of food animals suffer and die. Millions of unwanted companion animals are euthanized. Millions of acres of rainforest disappear. Tens of thousands of species of wild animals become extinct. Global warming runs rampant."

"What if I open the middle door?"

"In that case, you opt for a future that is speciesist, but less deeply speciesist. In this future, people hold that nonhuman animals have some moral standing, but not the same moral standing that human beings have. They treat nonhuman animals more humanely, but they fall short of embracing the principle of animal equality. They continue to eat nonhuman animals, use them in medical experiments, wear their skins and furs, and the like."

"And what about the right-hand door? What future do I support if I open that door?"

"Behind the right-hand door is Égalité, or something similar. If you open the right-hand door, you support a future that embraces the principle of animal equality. In such a future, people don't confine nonhuman animals in tiny cages, or in larger cages. All cages are empty. So what's your preference: tiny cages, larger cages, or empty cages?"

I reflect on my options. I now know the case for the principle of animal equality. I know why Égalitéans are vegetarians, and why they oppose experiments that cause harm to animals. I also have some idea how Égalitéans treat companion animals. The arguments that Safiya and her friends advance are powerful. I don't know how to refute them. But I still haven't made up my mind. I'm not yet ready to commit to Égalitéan ideals. I say to Peacemaker, "I'm sorry. I need more time to think about it."

"Think fast," Peacemaker replies. "You need to open one of the doors by July 4. No later."

"Why no later than July 4? What's significant about July 4?"

"Never you mind, son," Peacemaker says. "Don't be late."

A sound, barely discernible, rises above the pounding rain, roaring wind, and booming thunder. The sound is a knocking. The knocking comes from the other side of one of the three doors, but I can't tell which one. The knocking grows louder, more insistent. One of the three futures beckons me.

∘ ∘ ∘

A loud, insistent knocking wakes me up. I'm in my quarters, in bed, the white dog with the black button nose curled up next to me. I'm soaked with sweat, just as in my dream I was soaked with rain. Light streams in from the window. It's morning, bright and sunny. Last night's storm has passed. Today, I realize, is July 3. It's the day before the Égalitéan tricentennial.

The dog hops off the bed and runs to the door, where she cocks her head to one side and growls. I too feel like growling; I could use a little more sleep. When I finally open the door, Safiya and Blake tumble into the room. Safiya wears her usual creamy yellow robe, with her oboe in its pocket. Blake, by contrast, has exchanged yesterday's bright white outfit for a light gray shirt and dark gray pants and shoes. He looks sharp. Recognizing the two visitors, the dog abandons her growling and races around the room in an excited frenzy.

Safiya too is excited. Tripping over her words, she says she'd like to take Blake and me to a nearby village. At noon today, the Regional Planning Committee will meet in the dining hall of that village. Anyone who's interested is welcome to attend. The meeting will be an excellent opportunity for Blake and me to witness Égalitéan politics in action. After the meeting, Safiya continues, the three of us can go swimming. The village happens to be next to a lake. The lake, I surmise, is Hourglass Lake, where in my time Blake and Chaz like to show off in front of the pretty girls.

When Blake and I agree to Safiya's proposal, Safiya gives each of us a bear hug. Then, grasping me with one hand and Blake with the other, she leads us out of my quarters. Sensing adventure, the dog follows, her truncated tail in perpetual motion.

Despite her excitement, Safiya doesn't forget the dog. When we step outdoors, Safiya takes us to a spot specially designated for companion animals. Here the dog "leaves a present," as my mom would say. Following Safiya's instructions, I pick out a small plastic bag from a box that hangs on a tree, put the dog's "present" in the bag, and drop the bag down a pipe that sticks out of the ground. Safiya explains that the plastic bag is biodegradable and that the dog's dropping will be composted. In Égalité, she assures Blake and me, nothing goes to waste.

Our next stop is the clothing shop. If we're going swimming, I'll need swimming trunks, and I could use a couple of extra shirts and pairs of pants, socks, and underwear in any case. Safiya ushers us into the dining hall and down a ramp that leads to a large underground space. At one end of the underground space is the train station. Half a dozen people are unloading cargo from a small, sleekly designed train. They're putting the cargo into nearby storage rooms. One of the storage rooms, I notice, contains the fireworks that the villagers plan to set off tomorrow evening. At the other end of the underground space is a series of shops. The clothing shop sits between an art shop and a hair salon.

As we enter the clothing shop, two young women greet us with a smile and an embrace. They're the two young women who played the word game yesterday: the plump girl who chews bubblegum and the girl who flings back her renegade lock of hair like a horse shaking its mane. Safiya introduces us. I'm Phil, a visitor from the past, and Blake the two girls already know. The plump girl, Safiya says to me, is a tailor, and the girl with the renegade lock of hair is an image consultant.

I express surprise. In all the clothing stores I frequent, I see salespeople and rack after rack of clothes but never a tailor or an image consultant. Chewing her gum with gusto, the tailor explains, "In Égalité, every clothing shop has a tailor and an image consultant. Tailors are useful because they create clothes that fit each customer's unique body exactly. Before they cut any cloth, they obtain the customer's measurements to the nearest hundredth of a millimeter. Premade clothes, by contrast, even rack after rack of them, can provide only an imperfect fit. This is why Égalitéan clothing shops contain lots of cloth but no premade clothes."

The image consultant flings back her renegade lock of hair. She says, "An image consultant is useful because most people don't have the time to learn what clothes suit them best. I help my customers make good decisions. Take Blake, for example. He was here a few days ago. Doesn't he look fabulous?"

Blake twirls around, displaying his gray outfit. He likes the attention. I admit to the image consultant that he looks good.

The image consultant continues, teasingly, "Of course, not everyone seeks my services. For some people, looks don't matter much. This seems especially true of philosophers. Right, Safiya?"

Safiya blushes. She says, "I like my outfit. Yellow is a good color for philosophers. It symbolizes wisdom, enlightenment."

The image consultant replies, "But you look like you're ready for a toga party! Yellow's definitely not your color. You should wear cooler colors, such as lavender. These would go better with the sharp contrast between your dark hair and your light skin. For the sake of love, you don't have to wear yellow to look like a philosopher!"

"Maybe so," says Safiya. "Nonetheless, I think I'll stick with my robe."

"But what about salespeople?" I say, interrupting. "Who collects money from the customers? Is it one of you two?"

Safiya answers, "In Égalité, there are no salespeople, for the simple reason that nobody uses money. When we replaced capitalism with egalitarianism three centuries ago, businesses stopped seeking profits. Without the profit motive, money became unnecessary."

Blake interjects. "I've been in Égalité for a week, and I still don't understand your economic system. If you two girls don't make any money, what motivates you to do a good job? Or any job, for that matter?"

The tailor says, "I do a good job because I enjoy my work. I don't need a monetary incentive to do something I enjoy."

The image consultant says, "I agree with my partner. Our work is creative. When I look at you, for instance, I don't just see a person wearing a gray outfit. I see a work of art. I also see how much you enjoy your new look. These things give me great satisfaction. I don't need any further incentive to do a good job."

"Okay. Maybe you two enjoy your work," Blake says. "But surely some work in Égalité isn't creative or satisfying—mowing the community field, say, or waiting tables, or cleaning the dining hall. If people don't get paid for such work, why would they ever do it?"

"Actually," says Safiya, "our mower tells me he enjoys mowing the community field. He says it gives him a chance to think about things, to spend a little quality time with himself."

"Waiting tables, though, would be a horrible job. I'd never do that," says the tailor, making a face. "Luckily, nobody has to wait tables. Égalité has no restaurants. Everything we need is in the dining hall, and in the dining hall we serve ourselves."

"We do, however, have to clean the dining hall, and nobody finds that much fun," the image consultant says. "But people volunteer for the work readily enough. They do it in groups, so that the work goes quickly, and so that they can talk to each other. I often volunteer when Peacemaker is there. She tells stories about her childhood. Her stories are a lot like the latest village gossip: far-fetched, but just plausible enough to make people think there's a kernel of truth to them. I get a kick out of her—even if she dresses worse than Safiya does."

Ignoring the teasing, Safiya says, "As much as possible, we automate work that most people dislike. If we can't automate it, we divide it up. In this way, no one has to spend the bulk of her or his time doing what she or he dislikes. Thus, we've automated dishwashing, which nearly everybody hates, and we use a division of labor to clean the dining hall. We also educate our children to appreciate the social necessity of the less pleasant work that must be done. Our educational system is very effective."

"I don't know," I say. "It's hard for me to imagine loving work so much. I *like* working at my sporting goods store, but I don't *love* it. Sometimes it's boring. If I didn't get paid for my work, I don't think I'd do it."

"I'm with Philsbury," says Blake. "To get the most out of workers, you have to pay them."

"Perhaps," Safiya says, "you have a hard time imagining how creative and satisfying work can be because you live in a capitalist society. In your time, capitalists organized their businesses to maximize profits. Sometimes the way to maximize profits was to make work creative and interesting. But this wasn't always the case. Take assembly line production. Assembly lines proved highly profitable, but the work was repetitive and boring. In Égalité, production is organized differently. Instead of using a division of labor and automation to create profit, we use them to create enjoyable work. Creating enjoyable work, we've learned, satisfies interests better than does creating profit. If you stay in Égalité long enough, you'll see that this is so."

Blake snorts and rolls his eyes. "From what I've seen so far," he says, "Égalitéan egalitarianism is nothing more than communism. In the twentieth century, many people adopted communist ideals. Like you, they believed in equality and valued work. But communism wasn't exactly a smashing success. Capitalism beat it hands down. Égalité must suffer from the same defects that twentieth-century communist countries did."

Safiya says, "No. In many respects, egalitarianism differs from twentieth-century communism. In the first place, although communist nations of the twentieth century preached equality, they didn't practice it. They still had their poor and their wealthy—not, to be sure, wage-laborers and capitalists, as your capitalist society had, but instead peasants and members of the Communist Party. Égalité, by contrast, practices what it preaches. In Égalité, the interests of one individual are accorded the same value as the comparable interests of any other individual. Equality is a reality.

"In the second place, egalitarians preach a more thoroughgoing kind of equality than did twentieth-century communists. Some communists were openly sexist or racist, and most were openly speciesist. They preached equality for men, or for white people, or for all human beings, but almost never for all animals. Egalitarians are different. To be an egalitarian, one must advocate not only the principle of human equality, but also the principle of animal equality.

"There are other differences too. The next time we see Édouard, I'll ask him to tell you about them. As an economist, he knows more about communism than I do."

Blake snorts and rolls his eyes once more, but he says nothing. I also say nothing, but I don't snort or roll my eyes.

o o o

After the image consultant helps me make my choices, the tailor begins cutting cloth. She says she'll need about two hours to finish her work. In the meantime, Safiya, Blake, and I—and the dog—move to the dining hall to get some breakfast. The dog wolfs down her vegan meal—which looks and smells startlingly like dog food from my time—and then looks hopefully at Blake. Blake warns the dog to stay away from his home fries. He says that he's a meat and potatoes man, and, since he can't have meat, he'll at least have his fill of potatoes. Undeterred, the dog keeps an eye on Blake's plate.

Shortly after we start eating, Édouard and Franz join us. When Safiya tells Édouard that Blake was just asking about the differences between egalitarianism and communism, Édouard grins and—with his usual exaggerated enthusiasm, as if he's talking to a group of children—launches into an hour-long lecture on economics. It's like Sunday school all over again. Understanding scarcely a word of what he says, I keep myself occupied by rubbing the dog's belly. Once or twice, Blake tries to interrupt the monologue, but he can't get a word in edgewise. When Édouard finally runs out of steam, Franz announces, to no one in particular, "I love my Eddie—even though he multiplies words like bacteria in a Petri dish." Édouard blushes, and then, adjusting his oversized glasses, he replies, "I love my Franz—even though he has all the tact of a charging bull."

When we're finished with our breakfast, Safiya tells Édouard and Franz to go with love and wisdom, and then leads Blake and me—and the dog—back to the clothing shop. The tailor, chewing her gum at a frenetic pace, is still working on my new clothes. While we wait, I ask her partner whether Égalitéans ever wear leather or fur.

The image consultant says, "Never. We also avoid wool and silk, even though wool sweaters don't require the killing of any sheep and silk shirts don't require the killing of any silkworms. In our view, nonhuman animals should be treated as ends in themselves, not as mere means to human ends. Besides, human beings can dress warmly and stylishly without the use of leather, fur, wool, or silk. We have plenty of alternatives."

"Do you know anything about the use of animals for clothes in my time? How much or how little did these animals suffer?" I ask.

"I know a great deal," the image consultant says. The self-assurance with which she says this is partly lost when the renegade lock of hair falls across her face. "In your day, the use of nonhuman animals for their fur was especially controversial. In the United States alone, about four and a half million animals were killed each year for their fur. Furs were obtained in two ways: by trapping wild animals and, more commonly, by raising animals on fur farms."

Safiya interrupts. "Fur farms were similar to, though maybe slightly less horrifying than, the factory farms on which food animals were raised."

"That's right," the image consultant continues. "The most widely farmed fur animals were minks. In the wild, minks are solitary animals who range over hundreds of acres and love to swim. But on fur farms, they were crowded together in small cages. Under such conditions, they often mutilated themselves, biting their own skin, tails, or feet. When they reached a mere six months of age, they were slaughtered, struggling in vain as men wearing heavy gloves broke their necks and tossed them into pails. For a few minutes, they continued to wriggle as the men tossed more minks into the pails on top of them."

"Foxes were the second most widely farmed animals," Safiya says. "They lived, sometimes for several years, in cages less than one square meter, with up to four foxes per cage. Cages were often encrusted with dirt, fur, and excrement. Farmers had to kill the foxes without damaging their fur. Sometimes they would accomplish this by forcing the animals to inhale exhaust fumes from a truck. Other times they would insert a rod into the foxes' anuses and electrocute them."

"Trapping wild animals also caused suffering," says the image consultant. She reaches under a counter and brings out a foothold trap. "This is a relic from your time. I keep it here to help me teach my customers about the history of the clothing industry. Let me demonstrate."

The image consultant sets the trap and then touches the trigger with an ordinary wooden pencil. With a blur, the jaws of the trap clamp shut. The pencil snaps in two, the bottom half skittering across the floor of the clothing shop. The image consultant resets the trap and then touches the trigger with a sheet of plywood. Again, the jaws of the trap clamp shut. The plywood splinters. I imagine an animal stepping into the trap; I imagine myself caught in the trap. The pain must be excruciating.

"Why didn't trappers use padded traps?" I ask.

"Padded traps existed in your time," Safiya says. "But they were more expensive than unpadded traps and consequently were used less frequently."

"Suppose I want to use this trap to catch a coyote," I say. "How do I know that the animal that steps into the trap will be a coyote? Couldn't the trap catch a dog or some other animal instead?"

"Good question," says the image consultant. "Trappers varied the sizes of their foothold traps to catch only the kind of animal they wanted. Larger traps caught larger animals; smaller traps caught smaller animals. Despite this precaution, however, traps sometimes caught the wrong kind of animal. To the extent that this happened, animals suffered for no reason."

"Even when traps caught the right kind of animal," Safiya says, "the animal's fur was often severely damaged. Animals spent an average of fifteen hours, and could spend up to a week, caught in a trap before the trapper came by. During this time, some of the animals were attacked by other animals. The attack often damaged the fur of the trapped animals."

"Some trapped animals weren't attacked, but, in their desperate efforts to escape the trap, they frequently damaged their own fur," the image consultant says. "There were even reports of animals attempting to chew through their trapped leg."

"Trappers didn't always use foothold traps," Safiya says. "Other traps were available, such as the Conibear. The Conibear, used mostly to trap muskrats and beavers, was a body trap designed to fracture an animal's spinal column, so that the animal died quickly and with less suffering. Nonetheless, it normally took between three and eight minutes for the animal to die, and sometimes it took longer. All the commonly used traps caused at least some suffering."

"What about leather?" I ask. "Is wearing leather any better than wearing fur?"

"Not really," says Safiya. "Much of the leather that people wore, coming from cows and pigs, was a byproduct of the meat industry. You already know how food animals were raised and slaughtered. Every time you buy cowhide or pigskin, you support an industry that treats nonhuman animals abominably."

The image consultant says, "Some people wore more exotic skins. Sometimes goats were boiled alive to make kid gloves. Sometimes snakes and lizards were skinned alive in the belief that doing so resulted in more supple leather. Alligators were often raised in crowded sheds partially immersed in water. The water was polluted with rotting meat and the alligators' waste. Other animals didn't fare any better."

Blake, who has been listening quietly, can no longer contain himself. "I suppose Égalitéans wear faux fur and faux leather instead of the real thing. But isn't the real thing friendlier to the environment than are synthetic materials?"

The image consultant says, "Many synthetic materials—such as pleather, which is short for 'plastic leather'—are bad for the environment because they're not biodegradable. As much as possible, therefore, Égalitéans wear natural materials, such as cotton or linen. But we've also developed a number of biodegradable synthetic materials. These synthetic materials, however, bear little resemblance to fur or leather, since Égalitéans don't think it stylish to wear something that looks like a dead animal."

"Besides," says Safiya, "fur and leather were also bad for the environment. Furs were treated with chemicals to prevent them from biodegrading, and the tanning process kept leather from biodegrading. Furthermore, tanning and fur-making produced pollutants. Tanning in particular produced, among other pollutants, lime sludge, sulfides, and acids."

"And it gets worse," says the image consultant. "Tanneries produced arsenic and other carcinogens. Studies in your time found that workers in tanneries developed cancer at a twenty to fifty percent higher rate than the population at large."

"But doesn't the fur industry support Native Americans, many of whom trap for a living?" says Blake. "Since trapping and wearing fur are central to Native American cultures, wouldn't banning fur be tantamount to showing disrespect to Native Americans? Wouldn't it be a racist attitude, inconsistent with the Égalitéan principle of human equality?"

"The fur industry didn't support Native Americans; it exploited them," says the image consultant. "Native American trappers earned on average only between $200 and $300 per year from the sale of pelts. If the fur industry had truly wanted to support Native Americans, it would have helped them find alternative sources of income."

"Yesterday," Safiya says, "when we discussed vegetarianism, you defended meat-eating on the grounds that some cultures value meat. I replied that, insofar as a culture violates the principle of animal equality, we shouldn't respect that culture. No doubt, Native Americans were far less speciesist than the fur industry was. But insofar as they endorsed trapping, Native Americans were speciesist, and insofar as they were speciesist, we shouldn't respect them. Such a position isn't racist. It's the right thing to do."

"Can you say something about wool?" I say. "Do the sheep living in my time suffer as much as the animals from which people get fur and leather?"

"Sheep suffered more than most of your contemporaries realized," says the image consultant. "Consider, for example, the fate of merino sheep. Merino sheep were bred with wrinkled skin, because wrinkled skin, with its greater surface area, produced more wool than smooth skin. The wrinkled skin, however, rendered the sheep vulnerable to a potentially lethal condition called fly-strike. Blowflies laid their eggs in the moist folds of the sheep's skin, especially near the genitals, and when the eggs hatched the larvae started eating the sheep. Ranchers solved the problem with mulesing, the cutting away of the skin near the sheep's genitals. Mulesing was a painful procedure."

"So were other procedures that the sheep were forced to go through, including shearing," Safiya says. "The sharp razor that sheared off a sheep's wool also frequently cut the sheep's skin and damaged appendages, and a sheared sheep was more susceptible to sunburn and cold."

"When merino sheep no longer produced sufficiently high-quality wool," says the image consultant, "they were slaughtered for mutton."

Blake starts to object, but the tailor interrupts him. She announces that my clothes are ready. I try some of them on. They fit perfectly, and I like the way they look. The image consultant gazes at me with a critical eye and then smiles broadly. She says the sporty look suits me well and points out that the light colors and breathable fibers will keep me cool in the warm summer air. She adds that the light, warm colors complement the color of my hair and skin, and they match my gentle, soft-spoken demeanor.

Safiya says I look like a cuddly teddy bear. The tailor agrees and, with a wink, says that women love cuddly teddy bears. At this, Blake says to Safiya, "Looks like you have some competition."

Safiya ignores Blake. She smiles as she admires my new clothes.

Chapter 12
How Should People Treat Wild Animals?

The train rolls noiselessly out of the station. For several hundred yards it remains underground, but once outside the village it emerges into broad daylight. Safiya, Blake, and I—and the dog—are the only passengers aboard. We're finally on our way to the neighboring village where the Regional Planning Committee will meet.

Blake sits across from me, his legs sprawling in front of him. Pointing to the empty seats surrounding us, he comments that nobody else seems to be going to the meeting. Perhaps Égalitéans aren't so interested in politics? Safiya—who sits to my left and, in spite of the ample space in the compartment, presses her shoulder firmly against mine—replies that, on the contrary, Égalitéans are intensely interested in politics. Almost everyone from Safiya's village will participate in the meeting. Some are walking there; others will tune in via their PADs. We'd be walking too, Safiya continues, except that we're running late. We spent too much time at the clothing shop. Silently, I thank the tailor for taking her time with my clothes. I'm only too glad to have escaped the long, hot walk.

The dog stands on my lap, her front paws resting against my chest, so that she can peer out the window. I too peer out the window. The train is traveling inside a tube. The tube is transparent, allowing me to enjoy the view on the other side. I ask Safiya what the tube is for.

Safiya explains that the barrier, as Égalitéans call it, is designed to keep people and nonhuman animals away from the train tracks. In my time, automobiles struck a great many people, and an even larger number of nonhuman animals. Whereas the dead people were rightly considered tragic losses, the dead nonhuman animals were written off as mere roadkill. Such casualties appalled the founders of Égalité. To avoid them, they constructed a barrier around all train tracks. The barrier, Safiya adds, is transparent only from the inside. From the outside, it's opaque. Thus nonhuman animals standing on the outside are unable to see, and consequently are undisturbed by, passing trains.

I ask Safiya how people and animals are supposed to get from one side of the train tracks to the other. Doesn't the barrier restrict freedom of movement? No, Safiya says. At frequent intervals, the train tracks rise above the ground on small bridges. People and nonhuman animals can pass underneath.

It's interesting, I think to myself, how the vocabulary people invent reveals their values and biases. The term "roadkill" is a good example. Because it refers only to animals, the term suggests that animals and people belong to different categories. More than that, it suggests that animals belong to an inferior category. Roadkill may be repulsive, and it may be a nuisance to clean up, but, unlike a dead person, it can never be tragic. The term could catch on only in a speciesist society.

I've been driving for nearly half my life, and during that time I've run over three animals. Three instances of roadkill. Two of the animals were squirrels. The third was a groundhog. At least I think it was a groundhog. It's hard to be sure because I was driving at night. I passed over the crest of a hill, going sixty miles an hour. The speed limit was fifty-five. The groundhog—or whatever it was—was on the yellow line that ran down the middle of the road. It started to move to the other side of the road but, sensing an oncoming truck, reversed direction and ran directly into the front driver's side wheel of my car. I couldn't get out of the animal's way. I had time only to lift my foot from the gas pedal. After I hit the animal, I felt bad, but I never thought of the episode as a tragedy. I guess I had internalized the values and biases of my speciesist society.

Safiya takes her oboe from its pocket and entertains us with a melody taken from the second movement of Tchaikovsky's First Symphony. Titled "Somber Land, Misty Land," the second movement captures the feel of a Russian winter landscape. The melody is hauntingly beautiful, full of yearning. Then, as the train passes through a meadow dotted with the yellows and reds and blues of summer wildflowers, Safiya improvises a variation on Tchaikovsky's melody. The improvisation too is beautiful, but in a different way. It's verdant and joyfully serene. Safiya is trying to capture the feel of the meadow we're passing through. I suggest calling the piece "Heavenly Land, Colorful Land." Blake mutters that the music is a little *too* heavenly for his taste. From where he sits, heaven on earth is a contradiction in terms. He suggests calling the piece "Heavenly Land, Phony Land."

Setting down her oboe, Safiya gazes at the meadow outside, concern etched on her face. "Maybe the land isn't so heavenly," she says. Blake and I turn our heads in the direction of Safiya's gaze. In the distance, where the meadow merges with the surrounding forest, lies a tangle of twisted and toppled trees, a scab on the face of the earth. When Safiya asks her PAD what caused the damage, the androgynous voice replies that, during yesterday's storm, a tornado touched down at that spot. At one time, I think to myself, tornadoes in the area were unheard of. The first one—and the only one in my lifetime—came two days after my twenty-eighth birthday, tearing up the northern part of town, near the Dinosaur Eggs. The aberration was the talk of the town for weeks. But was the tornado an aberration? Or was it the start of a trend? Once again, I wonder whether the past has intruded into the future. Is my generation—a generation that knows about global warming, yet continues to contribute to it—responsible for the ugly scab I see before me? Like a judge reading out the charges against a defendant, Safiya's PAD lists the numbers of animals, species by species, that the tornado killed, injured, and displaced. A tear traces a crooked path down Safiya's cheek.

o o o

Like Safiya's village, the neighboring village has an underground train station, underground shops, and, directly above these, a dining hall. The dining hall is larger than its counterpart in Safiya's village, but it's packed with people nonetheless. Safiya, Blake, and I—and the dog—are sitting at a table in the middle of the throng. I'm trying to enjoy my lunch—pasta and artichoke in a tomato sauce, with crushed cashews sprinkled on top—but passersby keep inadvertently bumping against me. I feel vaguely like a hen in a battery cage.

Everyone is here for the big meeting. At one end of the dining hall, five people step up to a dais and take seats. Four of the five people I don't know. The fifth, sitting in the middle, is Peacemaker. As usual, she wears a T-shirt displaying a message. Today's message reads "I ♥ ARTICHOKES." Swallowing a mouthful of her salad and ginger dressing, Safiya tells Blake and me that the Regional Planning Committee consists of those five people. Peacemaker, who chairs the committee, represents Safiya's village. Each of the other four represents one of the remaining four villages in the region. The Regional Planning Committee is the closest thing the area has to a government.

Banging a gavel, Peacemaker calls the meeting to order. A few stragglers quickly find seats, and all talking immediately ceases. Peacemaker announces that two visitors from the past—Blake and I— are present at the meeting. After warmly welcoming us, she explains how the Regional Planning Committee functions. When a villager uncovers a problem that the region faces or has a proposal to improve the region, she or he contacts the Regional Planning Committee. The members of the committee discuss the problem or proposal until they're ready to make a recommendation. Peacemaker then calls a meeting, such as the one we're attending, where the recommendation is formally advanced, publicly debated, possibly modified, and voted on. All adult residents have the right to vote. Children and visitors, such as Blake and I, can't vote, but we're permitted to speak if we're so moved. Anyone who wishes to speak must either raise a hand or send a signal through Peacemaker's PAD, and then wait until Peacemaker recognizes her or him.

With these introductory remarks out of the way, Peacemaker turns to the first of the two items on the agenda. Several residents have complained about black bears. In the last fifteen years, the population of black bears in the region has increased by nearly thirty percent. Some villagers worry that this increase will destabilize an already fragile ecosystem, thereby threatening the interests of human and nonhuman animals alike. Other residents worry that sooner or later a black bear will attack a human being. Of course, an attack is unlikely as long as people wear their PADs, since PADs warn of approaching dangers. However, some people, especially children, sometimes forget to wear their PADs. These people are vulnerable.

Peacemaker states that the committee seriously considered three responses to these worries: first, relocate excess bears; second, give some bears food laced with a substance that renders them unable to reproduce but otherwise leaves them unharmed; third, continue to monitor the population of the bears but take no other action. After a spirited discussion of the pros and cons of each response, the committee unanimously agreed to recommend the first response. Peacemaker carefully explains the reasoning that led to the committee's recommendation. Then she invites discussion from the audience.

Several people raise their hands. Several more, who aren't in the dining hall, send signals through Peacemaker's PAD. Peacemaker calls on the mower from Safiya's village, the man who resembles the first officer from the science fiction program. He reminds the committee of Égalité's noninterference directive. Interfering with the course of nature, he says, usually makes matters worse, not better. Everyone knows, for example, of the disaster that took place a year ago in the Galapagos Islands. Relocating black bears could, for all anyone knows, be equally disastrous. What if the relocated bears destroy the habitat of another species? What if they eat the same food that another species eats? The other species might not survive. No, the mower concludes, it's best to let nature take care of itself. He supports the third response: continue to monitor the population of the bears but take no other action.

One of the committee members, who keeps the same watchful eye over the audience that my second grade teacher—what was her name? Ms. Harmon?—kept over her students, responds to the mower. She says that the committee is well aware of the noninterference directive and points out that, as useful as the directive is, it admits of exceptions. The committee carefully looked at several regions where excess bears might be relocated. It consulted eminent environmentalists, including Charlie Perkins-Goodman, as well as models produced by PADs. One region—about three hundred kilometers to the north—proved particularly promising, posing little risk to either the black bears or other species.

At this point, Peacemaker calls on Charlie Perkins-Goodman to testify. Stepping up to the dais and speaking in a quiet voice, Charlie defends the committee's recommendation. He outlines the causes of the increase in the bears' population, and explains how an understanding of these causes informed his support for relocation of some of the bears. Unlike Édouard, he doesn't multiply words like bacteria in a Petri dish. In less than five minutes, he returns to his seat.

Peacemaker calls on other people. Some are from Safiya's village; others are from other villages. Some of them, following the mower's lead, defend the third response. A few prefer the second. Most, however, agree with the committee; they support relocating some of the bears. Finally, Blake raises his hand. Peacemaker gives him the floor.

"For the last half hour," Blake says, "I've been hearing you all debate about which of three courses of action to take: relocate some of the bears, sterilize some of the bears, or do nothing. But these aren't the only alternatives. I'd like to suggest a fourth course of action. I think it's better than any of the other three."

"What fourth course of action would you like us to consider?" Peacemaker asks.

"Hunt some of the bears," Blake says.

Several gasps and murmurs reverberate through the dining hall. With a scowl, Peacemaker bangs her gavel. "Order!" she says.

"Speakers are not to be interrupted. The next person who interrupts Blake will find my sneaker print on his or her backside!"

Peacemaker glares at the audience, as if daring them to utter so much as a peep. When everyone keeps quiet, Blake continues: "I'm serious. Hunting prevents species from becoming overpopulated, and some people enjoy hunting. At least in my time they did. You should try it. You might like it too. There's nothing like a good hike through the forest on a clear morning, communing with nature, testing one's mettle against the speed and strength of an animal. Many hunters, including myself, find hunting to be a spiritual activity. It gives us a deeper understanding and appreciation of the cycles of nature, reminding us that death is the inevitable end of life and that some die so that others may live. As the Spanish philosopher José Ortega y Gasset puts it, hunters often experience a 'mystical union with the animal.' Besides, hunting the bears has got to be cheaper than relocating or sterilizing them."

"If I understand you correctly," Peacemaker says, "you support hunting some of the bears on a combination of four grounds: that hunting them prevents them from becoming overpopulated, that some people would enjoy hunting them, that hunting them would have spiritual value, and that hunting them is cheaper than other courses of action. Is this a fair statement of your position?"

"Yes," Blake says. "You understand me perfectly."

"Would anyone care to respond to Blake's arguments?" Peacemaker says.

Hands wave in the air like a field of grass blowing in the wind. Peacemaker calls on a young boy, aged six or seven, sitting at the table right in front of mine. It's the boy who reminds me of Gus Sherwood, the second-grader whom Chaz punched at the zoo so that Blake and I could slip away to the tiger's cage. Confident and articulate, the boy says, "Blake's logic is flawed. Even if hunting is one way to understand and appreciate the cycles of nature, it isn't the only way. It can't be, because I've never hunted, yet I know all about the cycles of nature. I learned about them in school. I'm glad I didn't have to kill any nonhuman animals so that I could learn about the cycles of nature."

Peacemaker's PAD produces a holographic image of an elderly man sitting in his quarters. The man says, "Blake is being disingenuous. If he's from the past, he's almost certainly a speciesist, and by definition speciesists have no interest in experiencing a union, mystical or otherwise, with nonhuman animals. To the contrary, they seek to distance themselves from nonhuman animals, asserting the superiority of human beings. It seems to me that, if Blake really wanted to experience a union with nonhuman animals, he could do no better than to adopt the principle of animal equality."

A tall, imposing woman says, "I don't understand what hunters enjoy about hunting. Do they enjoy, as Blake suggests, hiking through the forest on a clear morning and communing with nature? But they can do these things without hunting. Or do they, as Blake also suggests, enjoy testing their mettle against the speed and strength of nonhuman animals? But then why hunt rather than, say, play with a dog or run a hundred meter dash against a horse? Perhaps hunters enjoy hitting things with bullets. But if this is what they enjoy, they could shoot at bull's-eyes rather than at bulls. I suspect that what hunters really enjoy is killing. But receiving enjoyment from the death of another is morally repugnant. Surely people can find something more wholesome to enjoy than that."

"I don't know much about economics," says another woman, "but even if hunting bears would use up fewer resources than would the alternatives, the alternatives are morally better. Relocated or sterilized bears can still satisfy most of their interests. Dead bears can't."

Charlie Perkins-Goodman advances an ecofeminist critique of hunting. He argues that in my time hunters were overwhelmingly men and that hunting was primarily about machismo, the display of masculine power. Hunting had precious little to do with economic well-being, environmental health, or spiritual development—despite the rhetoric that Ortega y Gasset and other hunters used. The rhetoric that hunters used was merely a cover for baser motives, an artful attempt to lend legitimacy to a practice that had none.

Blake whispers in my ear, "Come on, Philsbury! Help me out. They're all ganging up on me."

I, however, don't know how to defend hunting against the powerful Égalitéan objections. Nor do I particularly want to defend hunting. I've never hunted, and I've only gone fishing once. My dad took me when I was ten years old. I swatted a lot of mosquitoes, but I didn't catch any fish. I was extremely bored. It seems to me that hunting is likely just as boring as fishing. Therefore, instead of supporting Blake, I merely shrug my shoulders. Blake shakes his head reproachfully.

Soon Peacemaker calls for a vote. Most people vote for relocating some of the black bears. Nobody—not even one Égalitéan—agrees with Blake.

After a short recess, Peacemaker turns to the second item on the agenda. As she speaks, I enjoy a bowl of fresh raspberries. I offer a raspberry to the dog. To my surprise, she gobbles it up. I didn't know that dogs ever ate berries. In a low whisper, I ask Safiya if raspberries, like chocolate, are poisonous to dogs. Safiya thanks me for my concern but assures me that raspberries are fine.

Blake's chair is empty. During the recess, he said he'd had his fill of Égalitéan politics. He was going to take a walk along the lake and maybe take a dip. I asked if he'd like some company, but he said he'd rather be alone for a while. He'd rejoin Safiya and me once the meeting was over.

The second item on the agenda concerns a missing stun gun. The stun gun is one of those defensive weapons Safiya told me about, the kind that can stun an attacking animal without harming it. Stun guns are also used when rescuing injured animals and relocating overpopulated animals. Stun guns will be used, for example, when relocating the black bears. Such weapons, however, are rarely needed. For this reason, only two stun guns exist in the entire region. Both are stored in the village up by the Dinosaur Eggs. That is where the missing stun gun was last seen.

Peacemaker announces that an investigation is underway. The investigators have determined that the weapon was stolen. Gazing at the audience through the trifocals perched on the tip of her nose, Peacemaker repeats the word "stolen." The word causes a collective gasp of astonishment to erupt in the dining hall.

"Stolen?" a flabbergasted member of the audience exclaims. "Such a thing is unthinkable. Égalitéans don't steal. What makes the investigators think the stun gun was stolen?"

Peacemaker explains that there are only two possibilities. Either the stun gun was stolen or it was misplaced. But it couldn't have been misplaced. If it had been misplaced, anyone's PAD should have been able to locate it. But when the investigators asked their PADs where the stun gun was, their PADs replied that that information wasn't available. No. Somebody must have stolen the weapon.

"But shouldn't a PAD be equally able to locate the stun gun if it was stolen?" the flabbergasted member of the audience says.

Peacemaker answers that a PAD would be fully capable of locating a stolen item, unless the thief took precautions. Hiding something in such a way that a PAD can't locate it isn't easy, but it's possible. If a thief is clever enough, she or he could pull it off. This must be what happened to the stun gun. There's no alternative explanation.

Another member of the audience, equally flabbergasted, asks, "Why would anyone go to such lengths to steal a stun gun? What's the motive?"

Peacemaker says that at this point the investigators have no motive, and no suspects. They have no leads of any kind. They've asked the Regional Planning Committee to recommend taking no action until they complete their investigation. After careful consideration, the Regional Planning Committee unanimously agreed.

A debate over gun control ensues. It begins with a holographic image of a woman sitting at a picnic table urging that stun guns be abolished. "Who knows," she says, "what the thief is capable of? How do we know, for example, that the thief won't use the stun gun to render people unconscious and then rape them?"

"Guns don't rape," retorts a young man sitting behind me; "people rape."

"True enough," the holographic woman shoots back. "But people can rape far more easily with a gun than without one."

"Maybe so," the young man says. "But people can also rape more easily with a knife or a length of clothesline. Do you suggest we abolish these as well? Where are we to draw the line?"

The debate continues, but I stop listening. I think about the missing fireworks in Safiya's village. Were they, too, stolen? If so, who stole them, and for what purpose? Are the missing fireworks in some way linked to the missing stun gun? How might they be linked? The mystery worries me. Maybe Égalité isn't as utopian as it appears. Maybe Égalité isn't a future that people from my time should strive to realize.

A vote is taken, but I pay no attention to the outcome.

o o o

As Safiya and I stroll toward the lake, the dog picks up a small branch that last night's storm tore from a tree. I take the branch from the dog's mouth, strip off the few leaves that cling to it, and toss it ahead of me. When the dog chases it down and brings it back to me, I toss it ahead of me again. Safiya and I laugh with delight as the dog, nothing more than a white blur, races after the stick again. The two of us seem to enjoy the game as much as the dog does.

When we reach the lake, Blake is nowhere to be seen. I inspect the lake carefully. Although it has the same hourglass shape that it did in my time, it's otherwise unrecognizable. In my time, the lake was crowded with sunbathers and swimmers, cottages and motorboats. By contrast, three centuries later, the human presence is scarcely noticeable. In the distance are a sailboat and a canoe. Nearby are a beach and a dock. Two people are swimming. A third, the young boy who reminds me of Gus Sherwood, is skipping stones. The boy is good at it, better than I am, and maybe as good as Blake is. I count the skips of a stone: one two three four five six seven eight nine ten eleven twelve thirteen fourteen. The boy lets fly another stone. I count again: one two three four five six seven eight nine ten eleven twelve thirteen fourteen fifteen sixteen.

Safiya and I have already changed into our swimwear. Safiya is stunning. Her one-piece suit—creamy yellow, of course—reveals a feminine as well as athletic body that the robe she usually wears keeps hidden. Standing next to her, with my bulging stomach and flabby arms and legs, I feel self-conscious. My self-consciousness, however, gradually fades, because my out-of-shape body doesn't bother Safiya. With one arm wrapped affectionately around my ample waist, she sets her beloved oboe down on the beach towel that she brought with her and leads me into the water.

When we're in up to our knees, something brushes against my ankle, something soft and feathery. What's that? Is it Safiya's foot? I look down into the clear water. No. It's a fish. I see lots of fish. The lake is teeming with them. When I was a young boy, as young as the boy skipping stones, the lake had a few fish. I remember them floating on the surface of the water. My dad explained to me that they were dead. When I asked him why they were dead, he said because the lake was polluted. Too many people were riding in motorboats. The motorboats left an oily slick on the water. A few years later, I stopped seeing floating fish. I didn't see any fish at all. The motorboats had killed all of them. My dad was sad, because he sometimes liked to go fishing.

I ask Safiya if Égalitéans ever go fishing. She says no, just as Égalitéans don't hunt, so also they don't fish. Safiya and I wade farther from the shore. We're now in up to our waists. The cool water is soothing. I begin to relax. The dog stands at the edge of the lake, cocking her head as she looks at us.

"But surely," I say, "fishing isn't as bad as hunting. When my dad went fishing, he never killed any fish. He simply caught them and then returned them to the water. What could be wrong with that?"

"Even catching fish and returning them to the water causes the fish discomfort. In the first place, the fish are dragged out of the water with hooks in their mouths. In the second place, during the time that the fish are out of the water, they can't breathe. Have you noticed that fish struggle when they're caught? Isn't their struggle a sign that they don't like being caught?"

"I don't know. My dad once told me that fish can't feel pain. Their brains are too primitive. Was he wrong about that? How can we know?"

"Yes, your dad was wrong. Even in your time, the scientific evidence was clear. There was, for instance, an interesting—albeit ethically dubious—study in which rainbow trout had bee venom and acetic acid injected into their lips. In response, the fish engaged in a rocking motion and rubbed their lips against the gravel at the bottom of their tank. When the fish were injected with morphine, they abandoned these behaviors and resumed feeding. The experimenters concluded that the bee venom and acetic acid caused pain and that the morphine relieved the pain.

"Other studies revealed that fish have many cognitive abilities that go beyond the ability to feel pain. For example, fish can remember events that took place months earlier, they can learn by observing other fish, they can cooperate with other fish to catch food, and they can know their social rank."

"Can all animals feel pain?" I ask. Safiya and I are now in the lake up to our chests. I luxuriate in the water, letting myself relax completely—perhaps for the first time since my arrival in Égalité.

"Possibly not. Yesterday, for instance, I mentioned that some Égalitéans eat bivalves, such as clams and mussels. They do so because, in their view, bivalves can't feel pain. Presumably, they claim, bivalves aren't conscious at all. If they're not conscious, they can't have preferences, any more than a stone can have preferences. Without preferences, they can't have preference-interests, and so we need not take their preference-interests into consideration."

"But didn't you tell me that, when we're deliberating about what to do, we should consider not only preference-interests but also welfare-interests?"

"That's right. We should consider not only what individuals prefer but also what's good for them. Even if bivalves have no preference-interests, they do have welfare-interests, since some things are good for them while other things are bad for them. Thus, although some Égalitéans eat bivalves, no Égalitéan believes that we may do anything we want to bivalves. For example, no Égalitéan would claim that we may stomp on a mussel just because we'd like to hear the sound of its shell crack."

"Aren't plants in the same category as bivalves? Even if they lack preference-interests, don't they have welfare-interests?"

"Correct. Just as Égalitéans consider the welfare-interests of bivalves, so we consider the welfare-interests of plants. The practical implications of this view are complex and vigorously debated. Égalitéans, however, widely agree that we may eat plants, and that eating plants is better than eating most animals, since most animals have both welfare- and preference-interests."

The water laps at my chin. Safiya, who's about four inches shorter than I am, can no longer touch the sandy bottom with her feet. She treads water, her arms and legs moving gracefully, rhythmically, effortlessly. In silence, we gaze into each other's eyes. Then, without warning, Safiya wraps her arms and legs around me and kisses me on the lips. The kiss is passionate. Caught off guard, I lose my balance. Safiya and I sink below the surface. Air bubbles tickle my face as Safiya, still kissing me, exhales. By the time I regain my balance and we rise above the surface, I'm kissing back. I feel Safiya's heart thumping as her chest presses tightly against mine.

A sound reaches my ears. The sound comes from the shore. Barking. The dog is barking. Breaking off the kiss but still embracing me, Safiya looks toward the shore. With a disappointed sigh, she tells me that she thinks the dog needs to relieve herself. She tells me further that she'll take the dog to the designated area and that I should stay right where I am. She'll be back in a jiff.

Safiya releases me from her embrace, swims to the shore, and disappears with the dog. I stand in the lake, the water gently lapping at my chin. I'm thunderstruck. I'm not sure just what Safiya's intentions are, but she obviously likes me. And I like her. I'm happy. Yes. *I'm happy!* I take a moment to let this knowledge sink in. *I'm happy.*

I turn toward the shore, where Safiya disappeared with the dog. Then I turn away from the shore, surveying the lake. Égalité is beautiful. I forget about the missing fireworks and the missing stun gun. A thought enters my head. What would it be like to live in Égalité? Would Safiya and the others allow me to stay with them? What would I do if I stayed? Would I be happier here than I would in my own time? No. I could never live in Égalité. The idea is crazy; I shouldn't even be thinking about it. Yet I continue to think about it. The idea puts a smile on my face.

Without warning, pain explodes in the back of my head. I lose my balance and sink below the surface. Air bubbles tickle my face as I exhale. I try to regain my balance, but I can't. I lose consciousness.

Chapter 13
Is Anything Wrong with Zoos?

I'm lying on my back. Massive pain engulfs my head, but even worse is the pain in my lungs. I must have taken a lungful of water. I try to inhale, but I get little oxygen. The attempt makes me cough and choke. Water dribbles out of my mouth and nose. I wonder if fish feel a similar pain when they suffocate on the deck of a fisherman's boat.

Kneeling over me, Blake shouts frantically into his PAD. He says I'm bleeding from the back of my head and need immediate medical attention. A reedy voice emanating from Blake's PAD says to calm down and asks what happened. Still frantic, Blake says he and I are on the beach. On his way back from a walk, he saw me standing neck-deep in the lake. He was about to shout hello when for no apparent reason I disappeared below the surface. He managed to fish me out of the lake, and since then he's been trying to resuscitate me.

I still can't get enough oxygen into my lungs. I black out.

o o o

I'm still on the beach, but now I'm lying on my side. Fingers probe the back of my head. The pain is awful. Most of the water, at least, is out of my lungs. I take deep, ragged breaths.

A few feet in front of me, Safiya, holding the dog with one hand and her oboe with the other, sits in the sand. Tears tumble from her eyes. She looks gravely worried. Standing behind her, Blake places a sympathetic hand on her shoulder. He rubs the hand awkwardly against the creamy yellow fabric of Safiya's swimsuit.

From behind me, a reedy voice announces that I was struck by a rock.

"A rock?" Blake exclaims. He removes his hand from Safiya's shoulder. A creamy yellow thread is caught between two of his fingers. He places his hand in his pants pocket. "Somebody threw a rock at Philsbury?"

"I saw a boy skipping stones. August. But I can't imagine he did it!" Safiya says.

The reedy voice says, "I need someone to find the rock that struck Phil. I mean to get to the bottom of this!"

The pain in my head is too much. I black out again.

○ ○ ○

I'm still lying on my side, but now I'm in a stretcher, riding on a train. Behind me, fingers work deftly on my head. In front of me sit Safiya and Blake. They're arguing.

"You saw the rock," Safiya says to Blake, clutching the dog with one hand and her oboe with the other. "It's too big and round. There's no way August tried to skip that rock."

"Maybe," says Blake, "the boy wasn't trying to skip it. Maybe he threw it at Philsbury on purpose."

"On purpose!" Safiya exclaims. "I'll never believe that. August is a good boy. He wouldn't hurt a fly."

"But if the boy didn't throw the rock, who did? The only other two people I saw were swimming, and, unless their arms are a lot stronger than mine, they were too far away."

Safiya thinks about this. Then, adjusting the swimsuit she's still wearing, she says, "I don't know who threw the rock. It doesn't make sense. Égalitéans don't do such things."

From behind me, a reedy voice breaks in. "Égalitéans also don't steal stun guns. Yet apparently one did."

"Stun guns? What's this about stun guns?" Blake asks.

"Somebody stole a stun gun from a village to the north," Safiya says. "That doesn't make sense either."

"Well, well, well!" says Blake with a grim smile. "Could it be? Something rotten in the state of Égalité?"

A wave of dizziness overwhelms me. I black out one more time.

○ ○ ○

I'm back in Safiya's village, in the bed in my quarters, lying on my side. Peacemaker is sitting in the plush chair, which someone has moved from the desk to the side of the bed. The dog is snoozing next to me. No one else is in the room.

"Good evening, son!" says Peacemaker in her reedy voice. I try to speak, but Peacemaker places a gnarled finger over her withered lips. "Hush! You just rest while I do the talking. First of all, you're going to be fine. You suffered a blow to the head. You have a concussion and eight stitches, but there's no permanent damage. I've removed the fluid from your lungs, and I've given you something to relieve the pain in your head. You'll need to take it easy for the next few days."

Peacemaker leans back in the chair, gathering her thoughts. At length, she says, "It appears, son, that somebody threw a rock at you, possibly on purpose. I've called for an investigation, but it may take time to complete it. In the meantime, I'm going to have someone accompany you at all times, someone both of us trust. Tonight, while you sleep, I'll be with you. I'll be with you the whole night. Tomorrow, Safiya and Blake will take over. For the remainder of your stay in Égalité, no one is going to harm you. I give you my word."

Exhausted, I soon fall asleep.

o o o

A clammy fog grips the zoo like a shroud. I step up to the tiger's cage. At least I think it's the tiger's cage. I don't see the tiger, though. I don't see anything at all. The fog is too thick. I pace from one end of the cage to the other, back and forth, half a dozen paces in one direction and half a dozen paces in the other direction. I press my face against the bars of the cage. I still see nothing.

Two soprano voices are nearby. I turn this way and that, but the fog prevents me from seeing who's there. The two voices might belong to young boys, or they might belong to young girls—I can't tell.

One voice says, "I dunno. Maybe tigers don't roar. Maybe they don't make any sound at all."

The other voice says, "Tigers do so roar, and I'm gonna prove it."

Without warning, pain explodes in the back of my head. One of the children has just thrown a rock at me. I turn to my left, but before I can take half a dozen steps, I run into a set of bars. Another rock bounces off my back. I turn to my right, but again I run into a set of bars. What's going on? Why can't I get out of here? Then it dawns on me. *I'm* the tiger, and I'm *inside* the cage! When a third rock strikes my shoulder, I retreat to the back of the cage.

The two children step closer to the cage. At first I discern only shadowy figures, but when the fog begins to lift I see that the two children aren't children at all. They're Safiya and Blake, speaking in soprano voices! Each accuses the other of throwing the rocks. When

Safiya protests that Égalitéans would never do such a thing, Blake retorts, "Right! Just as Égalitéans would never steal a stun gun!"

∘ ∘ ∘

I open one eye a crack. Darkness. It must be the dead of night. Am I still in my quarters? Yes, I'm in my quarters, lying on my side, the dog curled up next to me. In front of me, so close I could touch her, is Peacemaker, seated on the plush chair, her head thrown back and mouth agape. Beyond the walls of my quarters, providing harmonic accompaniment to Peacemaker's soft, melodic snoring, is the chirruping of a chorus of crickets.

My body pleads with me to go back to sleep. Under normal circumstances, I'd heed my body's pleas, but, having been struck with a rock, perhaps intentionally, I feel the tug of a matter more urgent than sleep. Fumbling, I grip my PAD between thumb and forefinger and, so as not to wake Peacemaker, address it in a bare whisper.

During the meeting of the Regional Planning Committee, Peacemaker said that, although it's not easy, it's possible to prevent PADs from being able to locate an object. How did the thief who stole the stun gun pull it off? My hypothesis is that she or he used her or his own PAD to hack into or disrupt other PADs. Would I be able to do the same thing? With some tinkering around, I think I would. I'm starting to feel comfortable with the PAD Safiya gave me—PADs are similar to computers and I know my way around computers. Maybe all those hours, starting in my early childhood, that I've spent on my computer socializing, playing games, and snooping around will prove not to be the waste of time my dad insisted they were.

∘ ∘ ∘

At last! Today is July 4, the Égalitéan tricentennial. As soon as the early morning fog lifts, the celebration begins. Safiya and I, along with other spectators, are sitting along the edge of the community field. We're about to watch an athletic event. I hold the dog tight against me, because she keeps trying to run onto the field to join the athletes.

I feel much better than I did yesterday. My headache is gone, and I'm breathing normally. The festive atmosphere puts me at ease. As the athletes warm up, I ask Safiya about zoos.

Safiya says that Égalité has no zoos. "The problem with zoos," she explains, "is that they confine nonhuman animals. In your time, the enclosures confining zoo animals were sometimes smaller and sometimes larger. To their credit, some zoos spent considerable sums of money to provide comfortable habitats for their animals. Nonetheless, a cage, no matter how large, is still a cage. Confined animals tend to have greater difficulty satisfying their interests than do free animals. Thus in Égalité there's a presumption against confinement."

"A presumption, you say? Under the right circumstances, presumptions can be overridden. Do Égalitéans believe, then, that confining animals is sometimes justified?"

"Of course—just as confining human beings is sometimes justified. Suppose, for instance, that an epidemic breaks out, or that we find a dangerous psychopath in our midst. Wouldn't we be within our rights to quarantine the sick? Wouldn't we be within our rights to lock up the psychopath until he or she's no longer dangerous? In general, Égalitéans believe that we may confine a human being, or a nonhuman animal, if doing so results in the greatest possible satisfaction of interests."

"So if an animal is injured, Égalitéans might confine it in an animal hospital until it heals?"

"Exactly. Similarly, when we relocate the black bears, we'll put them on a train. This too is a temporary but justified confinement."

"What, then, about zoos? Don't zoos satisfy a great many interests—nonhuman as well as human? In particular, they entertain visitors, they educate people about animals, they support scientific research, and they help preserve endangered species. Taken together, these four points seem to weigh heavily in favor of zoos."

As I say this, the athletic event begins. The event isn't a competition. Égalitéans dislike competition; they prefer cooperation. Thus the athletes on the field, ten altogether, form a single team. The object of the game is to keep a holographic ball inbounds—that is, within a large square drawn on the community field. The holographic ball—moving slowly at first but gradually picking up more and more speed—bounces off holographic barriers that move randomly inside the large square. Each athlete carries a paddle similar in size and shape to a tennis racket. If the ball threatens to bounce outside the large square, one of the athletes must block it with his or her paddle. Five of the athletes are men; the other five are women. One of the men is

Blake. Blake asked to participate because he wanted to prove that, as a meat-eater, he's more athletic than any Égalitéan.

Safiya says, "The four points in favor of zoos that you mention—amusement, education, research, and preservation—are probably the most important ones. Égalitéans, however, find them unconvincing."

"Why is that?"

The spectators cheer as one of the athletes stretches to block the ball from going out of bounds.

"Let's take them one at a time," Safiya says. "The argument that zoos are justified because they provide amusement is no better than the argument that meat-eating is justified because meat tastes good. The other day, we saw why the latter argument fails. First, the animals people eat suffer and die. Second, people can eat delicious food without eating meat. The former argument fails for similar reasons. First, the animals who entertain people at zoos often suffer, and sometimes die, as a result of their confinement. Second, people can amuse themselves without going to zoos. Clearly, whatever amusement zoos provide doesn't bring about the greatest possible satisfaction of interests."

"How do you know that zoo animals often suffer, and sometimes die, from their confinement?"

"We know because in your time studies were conducted in zoos. For example, polar bears who were confined in zoos spent a quarter of their time pacing back and forth, and their infant mortality rate was sixty-five percent. In contrast, during the late 1980s and early 1990s, the infant mortality rate of polar bears who lived in the wild was thirty-five percent—though fifteen years later, as global warming increasingly impacted the Arctic Circle, infant mortality in the wild increased to fifty-seven percent. Many other species confined in zoos also showed high levels of lethargy or repetitive behaviors, as well as high infant mortality rates and shortened life spans. A lot depended on the species, carnivores faring especially poorly."

I think about the tiger I saw when I was in the second grade. I remember its pacing. I remember the smell of its feces. The tiger must have suffered.

The holographic ball bounces toward Blake. As Blake runs to block the ball with his paddle, he slips on the dewy grass and falls to his knees. He makes a valiant effort but gets only the very tip of his paddle on the ball. The ball still threatens to bounce out of bounds. Coming out of nowhere, another athlete makes a brilliant diving save. The spectators roar like tigers. Jumping to her feet, the athlete who made the save helps Blake get up and then returns to her position.

"All right," I say. "Amusement probably isn't the most powerful argument for zoos. But what about the educational role zoos play? Isn't this a better argument?"

"No. It's also unconvincing. In the first place, although in your time employees at zoos often attempted to educate visitors about nonhuman animals, their attempts met with little success. Have you ever been to a zoo?"

"Yes. I visited a zoo when I was in the second grade, and then again a couple of years ago."

"What education about nonhuman animals did you receive?"

"I remember that my second grade teacher told us about the animals we saw."

"What do you remember your teacher saying?"

I think for a moment and then confess, "Not much. But that was a long time ago. When I visited a couple of years ago, I saw signs outside the enclosures containing information about the animals."

"Did you read the signs?"

My face turns red. "No, I didn't."

"Did you see other people read the signs?"

"Not many. Some did."

"Did the signs provide much information?"

"They didn't appear to. The signs were pretty small."

"How long did you spend at any one enclosure? Did you observe any animals carefully for a prolonged time?"

"Not really. I spent the longest time with the tiger. That was about five minutes."

"What about other people? Did they spend more time observing animals than you did?"

"Not that I noticed."

"So what did you learn at the zoo?"

"I remember that the animals were lethargic. Most of them didn't do anything."

"Do you think animals in the wild also tend to be lethargic?"

"I'm sorry. I don't know."

"Your experience, I'm afraid, is typical. Most people who visited zoos learned very little. They were more interested in amusement than in education. But this isn't the only problem. The other problem is that, even if zoos had been effective educators, there were other ways to educate people about nonhuman animals. In your time, for example, people could have watched nature programs on television or the Internet. In my time, children are taught about nonhuman animals at school, and people use their PADs to observe animals in the wild. We don't need zoos to educate people."

By now, the holographic ball has increased its speed. It whizzes about the playing field, little more than a blur as it bounces off paddles and holographic barriers. The athletes run to and fro at a frenzied pace. Whereas Blake's chest heaves as he tries to keep up, the other athletes look remarkably fresh.

"But aren't zoos useful for conducting research?" I say. "I'm not talking about research that harms animal participants. Peacemaker has already explained to me that Égalitéans disapprove of that kind of research. I have in mind research that doesn't harm animal participants. Such research could benefit people and animals, or simply provide knowledge for its own sake. Might not these benefits and knowledge outweigh the costs of keeping animals in captivity in zoos?"

"No. Many zoos didn't support research at all, including research that didn't harm animals. Those that did supported research of two kinds: research conducted on animals in the zoos and research conducted on animals in the wild. The latter research, however, didn't have to be funded by zoos. It could equally well have been funded by, say, a government agency. To conduct research on animals in the wild, zoos are unnecessary."

"Granted. But if we're going to conduct research on animals in zoos, surely we need zoos. And surely such research confers benefits."

"Research conducted on animals in zoos had two aims. Some of it aimed at increasing knowledge of animal behavior; some of it aimed at improving conditions for zoo animals. Both aims were misguided."

"How so?"

"Let's take the first aim first. When we seek knowledge of animal behavior by studying zoo animals, what knowledge are we seeking? Are we seeking knowledge of the behavior of animals in zoos, or are we seeking knowledge of the behavior of animals in the wild? No doubt, knowledge of the latter sort is a good thing. But in many respects, the behavior of animals in the wild differs from the behavior of animals in zoos. Thus the best way to gain knowledge of the behavior of animals in the wild is by studying animals in the wild. Studying zoo animals is apt to lead us astray. As for knowledge of the behavior of animals in zoos, it's not clear that such knowledge is worth acquiring. It might be worth acquiring if we were going to have zoos in the first place. But that begs the question at issue. Should we have zoos in the first place?"

"I understand. What about the second aim—improving conditions for zoo animals? This aim seems laudable enough."

"So it is. But this aim, too, presupposes that we're going to have zoos. The question is whether we should. Possibly—just possibly—we should have zoos if we can design them such that zoo animals lead better lives on average than do their wild counterparts. The history of zoos, however, suggests that this almost certainly won't happen."

I return my attention to the playing field. Blake is doubled over, hands on knees, sucking air. Bouncing off a rotating barrier, the whizzing holographic ball takes dead aim at Blake's face. Only at the last second does Blake manage to lift his paddle for a block. The effort makes him stagger backward and fall on his rear end. Seeing Blake struggle to get back on his feet, the athlete next to him, the woman who earlier made the spectacular diving save, moves a few paces in his direction, ready to cover for him in case the ball comes back his way.

"This leaves only one more defense of zoos," Safiya continues. "Through breeding programs, zoos sometimes helped preserve endangered species. In your day, the most talked about case was the California condor. In 1982, by your calendar, only twenty-two California condors existed in the wild. Thirty-two years later, thanks to breeding programs funded partly by zoos, the population increased to four hundred twenty-five, two hundred nineteen of which were living in the wild. A happy ending, wouldn't you say?"

"Yes, but I think I know what you're going to say next."

"What am I going to say next?"

"That we don't need zoos to save endangered species. That a government agency or some other organization could undertake the task instead."

Safiya smiles. "You're getting to know me well, Phil. Yes, that's one thing I was going to say. But I want to say something else as well."

"What's that?"

"That most attempts to preserve endangered species through zoos were far from stellar successes. In your time, there was a review of one hundred forty-five attempts to reintroduce one hundred fifteen species into the wild. The review showed that only sixteen of these attempts produced self-sustaining populations, and of these sixteen only half involved endangered species. Even the attempt to save the California condor had its share of problems. For example, in the first dozen years of reintroduction into the wild, most condors died. Only six eggs were laid in the wild, and only one chick fledged. It wasn't until the founding of Égalité that the California condor rebounded. Today, more than ten thousand of the birds thrive in western North America."

Once again, the holographic ball whizzes toward Blake. Blake lunges at it with his paddle but misses. The woman positioned next to Blake also lunges and gets a piece of it. As Blake and the woman crash into each other, the ball bounces off a barrier and back toward Blake and the woman. Both scramble to get to the ball but, because they're lying on the ground in a tangled heap, they can't reach it. Another athlete, seeing his helpless comrades, tries to come to the rescue, but he's too far away. In desperation, he throws his paddle toward the ball. He misses by less than an inch. The ball bounces out of bounds. The game is over.

The spectators cheer the athletes with enthusiasm. We appreciate their effort and good play. It was an entertaining show, more entertaining than the zoos I visited.

o o o

While Blake showers, Safiya and I continue to chat.

"If Égalitéans oppose zoos," I say, "I guess I don't need to ask what they think of bullfighting, cockfighting, and dog fighting. They must oppose these too."

"Yes. We also disapprove of greyhound racing and rodeos. All such spectacles use nonhuman animals as mere means to human ends. They're about entertaining us rather than doing what's best for them."

"I imagine Égalité has no circuses either." I say this with a touch of sadness. When I was a kid, my mom and dad often took me to the circus. It was fun. I especially liked the magic shows, and the cotton candy.

"No, we have circuses. I've been to a lot of them. I especially enjoy the magic shows. I'm fascinated by the art of illusion."

"Really? Surely, though, you don't have lion tamers placing their heads inside the gaping mouths of lions, or chimpanzees riding about on tricycles?"

"That's right. No nonhuman animals perform in our circuses—no lions, tigers, or bears, no chimpanzees, elephants, or horses. We also don't have bearded ladies, little people, or Siamese twins. We find such uses of human and nonhuman animals demeaning."

"So what do you have—besides magic shows?"

"Oh, lots of things! We have clowns and rides and games and food—healthy food, not cotton candy or candied apples, as circuses from your time had. We also have caricaturists and storytellers and actors and musicians and gymnasts."

"Hm."

"What? Is something wrong?"

"No. I just never thought a philosopher would enjoy the circus."

"Why not? Some of the games our circuses have are logic puzzles. Philosophers love a good logic puzzle. Besides, I'm a musician as well as a philosopher. I like the music too. A couple of times I've performed at a circus."

"So we both enjoy the circus. It looks like we have something in common."

o o o

When Blake returns, Safiya leaves. She says she needs to put on her costume for the parade. She, Franz, and Édouard are planning to participate as the Statues of Wisdom, Love, and Equality, respectively. They'll join the other participants as soon as the parade, coming from the village near the Dinosaur Eggs, enters Safiya's village, and together they'll walk all the way to the village by Hourglass Lake.

As soon as Safiya is gone, Blake grins, poking me in the stomach with a forefinger. "Did you see that, Doughboy?" he says. He looks sharp again today, but instead of wearing gray, as he did yesterday, he's dressed in black from head to toe.

"See what?" I say.

"My performance on the field, of course! It was great, wasn't it? I showed those vegetarians a thing or two!"

"Yes, I'm sure everyone was impressed. Too bad you couldn't get to that last one."

"Yeah, I know. I would've, though, if that woman hadn't crashed into me. Did you notice how bad a player she was? I had to keep covering for her."

My PAD bleeps three times, preventing me from answering Blake. Peacemaker is calling me. She says, "I have an update for you, son. It's about yesterday's incident."

"Yes," I say. "What is it?"

"According to the testimony that Blake and Safiya gave me, three people were near the lake when you were struck by the rock. Two of the three were swimming. I've concluded that neither of them threw the rock. First, they were too far away. Second, even if they'd been close enough, they would, given their position relative to yours, have hit you in the side of the head, not the back of it. The third person was a young boy skipping stones. His name is August. He didn't throw the rock that hit you either."

"How do you know that?" Blake interrupts.

"Who's that? Blake?"

"Yes. How do you know the boy didn't throw the rock?" Blake repeats.

"Unlike the two swimmers, he was close enough to hit Phil, and he could have hit him in the back of the head. But the wound Phil received suggests that whoever threw the rock was standing directly behind him. The boy, however, was standing off to one side. If he had thrown the rock, Phil would have received a glancing blow, and a different wound. The boy is innocent. I have no doubt in my mind."

"Then who threw the rock?" I ask.

"I don't know. Blake, of course, was also on the beach. But according to his testimony he, like the two swimmers, was too far away and not directly behind you. Besides, Blake's your friend, and he's the one who dragged you out of the water. It hardly makes sense to harm someone and then save his life. I believe Blake is innocent as well."

"But nobody else was on the beach," Blake says.

"Nobody we know of," Peacemaker replies. "Somebody could have been hiding in the edge of the woods directly behind Phil. From there, it would be possible to give Phil the kind of wound he received. That'll be the next thing I investigate. I'll keep the two of you posted."

Chapter 14
Are All Animals *Really* Equal?

"Not exactly Macy's Parade, is it?" Blake remarks when the parade participants come into view. Blake and I stand next to the dining hall, observing the spectacle from the shade of a giant oak tree. The dog cocks her head to one side as she too watches. Despite the shade, she pants heavily. Saliva drips from her tongue, moistening the grass below.

"No. It isn't," I agree. It's more intimate and less ostentatious. Half a dozen school children walk behind a banner that reads, "HAPPY BIRTHDAY, ÉGALITÉ." A quartet of musicians plays a dignified tune. With long sticks, three people hold up a large, white dove. The dove, symbolizing peace, is made of bed sheets wrapped around a wire frame. Some parade participants wear costumes that have symbolic meaning; others join the march simply for the joy of marching. I like the cozy feel of the parade, better than I like the pomp and circumstance of the bigger parades I see on TV.

In less than twenty minutes, the entire procession passes by. Safiya, Franz, and Édouard bring up the rear. Safiya's costume, scarcely different from the robe she customarily wears, is creamy yellow. In her left hand she grips her oboe, while in her right she holds aloft a torch. The torch represents the all-encompassing light that wisdom sheds. I don't know what function, if any, the oboe serves. Perhaps at some point Safiya will join the quartet of musicians. As she passes, I applaud and wave. She waves back and blows me a kiss. Blake stands stiffly, arms folded across his muscular chest.

Once Safiya and the others are out of view, Blake and I, with the dog following close behind, wander into the dining hall. The people inside are playing games. Many of the games are intellectual. Some people, for instance, are working on logic problems, while others are playing the word game that the tailor and image consultant played the other day. None of the games is a competition. All require cooperation.

Blake and I stop by a table where four people, including Charlie, are about to play a game of cooperative poetry. As Charlie quietly explains to us, the four of them will together compose a poem, taking turns adding a line until they agree the poem is complete. One of the players asks me if I'd like to suggest a topic for their poem. Because I have no experience with poetry, I'm uncertain what to suggest, so I point to the first object I set my eyes on, a bowl sitting on the edge of the table. The bowl is filled with salad greens and has a small crack on its side. "Perhaps your poem could be about this bowl."

Blake, who evidently doesn't want to hear a poem about a bowl, says, "I'd like your poem to be about the twenty-first century."

After a brief discussion, the four Égalitéans agree to compose a poem that is about both the bowl and the twenty-first century. They record the poem on one of their PADs, dedicate it to Blake and me, and, once it's complete, give it the title "The Parable of the Bowl":

The bowl, like me, is made of clay,
Its verdant bounty on display.
It gives without expecting pay,
A mom who feeds me ev'ry day:

Green beans and peas and leeks and beets,
And cheese and eggs and seasoned meats,
A loaf of bread and sav'ry treats,
Pecans and pears and sundry sweets.

"You have dominion," says the Lord,
Which means, I think, I can afford
To treat the bowl in ways untoward:
To batter, tatter, waste, and hoard.

On corn, not grass, my burgers graze,
My scrambled eggs the caged hen lays,
In filth my bacon sleeps and plays —
Yet ere each meal the Lord I praise.

The forests I have set ablaze,
The air I've made a smoggy haze,
In many ways I daily raze —
Yet for his gifts the Lord I praise.

My highways are a tangled maze,
My trash abounds where'er I gaze,
All round me lurks a deep malaise —

Yet piously the Lord I praise.

The bowl is cracked, I now detect,
The cause of which I recollect:
In part my greed, in part neglect,
In part my hubris — no respect.

The crack keeps growing, long and fat,
So slowly I don't notice that
The bowl and all therein are at
The breaking point and soon will shat-
*   ter.*

Then fields no more will bloom and grow,
And streams, once pure, will stop their flow.
'Tis I alone who'll sow such woe:
The bowl forever will be bro-
*   ken.*

Is this the fate that I await?
Is it too late to set things straight,
To seal the crack, get back on track?
My brain I rack to heal the frac-
*   ture.*

I must obey this rule today:
"The biosphere thou shalt protect —
From tallest tree to small insect,
All living things deserve respect."

I'll end the harms of fact'ry farms,
Reverse the dang'rous climate change,
Replant the forests, lush abode
Of bear and boar and bird and toad.

I'll take a stand to save the land,
With utmost care I'll clean the air,
Pollution-free shall be the sea —
With all my soul I'll love the bowl!

Charlie quietly asks if we'd like to participate in the creation of the next poem. Blake, however, declines. He has no interest in cooperative games; he thrives on competition. He says he'd like to show them a game people play in my time. The game is chess. He promises that they'll enjoy the game, because, like Égalitéan games, chess is intellectual. He neglects to mention that it's a competitive, not a cooperative, game.

When the four people agree, Blake uses his PAD to set up a holographic chessboard. He takes the white pieces; I take the black. When we were in high school, Blake and I played a lot of chess. He was no grandmaster, playing too impatiently and aggressively, but he was a stronger player than I was. I was never able to beat him, though I came close once. That was the last time we played. We haven't played in some years.

For the benefit of the four Égalitéans, Blake briefly reviews the rules of the game. Then he announces, "e4." Without anyone touching it, the holographic pawn in front of Blake's holographic king slides forward two holographic squares.

I reply, "d6."

Blake rolls his eyes and makes a face. He says, "The Pirc Defense? You've got to be kidding! This has always been your problem, Philsbury. You're too passive. I'm going to enjoy crushing you like a bug!"

Two of the Égalitéan onlookers gasp. In his quiet voice, Charlie says, "Égalitéans don't crush people, and we don't crush bugs." Uncrossing his thick legs, he gets up from his chair and walks away from our table. Blake ignores the departure. He and I play our next several moves rapidly: d4 Nf6, Nc3 g6, f4 Bg7, Nf3 0-0.

As Blake mulls over his next move, one of the three remaining Égalitéans shrugs her shoulders. The other two exchange perplexed glances. Thirty seconds later, Blake says, "h3."

This move is new to me. I was expecting the more common e5. What could Blake have in mind with h3? After some hesitation, I make my move: c5. Blake replies immediately. "g4," he says.

Now I know what Blake is up to. He means to storm my king with his pawns. The attack, I realize, is premature. As usual, Blake is recklessly aggressive. But what is the best way to respond? After thinking for several minutes, I say, "Qa5." I'm threatening Nxe4. Perhaps this threat will distract Blake from his intended pawn storm.

One of the Égalitéans—the one who shrugged her shoulders—says she needs to talk to her daughter about something. With a polite apology, she excuses herself. The other two Égalitéans tell her to go with love and wisdom.

Blake says, "Bd2." What's this? Did Blake just make a mistake? My heart skips a beat. I can no longer win the pawn on e4, but now I can take the pawn on d4. It's not like Blake, though, to make such an obvious blunder. What's he hoping to accomplish? Figuring there's only one way to find out, I take the bait. I say, "cxd4."

One of the Égalitéans says, "Excuse us. I hope we're not being rude. However, your game is too ... how shall I say? Your game is too *military* for our taste. Please go with love and wisdom." He and the other Égalitéan abruptly depart. Now only the dog, loyal to the end, accompanies Blake and me.

His voice just above a whisper, Blake says, "It's just as well they're gone. It gives me a chance to talk to you—in private." A little more loudly, he says, "b4."

"Would you like to go to my quarters? Or yours?"

"No. We'll be fine here. As long as we're playing this *military* game, no one's likely to bother us."

I examine the holographic chessboard. If I take the pawn on b4, Blake can move his knight to d5, with more threats than I can counter. I opt for a prudent retreat instead. "Qb6. So what would you like to talk to me about?"

Blake inhales slowly, until his chest reaches maximum expansion. Just as slowly he exhales. At length, he says, "I'm planning to leave Égalité. Today. I'd like you to leave with me. Nd5."

I shouldn't be surprised. Blake belongs in Égalité as much as a fish belongs on dry land. But I am surprised—shocked even. "You want to leave? Why? Nxd5."

Blake glares at me, incredulous. "Isn't it obvious? Égalité is dangerous. Somebody stole a stun gun, and somebody hit you with a rock. Of course I want to get out of here. Our lives could be at stake. exd5."

I'm torn. Part of me shares Blake's worry. For all I know, somebody tried to kill me. But another part of me wants to believe in Égalité. The equality that Égalitéans have fashioned is a beautiful ideal; it tugs at my soul. Staring blankly at the chessboard, I say, "I don't know. Maybe we shouldn't do anything just yet. Maybe we should wait for Peacemaker to conclude her investigation first. d3."

"No. It's time to act." Blake pauses, waiting for me to respond. When I don't, he says, "Do I have to spell it out for you? Look, Philsbury, an awful lot of strange things are going on. Haven't you noticed? Bxd3."

Of course I've noticed. But I pretend I haven't. "What strange things are you talking about? Bxa1."

"The physical appearance of the Égalitéans, for starters. They look familiar, don't they? Almost exactly like people from our time. Do you have any idea how such a thing could happen? Qxa1."

"No. You're right. I admit that's odd."

"And what about their names? Compare Bach-Kuhn with Bhayq, Bel-Ami with Bell, and Charlie with Chaz. Surely you don't think this is a coincidence?"

My position on the chessboard is growing worrisome. Although I've won a rook for a bishop, Blake's pieces are poised for an assault on my king. On the defensive, I say, "Nd7. So Égalitéan names are similar to the names of people from our time. Is this a problem? I don't see anything sinister here."

"No? What about dishonesty, then? Wouldn't you agree that dishonesty is sinister?"

"I suppose it could be. Is somebody being dishonest?" I think of Safiya. I think of how she's been hiding something from me. What's her secret? Does she pose a threat? No. Impossible. She seems genuinely to care for me.

"Everybody's being dishonest—the whole lot of them. You've heard the boasts they make. How they all love the work they do. How they produce no garbage. How they've eliminated all prejudices. One big happy family! Do you believe a word of it, Philsbury? I don't. No society has ever achieved such results. No society ever will. f5."

I too harbor doubts about the possibility of creating a utopia. However, I play devil's advocate. "I'm sure Égalité has its flaws. But Égalitéans—at least the ones I've met—seem to enjoy their work. And in the several days I've been here, I haven't noticed any garbage or any prejudice. Maybe Égalitéans have solved some of the problems that plague our own society. Nf6."

"Égalitéans haven't solved anything. On the contrary, they threaten everything our society holds dear."

"Such as?"

"Such as religion, for one. There's no room for God in their hearts. I know you, Philsbury. How could a good Christian like you defend a pack of atheists like them? Bh6."

"Some atheists are decent people."

"Then there's capitalism. There's no room for entrepreneurial spirit in their hearts either. And what about the God-given right of a man and a woman to have children? Do you know how many people inhabit the globe in 2376? Only half a billion. Half a billion! I looked it up. To reduce the population so drastically, the Égalitéan government denied people the opportunity to reproduce."

"I looked it up as well. From what I understand, the decision to reduce the population originated with the people rather than the government. They were concerned that too large a population would adversely affect the environment. Thanks to human overpopulation in our time, many species are becoming endangered or extinct. Qxb4+."

"But that's just it. Égalitéans care more about other species than about our own. Their values are warped."

"Not true. According to the principle of animal equality, the interests of a human being have the same value as the comparable interests of a nonhuman animal. Human interests count too."

"C'mon, Philsbury. Do you really believe in this principle of animal equality? Ke2."

"I don't know. I've heard the arguments in its favor. I don't know how to refute them. Re8."

"Well, I do. Suppose three individuals are dying: your mom, me, and that dog you're petting right now. You can save only one. Which one would you save? Hmm? Be honest now. Even if all three of us have an equal interest in living, wouldn't you save your mom? Nd2."

"Yes, I'd save my mom. If I could save a second individual, it'd be you. The dog would come last."

"Or suppose your mom and I and the dog are each suffering from an equal amount of pain, and you can help only one of us. Which one would you help?"

"Again, my mom would come first, and then you, and then the dog."

"Even if we all have an equal interest in eliminating our pain?"

"Yes. Bd7."

"So your mom's interests have greater value, at least to you, than do my comparable interests? And my interests have greater value, at least to you, than the dog's comparable interests? Ne4."

"So it seems."

"Well, then. So much for the principle of animal equality. So much even for the principle of *human* equality. No one in his right mind is an egalitarian. We all favor family first, and then friends, and then acquaintances, and then strangers. Animals don't even make the list, unless they're pets. And even then, they come after human beings—or they should. Do you know why this is?"

"No. Why? Rac8."

"Biology. Whether we realize it or not, we're all striving to get our genes into the next generation. The laws of evolution mandate as much. We favor family because they share many of our genes. By helping them get their genes into the next generation, we simultaneously pass on many of our own genes. We also favor friends. We do so because friends form alliances, thereby helping each other live long enough to get their genes into the next generation. But why on earth should we ever favor a cow? We have no good reason, since cows aren't going to help us get our genes into the next generation. Unless, of course, we eat them or wear their skins. The nourishment and warmth they provide might help us live longer so that we can pass on our genes. But eating them and wearing their skins is hardly favoring them. No. Human beings are biologically incapable of equality. For us, equality is, and will always be, morally repugnant. Kd1."

Blake's argument is powerful. Whereas a moment ago equality seemed a beautiful ideal, now it seems a grotesque caricature. Equally powerful is Blake's position on the chessboard. It's only a matter of time before Blake crashes through my defenses on the kingside. I expect that I'll soon be forced to resign.

After a long pause, I say, "All right. You've convinced me. We'll leave Égalité together. Do you know how to get back home? Ba4."

Blake smiles. He knows he's winning. "Yes. Do you remember where you were when you first arrived in Égalité?"

"Of course. The place is a few miles from here. There's a river, and a cave."

"Right. It's the same place I was when I first arrived in Égalité. According to my PAD, all we have to do is walk into the cave. Then we'll be home again. fxg6."

"Don't forget that I'm recovering from a concussion. I shouldn't walk such a long distance."

"Don't worry, buddy. We'll take it nice and slow. I won't let anything happen to you. Not on my watch."

I pause again. I'm going to miss Égalité. I'm going to miss Safiya. My voice quavers as I say, "I suppose I should say goodbye to Safiya. hxg6."

"No! I don't want anyone to know we're leaving. It's too risky. No one is going to throw another rock at you."

"But surely Safiya's all right. She cares about me. I know."

"No! I'm not taking any chances. We're leaving without a word to anyone. And we're leaving now."

"It won't work. Somebody will notice us missing, and somebody will find us. A PAD could easily locate us."

"Not to worry. I have it all planned out. It's possible to hide things even from PADs. I've learned how to do it. Nobody will detect us. Rf1."

A shiver runs down my spine and to the core of my being. I can no longer sustain my knight on f6. Once that's gone, my king will be defenseless. I have only one chance to save myself. Counterattack. I must get to Blake's king before he gets to mine. But can I pull it off?

"Very well. If you'll just let me use the restroom for a minute, I'll be ready to go."

∘ ∘ ∘

I sit on the toilet, hesitating. I know what I must do; I have, however, no desire to do it—I've always disliked confrontation. My hand reaches for my PAD, hangs in midair, and then drops back to my side. I reach for my PAD again, but, before I can grasp it, it bleeps three times. Peacemaker is calling me with an update.

"I'm at the lake, son. I've examined the edge of the woods by the beach, and I've found something. You're not going to like it."

"What is it, Peacemaker?"

"I found a thread and a hair. The hair is white and comes from a dog. The thread is creamy yellow."

"Safiya?"

"Yes. Safiya. I'm going to detain her for questioning. I'm sorry, son."

I hesitate again. My heart thumps sorrowfully in my chest. At length, taking a deep breath, I say, "That's all right, Peacemaker. No need to apologize. I know who threw the rock, and why. I also know what I'm going to do about it."

"Really? And what's that?"

"Counterattack."

I think about the chess game. Yes. I can beat Blake. After all these years, I can finally beat him. The winning move is Bxc2+. I picture how the game might conclude: Bxc2 Rxc2, Nxf6+ exf6, Kxc2 Qc4+, Qc3 Qxf1, white resigns.

o o o

Blake and I trudge in silence, while the dog scampers ahead sniffing this and that. The going is slow because I rest frequently. Every time I rest, Blake rummages through the capacious knapsack he brought and hands me a cool bottle of water or a juicy piece of fruit. Although he's eager to reach the cave, he graciously waits for me to catch my breath. I don't, however, need to rest. On the contrary, I feel fine. I rest only to bide time. I want to make sure everything is ready. I don't want any surprises.

Blake doesn't want any surprises either. He adjusts his PAD so that it warns him any time an Égalitéan approaches us on the footpath. Evidently most of the villagers are celebrating in their villages, so not many Égalitéans pass by. When one does, Blake and I pick our way a hundred yards into the woods and hide in the foliage. I hold the dog in my arms, stroking her gently to keep her quiet. As soon as the coast is clear, the three of us return to the footpath.

Because of the delays, we don't reach the cave until dusk. The cave looks the same as it did when I arrived in Égalité a few days ago, except that, in the dim light, it has taken on a sinister gloom. As I plop down on a nearby rock, Blake places his knapsack at the mouth of the cave. The dog, sitting at my feet, cocks her head, gazing intently at the objects Blake takes out of the knapsack. I gaze intently too. Despite the growing darkness, I recognize the objects immediately. They're the missing fireworks.

I ask Blake what he's doing. He replies that he's going to blow up the entrance to the cave. When I ask him why he wants to do that, he says, "To prevent the Égalitéans from following us. In my knapsack, I have a delay detonator. We'll enter the cave and return safely home. Then these fireworks will go off. The explosion will collapse the entrance to the cave. The Égalitéans will have no way to travel to our time, or to any other time. They'll never bother anybody again."

A swirl of questions crowds into my mind. Are fireworks, which are low-explosive devices, powerful enough to collapse the entrance to the cave? If they are, why can't the Égalitéans simply clear away the rubble and then follow Blake and me into the cave? Is the cave really a passageway from the future to the past? Is it the only passageway the Égalitéans have? Is time travel even possible? I decide, however, not to press Blake on these matters. There isn't much point, because I have no intention of following him into the cave.

"I've been thinking, Blake," I say. "When we were in high school, we played a lot of chess. Then we suddenly stopped. Why did we stop?"

"I don't know," Blake says absently. His attention is focused on setting up the fireworks. "We became too busy, I suppose. Why do you ask?"

"Because the last time we played, I nearly won. Do you remember? I was ahead a knight for a pawn, and then I lost my knight when I let it get trapped."

"I'm sorry, buddy. I don't remember."

"Well, I do. I'm wondering if we stopped playing because you were afraid you might lose. You never liked to lose at anything."

Blake laughs. "Afraid to lose? To you? I could beat you with my eyes closed."

I drop the subject. Taking a deep breath, I move on. "What about when we were in the ninth grade? Do you remember those bullies who tried to get my lunch money?"

"Now *that* I remember! You were lucky I was nearby. I saved your hide that day."

"Yes. And you were lucky Chaz was nearby. He made sure everybody knew what happened. If Shakin' Bhayq hadn't heard the story, she'd never have agreed to go out with you."

"I know. She didn't like dating younger boys. They were too immature, she thought. Good ol' Chaz! He's always been a loyal friend, as loyal as a dog."

"Yes, he has. He does everything you ask. I think, on that day, you asked him to be in the hallway just as the bullies showed up, and I think you asked him to tell everyone what a hero you were."

Blake looks up from his work and furrows his brow. "I beg your pardon?"

"I also think you paid the bullies to go after me, and then to run away when you came to the rescue. There's no other explanation. You could never have whipped those five kids on your own. It was all a setup. You used me to get to Shakin' Bhayq." I should have thought of this years ago. Why didn't I see what Blake was really up to? Perhaps Mr. Bhayq was right: although I have a good head on my shoulders, I hardly ever use it.

"You have a strange sense of gratitude, Doughboy," Blake says, his voice becoming tense. "I rescued you because that's what friends do. That time in high school wasn't the only time I bailed you out, you know. Just a few days ago, when you passed out in the dining hall, I carried you to your quarters, and yesterday I dragged you out of the lake. Each time I come to your rescue, it's because I'm your friend. It's that simple. I don't have any ulterior motives."

"I think you do—you did in high school, and you do now in Égalité. You've been plotting against the Égalitéans for some time, haven't you? Several days at least, possibly from the moment you arrived. You must have recognized right away that Égalité is a threat—not just to our society, but to you personally. If our society were to adopt Égalitéan ideals, the pharmaceutical industry would shrink and animal testing would disappear. You'd be out of a job. You were worried that Égalitéans would travel back in time to influence our society. So you decided to blow up the entrance to the cave. To do that, you stole some fireworks. At some point—perhaps after you stole the fireworks?—I arrived in Égalité, and when I passed out you carried me to my quarters. I've been wondering why you did that. You say you did it because you're my friend, because you care about my well-being. I'd like to believe you. I really would. But I don't. I think you carried me to my quarters for more self-serving reasons. I think you were hoping to persuade the Égalitéans—and me—that you're a fine, upstanding fellow, not the sort of person who commits acts of sabotage. That way, if the Égalitéans ever detected that some of their fireworks were missing, they'd be less likely to suspect that you were the thief and I'd be more likely to stand by your side."

My voice quavers, because I'm about to end a lifelong friendship. Taking a moment to recover my poise, I forge ahead. "But you also rescued me from the lake. Wasn't that, at least, a noble deed? Shouldn't I be thanking you for saving my life? Shouldn't I be showering you with praise and gratitude? No, I shouldn't, and for one very good reason: you were the one who threw the rock at me."

"What? Why are you making vicious accusations? What's gotten into you?"

"I've finally figured out a few things. You're not the good friend you seem to be. Rescuing me from the lake was no different from rescuing me from the bullies. In both cases, you were using me as a mere means. Yesterday, at the meeting with the Regional Planning Committee, I didn't help you defend hunting. Shortly after, you saw me kissing Safiya in the lake. You were afraid that I was going to side with the Égalitéans. You were afraid that you were going to lose your only ally. That's when you threw the rock at me. You wanted to convince me that Égalité is dangerous. You wanted to convince me to return with you to our time. You wanted me to let everyone back home know what a hero you were. Just as Chaz told how you singlehandedly chased the bullies away, so I would tell how you singlehandedly stopped the Égalitéan threat. Maybe you're hoping to win Shakin' Bhayq's heart again. Maybe you have your eye on someone else. Or maybe you just want people to admire you. Whatever you're hoping to gain, I'm not going to be your dupe. Not this time."

"If you're going to turn against a friend," Blake says, "you'd better have powerful evidence to back you up. But you have no evidence."

"Indeed, the evidence points to Safiya. Earlier today, Peacemaker found a white hair and a yellow thread in the woods near the lake. The yellow thread is from Safiya's swimsuit. The white hair is from the dog, who was with Safiya at the time I was struck with the rock. Pretty damning evidence—except that you were the one who placed it there."

"And what makes you think that?"

"When I came to on the beach, I saw Safiya kneeling in front of me. You were standing behind her, with your hand on her shoulder. You appeared to be offering her comfort. But you weren't. In fact, you were surreptitiously removing a loose thread from her swimsuit. I saw you put the thread in your pants pocket. I think you did something similar with the dog, perhaps when we were in the lounge a couple of days ago talking about companion animals. I remember you petting the dog on the head, snagging some of her hair between your fingers, and then putting your hand in your pocket."

"Are you sure that's what happened? When you were on the beach, you were fading in and out of consciousness. You were in a great deal of pain. I think your mind was playing tricks on you."

"That's a clever explanation," I say. "But it's not the right one. Would you like to know what finally tipped me off—what clue finally gave your scheme away? It was when we were playing the chess game. You said you'd figured out how to hide things from PADs."

"So?"

"At the meeting with the Regional Planning Committee, I learned—after you left—that someone had stolen a stun gun. The investigators tried to locate the stun gun, but their PADs couldn't find it. Whoever stole it knew how to hide things from PADs. You're the thief, aren't you? I'm guessing you have the stun gun with you right now. Maybe it's in your pocket, or maybe it's in your knapsack. Why did you steal it, Blake? Because you wanted a weapon—in case the Égalitéans tried to detain you before you could blow up the entrance to the cave? Or were you hoping that I'd believe the thief was an Égalitéan rather than you—so that I'd be eager to leave this dangerous place with you? But Égalitéans aren't thieves, and they're not dangerous. The only dangerous person here is you."

Blake shakes his head. "You're wrong, Philsbury. You've got it all wrong. The Égalitéans are the dangerous ones. Their principle of animal equality isn't just mistaken. It threatens you and me and our whole society. I proved this to you when we were playing the chess game. Surely you haven't forgotten my argument?"

"Of course not. I was thinking about it the whole time we were walking to the cave. On the surface, it seems convincing. Ultimately, however, it's flawed."

Blake's teeth clench. "What do you think the flaw is?"

"Do you recall the debate over diet that you and Safiya had? You argued that meat-eating is justified because it's natural. In response, Safiya accused you of committing the naturalistic fallacy. I too accuse you of committing the naturalistic fallacy. When we were playing chess, you argued, in essence, that inequality is natural. It's natural, you suggested, in the sense that believing in it helps us get our genes into the next generation. And from the claim that inequality is natural, you inferred that inequality is good. Just because something is natural, though—just because it helps us get our genes into the next generation—doesn't necessarily mean that it's good. An act of rape may help a rapist get his genes into the next generation. But it doesn't follow that rape is good. Similarly, wiping out a neighboring tribe isn't necessarily good, even if doing so increases our territory and food supply, thereby helping us get our genes into the next generation."

"You misunderstand my argument," Blake protests. "I don't claim that what's natural is good. What I claim is that 'ought' implies 'can.' If you can't do something, it makes little sense to say that you ought to do it. Suppose, for instance, you agree to meet me an hour from now for dinner. On your way, however, a kidnapper kidnaps you, so that you can't keep your promise. How ridiculous I'd be if, upon your release a week later, I say to you, 'Shame on you! You ought to have kept your promise.' My contention is that Égalitéan egalitarianism is no less ridiculous than this. Given our biological drive to get our genes into the next generation, we can't be egalitarians. We'll always favor some over others. To say we ought to be egalitarians is to speak nonsense."

"I've thought about this too, and I disagree. The principles of human and animal equality aren't nonsense. I believe we *can* adopt them, and I believe we *ought* to adopt them."

"How? How are we going to pull it off?"

"You claim that we all play favorites. You're right. We do. I certainly do. I run errands for my mom, but I don't run errands for strangers. I'll raise my own children, if I ever have any, but I won't raise your children. Such favoritism is, perhaps, harmless enough. Some of it may even be inevitable. I suppose it has a biological basis, as you argue. All of this I grant. To these claims, however, you add that the presumably harmless favoritism we all engage in is incompatible with the principles of human and animal equality. This I don't grant. I believe that Égalitéan egalitarianism can accommodate such favoritism."

"Again, I ask how?"

"Consider my mom and your mom. Should I help my mom satisfy her interests, or should I help your mom satisfy her comparable interests? Initially, it seems that, from an Égalitéan standpoint, it makes no difference. Since your mom's interests have the same value as my mom's comparable interests, I seem to have no basis for favoring my mom. But this is false. I have, if you're correct, a strong, biologically based interest in my mom's interests. My interest in your mom's interests isn't nearly as strong. Therefore, when I help my mom rather than yours, I don't just help my mom satisfy her interests. I also satisfy my interests. Similarly, when you help your mom rather than mine, you don't just help your mom satisfy her interests. You also satisfy your interests. Moreover, since I'm more motivated to help my mom than yours, I'll as a rule do a better job of satisfying my mom's interests than satisfying your mom's interests. And since you're more motivated to help your mom than mine, you'll do a better job of satisfying your mom's interests than satisfying my mom's interests. Thus, as a rule, if we want to satisfy the greatest possible set of interests, I should help my mom and you should help yours.

"While we were walking to the cave, I was thinking about what the principles of human and animal equality mean. As I'm inclined to interpret them, they don't assert that we ought to satisfy the greatest set of interests. More precisely, they assert that we ought to satisfy the greatest set of interests *that we can*. Suppose, then, that you're right, that we can't help but give at least some preference to friends and family. This being so, it follows that, if we're going to satisfy the greatest set of interests *that we can*, we must give at least some preference to friends and family."

"But if Égalitéan egalitarianism is compatible with favoritism," Blake objects, "what's so great about being an egalitarian? Why not believe instead that the interests of some have greater value than the comparable interests of others? What's the difference? We'll favor some over others in either case."

"The advantage of Égalitéan egalitarianism is that it places strict limits on how far we may take our favoritism. While it allows us to run errands for our respective moms, it forbids prejudices such as racism, sexism, heterosexism, and speciesism. It forbids these prejudices because it forbids what they by definition involve—the discounting of interests. Thus, from an Égalitéan perspective, we shouldn't deny people housing because of their race. We shouldn't deny people promotions because of their gender. We shouldn't deny people the right to get married because of their sexual orientation. We shouldn't eat meat, support animal testing, or hunt or fish.

"Perhaps you'll object that racism and other prejudices, however ugly they may be, are inevitable, because they help us get our genes into the next generation. Or maybe they're inevitable because they helped our ancestors get their genes into the next generation, and we, for better or worse, have inherited their prejudices. No doubt, racism and other prejudices are deeply ingrained in our species. But they're not as deeply ingrained as the favoritism we show family, and they're not inevitable. Prejudice is like handedness. Some people have a genetic predisposition to write with their left hand, but end up writing better with their right hand. Why? Because they're taught to write with their right hand. Similarly, prejudice may have a genetic basis, but people can be taught to avoid it. One way to teach people to avoid prejudice is to inculcate in them the principles of human and animal equality. This is what Égalitéans have done, and we should follow their lead."

I pause to give Blake a chance to respond. By now, dusk has transformed into night. The stars and moon shine from above, providing scant light. Blake, dressed in his black clothes, is no more than a dark shadow, barely visible even though he stands just a few yards from me.

At length, Blake says, "I'm disappointed in you, Philsbury. I thought I could count on you, but I guess the Égalitéans have brainwashed you. Too bad. You could've shared in my glory."

As Blake speaks, five colorful bursts of light rise simultaneously into the sky from five distant locations. The five locations must be the five villages in the region. Each village has started its fireworks display.

For a few minutes, Blake and I watch the five shows. Then Blake continues, "I'm still going to return home, and I'm still going to blow up the entrance to the cave. You, however, won't be coming with me. I'm sorry, Philsbury, but I'm going to strand you here. I wish I didn't have to. But I can't trust you. If I were to bring you home with me, you might tell people what you think of me. I'm not going to risk my reputation. If only you were as loyal as Chaz! Then I could count on you to testify that we were really in the twenty-fourth century. People back home would be more likely to believe. But I'll do my best without you. I have my PAD, as well as a few knickknacks in my knapsack. Maybe those will convince people. If they don't, I can always take apart my PAD and figure out how it works. I'm sure it's a complicated device. It might take me years. But I'm a smart guy. I'll figure it out eventually. Then I'll start constructing PADs. I'll be the guy who invents them. This PAD will make me rich and famous."

"No, Blake," I say, standing up. "I can't let you do that."

Blake chuckles. "How are you going to stop me?"

"With the help of my friends."

At this signal, five shadowy figures emerge from the foliage that lines the footpath. In front is Peacemaker, who as usual wears a T-shirt. Its message, barely discernible in the darkness, reads "I ♥ ÉGALITÉ." Behind Peacemaker are Franz, Édouard, Charlie, and Safiya. Safiya steps up next to me, giving me a kiss. I return the kiss and encircle my arm around her waist.

Blake's eyes widen, the whites standing out against the blackness of his clothing. "What the hell?" he says. "Why didn't my PAD detect these people?" He removes from his neck the necklace to which his PAD is attached and checks to see if his PAD is malfunctioning.

"You're not the only one who's figured out how to hide things from PADs," I say. "It's over, Blake—unless you'd care to take on these five people the way you took on the five bullies. I'm pretty sure, though, that my friends won't run away."

Blake takes a moment to recover his composure. Then, with the speed of a striking rattlesnake, he reaches into his knapsack, still lying near the mouth of the cave. When he straightens up again, he holds his PAD in one hand and the stolen stun gun in the other.

"You're not very bright, Philsbury," he says. "You knew I had the stun gun. Yet you did nothing to prevent me from using it. By the time you all wake up, I'll be gone, and the cave will be nothing but debris. I hope you like Égalité, Philsbury. You'll be spending the rest of your life here."

Blake aims the stun gun at my chest. I hold Safiya close to me. She trembles in my arms, but I remain calm. Just as Blake is about to fire, a large, dark mass comes crashing through the woods and onto the footpath. It's a black bear, moving fast and heading in our direction. The dog barks fiercely, but only after taking cover between my legs. Franz, Édouard, and Charlie all flinch and step away from the footpath. Safiya too flinches, gripping me tightly. Peacemaker, though, holds her ground. She grins, revealing her well-preserved teeth.

Blake's eyes widen again. Remembering that he's holding a weapon, he shifts his aim from me to the bear and pulls the trigger. His aim is true. He hits the bear squarely in the chest. The bear, however, doesn't even slow down. It charges past me and the five Égalitéans, aiming directly at Blake.

Blake panics. Dropping his stun gun and PAD and stumbling over his knapsack, he flees into the cave. The bear comes to a skidding halt at the mouth of the cave, stands on its hind legs, and roars menacingly. I let go of Safiya and stroll to the mouth of the cave. Standing side by side with the roaring bear, I peer inside.

"Blake?" I shout. "Are you in there?"

No response.

"Blake!" I shout again. "Can you hear me?"

Still no response.

Placing my thumb and forefinger around my PAD, I say, "Discontinue the holographic image."

The black bear vanishes into thin air.

Chapter 15
How Can One Person Make a Difference?

"Bravo!" Peacemaker says, still grinning. "Well done, son. Well done!"

For a moment, Édouard, Franz, Charlie, and Safiya stand in stunned silence. Then, realizing what just happened, they all gather around me. The three men congratulate me, shaking my hand or slapping me on the back. Safiya wraps her arms about my neck and kisses me all over my face. Not wanting to be left out, the dog jumps up against my legs and barks.

Gently, I disengage from Safiya's embrace. Looking Peacemaker in the eye, I say, "Don't congratulate me yet. I'm not finished."

"Why?" Charlie says quietly. "Is something wrong?"

I don't so much as glance at Charlie. My eyes focus solely on Peacemaker. "Yes. Something's wrong. Blake was just one problem that needed solving. There's another."

"What problem is that?" Safiya asks.

"I feel as though I'm nearing the end of a utopian novel," I say. "Much of the novel is realistic. Very much so. The landscape, the villages, the customs, the characters—all are vivid, all are compelling. The characters are so compelling that I'm falling for one of them. Yet, in places, the novel isn't realistic at all. Strange things keep happening. Too many strange things. The effect is jarring."

"What on earth are you talking about?" Édouard says. He adjusts his glasses, smudging the lenses with his fingers.

I say, "Let me give you two examples. Two examples that have especially occupied my thoughts. First, there are the names and physical appearance of several Égalitéans, including the five of you. All of you look almost the same as people from my time, and your names are similar to the names of the people you look like. What could possibly account for this? What's the rational explanation?"

"A curious coincidence," Franz admits, stroking his massive beard. "I'm confident, though, that together the six of us can solve the mystery. We all have good heads on our shoulders. We need only use them."

"Second," I say, "there's Safiya. I keep hearing how honest Safiya is. For instance, you, Peacemaker, said she's the most honest person you know. And Safiya said she doesn't lie, adding that, as a student of philosophy, she values the truth above all else. Yet on two occasions she averted her eyes, as if she had something to hide. The first time was just after I arrived in Égalité. I asked Safiya if Égalité is real. The second time was when I saw the play that critiqued Plato's true city. I asked Safiya how Égalité, or any other utopian society, could exist. On both occasions, Safiya's answers were evasive. She held something back. Why would someone who values the truth above all else hide the truth?"

"If you give me a chance," Safiya says, "I'll be happy to explain."

"That won't be necessary," I say. I still look only at Peacemaker. "I now know what Safiya was hiding. What she didn't tell me is that *Égalité doesn't exist*. The people, the culture they've fashioned, the villages in which they live, even the blades of grass they walk on—all are illusions, as much illusions as the black bear I conjured up."

Édouard, Franz, Charlie, and Safiya try to interrupt, but Peacemaker cuts them off. "It's all right, sons. It's all right, daughter. Let Phil speak."

"Ever since I set foot in Égalité," I continue, "I've been puzzling how it could exist. How did Égalitéans eliminate all cities, all garbage, and all automobiles? How did they so drastically reduce their population, and how did they so drastically reduce crime? How did they provide creative work and quality health care for all? In short, how did they create a utopia? A utopia, after all, is an ideal. It's not real. It doesn't exist in my time, and there's no reason to think it'll exist in the twenty-fourth century either. At most, the real world will adopt parts of Égalitéan culture. No. Égalité isn't a society that *will* exist. It's a society that *should* exist.

"So here I am, feeling as though I'm nearing the end of a utopian novel. At first, I couldn't make sense of the unrealistic parts of the novel—including the two strange things I mentioned. They appeared to be defects in the story. But now I realize they aren't defects at all. They're *hints*—subtle, carefully crafted messages. Somebody wanted me to know that Égalité doesn't exist, but without coming right out and saying so. Somebody wanted me to figure it out on my own.

"Take Égalitéans' names and physical appearance. Why do Égalitéans, in name and appearance, closely resemble people from my time? Such a thing could never happen in the real world—the coincidence is too far-fetched. But it could happen in a utopian novel. Somebody was hinting that I'm like Dorothy encountering characters in Oz who closely resemble people from Kansas. Just as the characters in Oz, and Oz itself, are unreal, so Égaliteans, and Égalité itself, are unreal.

"Or take Safiya's evasiveness. Why did Safiya avert her eyes when I asked her if Égalité is real? Why did she avert her eyes again when I asked her how Égalité could exist? Why did she hide the truth when, as a student of philosophy, she values the truth above all else? Because somebody wanted me to experience Égalité. If Safiya had been completely honest, if she had told me from the beginning that Égalité doesn't exist, I wouldn't have had any interest in experiencing Égalité and would have insisted that Safiya end the charade and return me to my home immediately. Hence somebody made sure that Safiya didn't tell me the truth. Somebody made sure that instead Safiya averted her eyes and avoided answering my questions, leaving me with no more than a hint that all was not as it appeared to be.

"These hints leave me with a host of questions. Who is the one dropping the hints? Who gave Égaliteans their names and physical appearance? Who made Safiya avert her eyes? Who is the author of the utopian novel I'm experiencing? And why? Why is this author showing me a fictional society?"

The five fireworks displays are reaching their climax. Brilliant greens and reds and yellows simultaneously light up the sky. Peacemaker and the others become clearly visible.

Still grinning, Peacemaker says, "Very good, son. Do you know the answers to your questions?"

"No," I say. "But if I had to guess, I'd guess the utopian novelist is you, Peacemaker. You're different from everyone else. For example, when the black bear chased Blake into the cave, everyone else was frightened. But not you. You alone held your ground; you alone grinned. You're still grinning. You knew the black bear wasn't real, even though I never told you, or anyone else, about my plan to create it. Somehow, you knew what I was up to, much as a novelist knows what will happen next in her novel."

Peacemaker grips her PAD between her gnarled thumb and forefinger. She says, "Discontinue all holographic images—except for the fireworks displays, the cave, and Peacemaker."

One by one, objects disappear—Blake's PAD, the stolen stun gun, the stolen fireworks, the knapsack, Safiya's oboe, the footpath, the river, the surrounding trees, the dog, Édouard, Franz, Charlie, and Safiya. When Safiya disappears, I wince. A lump wells up in my throat. I also notice that I'm no longer wearing my Égalitéan clothes. Instead, I have on my old clothes—the rumpled T-shirt, the jeans, and the paint-spattered tennis shoes. I reach into my pockets. The wallet that Peacemaker gave me—with the cards labeled DIET, EXERCISE, and STRESS REDUCTION—is gone. My PAD too disappears, as does Peacemaker's. Even the wound and eight stitches in the back of my head vanish. The last things to disappear are the moon and the stars. Only the fireworks displays, the cave, Peacemaker, and I remain.

∘ ∘ ∘

"Who are you?" I ask. Fireworks continue to illuminate the sky, but now only at irregular intervals, much like the intervals between flashes of lightning during a thunderstorm. Between the flashes is an impenetrable inky blackness.

"I'm not really Peacemaker, of course. Neither am I Mrs. Shoemaker. I'm a daimon."

"A daimon? What's that?"

"A daimon is an attendant spirit. Many centuries ago, I came to Socrates. Socrates knew me as his inner voice. Whenever he was on the verge of making a wrong choice, the voice intervened. I never told him what he should do; I only steered him away from what he shouldn't do. Thus, when Socrates was a young man and considered a life in politics, I told him to stay away from politics. He trusted me implicitly. And a good thing too. Had Socrates gotten involved in politics, he would have made many enemies and wouldn't have lived long enough to do all the remarkable things he did."

"And now, all these centuries later, you've become my inner voice?"

"That's right. Of course, you're no Socrates. Although you have a good head on your shoulders, you hardly ever use it. That's why I showed you a fictional society. I needed something dramatic, something that would shake you up, that would rouse you from your dogmatic slumber and force you to think critically. But I've now shown you enough. From this point on, I'll treat you the way I treated Socrates, telling you only what *not* to do. Don't support the meat industry; don't support the pharmaceutical industry; don't support the fur industry; don't support the animal entertainment industry. Don't support anything that discounts the interests of nonhuman animals. If you ask me what you *should* do, as opposed to what you *shouldn't* do, I'm not going to answer. If you'd like to adopt the Égalitéan lifestyle, you're welcome to do so. If you'd rather do things a little differently, that's fine too. Would you like to be religious? Or live in a city rather than a village? Or drive a car rather than walk? Or play competitive rather than cooperative games? I'll let you figure those things out for yourself. But don't be a speciesist. I hope you trust me as implicitly as Socrates did."

"I'm not sure that I do. I doubt there are such things as daimons."

"Really? You surprise me, son. If you can believe in the Father, the Son, and the Holy Spirit, I don't see why you can't believe in daimons too. But it doesn't really matter one way or the other. If you'd rather not think of me as a daimon, perhaps you can think of me as your conscience."

"My conscience? Could my conscience have invented Égalité? Could it have taught me about factory farming, the Draize test, puppy mills, and other things that, as of a few days ago, I knew almost nothing about? I doubt you're my conscience either."

"You're missing my point. The point is that it doesn't matter who or what I am. What matters is that I've given you a wonderful experience. You've heard the arguments for the principles of human and animal equality. You've seen a society that comports itself in accordance with these principles. The question, then, is what you're going to do with this experience. Are you going to ignore it? Are you going to carry on business as usual, eating meat and wearing leather and frequenting zoos and buying products that are tested on animals? Or are you going to let the experience change you? If you let the experience change you, how profound will be the change? Will you merely support larger cages, or will you go further and support empty cages?"

I recall the dream I had the other night, in which I had to choose from three doors. Each door had a cage etched on it. Should I choose the tiny cage, the larger cage, or the empty cage? I say, "I guess you're right. The question is what I'm going to do with the experience I've had. I don't think I can any longer support tiny cages. I don't think I can support larger cages either. The cages should be empty. But what can I do? I'm just one person, one ordinary person. The cages will never be empty. Égalité doesn't exist; it'll never exist."

"Don't lose hope, son. You may not be able to create a utopia, either singlehandedly or with the help of others. But you can make a difference, maybe a larger difference than you would ever imagine."

When, feeling unconvinced, I don't respond, Peacemaker adds, "Remember, son, the people of Égalité look much the same as people from your time."

"Excuse me?"

"What I mean is that moral progress is possible. To get people to behave more ethically, you don't need to do anything as radical as alter human nature. All you need to do is change some attitudes."

"But how can I change people's attitudes? Tell me what I should do."

"I'm sorry, but, as I said, I'll tell you only what you *shouldn't* do. As for what you *should* do, you'll have to figure that out without my help. But don't worry. You now know everything you need to know. You're ready to go home. You're ready to make a difference."

"I don't want to go home. I want to live in Égalité."

"But Égalité doesn't exist. You have to go home."

"Yes. Yes, you're right, of course. How do I get back home?"

"It's very simple. All you need to do is step into the cave."

"I have to step into the cave?"

"Well, if you'd prefer, I could put a pair of ruby slippers on your feet, and you could click your heels together three times. But personally, I like the symbolism of the cave."

For a moment, the fireworks cease. Blackness envelops me. Then one more firework: a whistling sound ascends into the sky, followed by a burst of color. The cave, just a few yards from me, becomes visible. Peacemaker, however, has vanished. I look about and then, shrugging my shoulders, I step into the cave.

∘ ∘ ∘

"Empty cages," I say aloud. "What can I do to empty the cages? How can one person make a difference?"

I'm in my apartment, sitting on my worn leather couch. The TV is on. I see the first officer from the science fiction program. He's talking to an alien. He says, "We no longer enslave animals for food purposes." The alien objects, "But we have seen humans eat meat!" The first officer replies, "You've seen something as fresh and tasty as meat, but inorganically materialized out of patterns used by our transporters." The alien is mortified. He says, "Sickening! Barbaric!" The first officer furrows his brow.

I reach for the remote control and hit the power button. To my relief, the TV turns off. I notice that my belt is unbuckled and my pants are unbuttoned. I refasten them, even though my stomach is full of veal.

I get off the couch and wander through my apartment. So many of my possessions are made of leather: my leather couch, my leather wallet, my leather jacket, my several leather belts and several pairs of leather shoes, even my autographed baseballs. I step into the kitchen and open the refrigerator. Staring back at me are a pound of hamburger, several slices of bacon, a package of chicken nuggets, a carton of milk, a stick of butter, a block of cheddar cheese, a dozen eggs, and a lemon meringue pie. Disgusted, I slam shut the refrigerator door. I rummage through cabinets and drawers. Inside are numerous household products: shampoo, conditioner, dish soap, laundry detergent, all-purpose cleaner, and other such things. None of these has a label stating, "This product not tested on animals."

Anguish rises from within my chest. How could I have bought all these things? How could I have participated in the suffering of so many animals for so many years? I grab two large garbage bags and stride to the refrigerator. Into one of the bags go all of the meat, eggs, and dairy. Then I return to my cabinets and drawers. In a frenzy, I snatch up all of my household cleaners and other such products, and I dump them into the other garbage bag. I also toss in my leather wallet, leather jacket, leather belts, and leather shoes. The bags are full. I carry them outdoors and heave them into the dumpster. They join the chicken bones I threw out earlier.

When I'm back in my apartment, I walk past my leather couch. The mere sight of it sickens me. I drag the couch through the living room and through the door to my apartment. Once I'm outside, I lift the couch over my head, and, letting out a primal scream, I run to the dumpster and throw the couch into it. Startled by the scream, a few of my neighbors peer out of their windows.

Returning to my apartment once more, I grab more large garbage bags. I pick up every autographed baseball—more than two thousand of them—and shove them into the bags. I heft one of the bags over my shoulder and stagger to the dumpster. More neighbors peer out of their windows. I'm about to hurl the bag into the dumpster, but a voice stops me short. The voice is reedy, with the same tone color as Safiya's oboe. It says but a single word: "No!" I put the bag down. The voice is right. Perhaps I can sell the baseballs and donate the earnings to an animal rights organization. I drag the baseballs back to my apartment.

I plop down on my bed. As soon as my head hits the pillow, I realize how sleepy I am. I set the alarm clock so that I can be on time for work tomorrow. But do I want to go to work? I work at a sporting goods store, where I sell footballs, baseball gloves, soccer cleats, and many other products made of leather. No. I can't work at the sporting goods store anymore. I'll quit tomorrow and start looking for another job. What kind of job will I look for? Probably Blake could get me a job at the pharmaceutical company where he works. A bookkeeper perhaps—I've learned a little about bookkeeping while working at the sporting goods store. But I don't want to work at a pharmaceutical company either. I'm not sure what kind of job I should get. I'll have to give it some thought.

I'm also not sure what I should do about Blake. I don't for a moment believe he was with me in Égalité. He therefore didn't really throw a rock at me, and he didn't really steal a stun gun and fireworks. He is, however, a thoroughgoing speciesist. I'm also convinced that, when we were in the ninth grade, he paid those bullies to come after me. He isn't the good friend he seems to be. I think I should stop hanging out with him.

Why did Peacemaker—or whoever she is—use Blake as a character in Égalité? Did she put him in Égalité so that I could figure out what kind of person he really is—that he isn't really my friend but only pretends to be? Or did she have a different motive? Did she use Blake's character so that I could understand that some people's speciesism runs so deep they'll never overcome it? Did she want me to understand that trying to convince some people to adopt the principle of animal equality is a waste of time, that I should instead focus my energies on people whom I can convince? Or maybe Peacemaker had something else in mind. Maybe Blake was there to play devil's advocate, to force me to think hard about whether or not speciesism is justified.

I can't think clearly anymore. I'm too tired. I fall asleep.

o o o

From hidden outposts, cicadas thrum an insistent melody. High in a maple tree, baby birds, vying for mama's attention, cheep-cheep. Daylilies whisper in a hot, breathy breeze, while a meandering stream gurgles languidly. Where the stream widens into a sandy wading pool, children—no less a part of nature than the baby birds and daylilies—splash and squeal with laughter. Thrum, cheep-cheep, whisper, gurgle, splash, squeal. Nature is performing a summer symphony.

"Mind if I join you?"

Blake stands in front of me, holding a grilled vegetable wrap, fresh strawberries, and a glass of ice cold water. I too have selected a grilled vegetable wrap, strawberries, and water. I'm sitting at a picnic table, just outside the dining hall in Safiya's village. It's good to be back in Égalité.

I look up at Blake, but I don't invite him to sit down with me. He sits down anyway. Taking a bite out of his wrap, he says, "You know what your problem is, Philsbury? You didn't look both ways before crossing the street."

I furrow my brow. "I beg your pardon?" I say.

"You jumped on the animal rights bandwagon before you knew what you were getting yourself into. Do you really think you can be a vegetarian?"

"Vegan. I'm going to be a vegan."

Blake shrugs. "Even worse. Aren't you going to miss steak, the juice dribbling down your chin? Or bacon, nice and crisp, just the way you like it? And what about ice cream? What's your favorite flavor? Rocky road? On a hot day like today, a bowl of rocky road sure would hit the spot! You'll never last. I bet you don't even make it past the Fourth of July. You'll be grilling burgers with the rest of us!"

When I don't respond, Blake continues. "Then there's your job. Are you really going to quit? How will you make a living? You only have a high school degree, and the economy's still in a slump. Who's going to hire you? Let's face it. You haven't thought things through."

I still don't respond. Blake says, "I'll tell you what. Since I'm such a good friend to you, I'm going to give you some advice. If you're determined to become an animal rights advocate, go talk to Safiya. I don't mean the Safiya who lives in Égalité. I mean the Safiya from our time—the real Safiya. If anyone can help you, she can."

"I don't want your advice," I say. "I just want you to go away."

Blake shrugs again. Swallowing the last of his wrap, he says, "Suit yourself. But don't say I didn't warn you." Blake gets up and walks away from the picnic table.

Thrum, cheep-cheep, whisper, gurgle, splash, squeal. I love the sounds of Égalité. It's so peaceful here.

o o o

Across the street from the library, a neon sign hums, the *G* in "Giovanni's Pizza" flickering uncertainly. The traffic at the intersection is thick: cars beep-beep with irritation at the fellow who fails to notice that the light has turned green. An exasperated mother grips her son by the hand as she marches down the sidewalk. "I'm hot, Mommy!" the son whines. "When are we gonna get some ice cream?" The boy isn't watching where he's going. The mother has to yank him out of the way of a brown, oily puddle. Drop by drop, the oily goo dribbles down a drain by the edge of the street. Just behind the mother and son, a teenage boy, his arm wrapped around his girlfriend, passes the puddle. The boy turns his head; a moment later, a wad of spit splats against the surface of the oily liquid. In the distance, a police siren wails. Hum, beep-beep, whine, dribble, splat, wail. I'm not in Égalité anymore.

"Mind if I join you?"

Safiya is sitting at a picnic table just outside the public library. Her black hair is tied up in a bun. Her clothes, similar to the clothes she wore on our blind date, consist of black high-heeled shoes, a black skirt, and a blouse covered with white triangles and gray squares. In front of her is a laptop; to one side, in its case, is her oboe.

Safiya glances up from her laptop, appraising me with her penetrating steel gray eyes. I'm wearing a sporty outfit that I bought earlier this morning. It looks much like the outfit that the tailor made for me in Égalité. I'm holding two grilled vegetable wraps, a quart of strawberries, and two bottles of ice cold water. Safiya doesn't invite me to sit down with her, but I sit anyway. I offer to share my food with her. She hesitates, but accepts my offer.

"First off," I say, clearing my throat, "I'd like to apologize. I regret taking you to a beef joint last night."

When Safiya doesn't respond, I continue. "I'd also like to ask you something, if you don't mind. I want to help animals. They deserve better lives, less suffering. But I'm not sure of the best way to help. I thought you might know more than I do. Can you give me any insights?"

Safiya glares at me coldly. She says, "Don't eat veal!"

"I know. I won't. But what else should I do? Please. I'm serious about this."

Safiya's glare softens. She looks into my eyes, trying to determine whether I'm sincere. She evidently decides that I am. She tells me that there are many ways to help animals: become a vegetarian or vegan, stop wearing fur and leather, purchase household products that aren't tested on animals, give donations to animal rights organizations, participate in demonstrations against animal research labs, organize vigils, write letters to lawmakers, and many other things besides. What I should do depends on my interests, as well as on my strengths and limitations. If I'm interested in controlling the population of companion animals, I might pass out pamphlets about spaying and neutering. If I'm better at writing than organizing, I might write letters to lawmakers rather than organize vigils.

I ask Safiya what she does to help animals. She begins by telling me about her conversion to the animal rights philosophy. She speaks cautiously at first, but with gradually increasing enthusiasm.

She became a vegetarian, she says, eight years ago, shortly after she got her cat—the black and white one I saw when I took Safiya home after our blind date. She fell in love with the cat instantly. When he hopped on her lap, the cat would wrap his front paws around her neck, always careful not to scratch her, and rest his head under her chin. How he purred when he did that! Then one day she learned that, in China, some people eat cats. That got her to thinking. She could never eat her cat, or any other cat. Cats have personalities. They have likes and dislikes. They can suffer and enjoy. But in these respects cats are no different from cows, pigs, chickens, and other animals that, at the time, Safiya ate with relish. If it's wrong to eat a cat, Safiya reasoned, it must also be wrong to eat other animals; it's wrong to eat a cat; therefore, it must also be wrong to eat other animals. At that moment, Safiya stopped eating animals.

For a time, Safiya continued to eat eggs and dairy products. After all, one doesn't have to kill a hen to get her eggs or kill a cow to get her milk. Then Safiya discovered that most hens are confined in battery cages. She started buying cage-free eggs, but that didn't last long. Cage-free hens may not live in cages, but they do live in sheds, in horribly crowded conditions. Free-range hens, hens that are allowed outdoors, though more common than they once were, are still rare in the United States. In addition, the label "free-range" means different things on different farms. Free-range hens might be allowed to roam in wide-open spaces, or they might be confined in crowded outdoor mobile pens. They might live in any number of inhumane conditions, and they might be slaughtered inhumanely. Safiya decided that the simplest thing would be to give up eggs altogether. At the same time, she gave up dairy products as well—like laying hens, dairy cows suffer a great deal. That was six years ago. Safiya's been a vegan ever since.

I ask Safiya if she ever misses eating animal products. Does she ever crave an omelet, a milkshake, or a pepperoni pizza? She says she doesn't. On the contrary, being a vegan has only enriched her life, leading her to try a wide variety of foods from a wide variety of cultures. Before she became a vegan, for instance, she'd never eaten Indian food, but now Indian food is among her favorite choices. She adds, though, that, if I ever decide to become a vegan, I should take care to get all of the nutrients I need, including vitamin B_{12}. This isn't hard. These days, many vegan foods—such as many breakfast cereals and breakfast bars, and many brands of rice milk and soy milk—are supplemented with vitamin B_{12} and other nutrients.

Safiya says that changing her diet was only the start. About the time she became a vegan, she stopped buying household products that were tested on animals, and she stopped buying clothes made of fur, leather, wool, or silk. She also stopped frequenting zoos and aquaria, and she stopped going to circuses that feature animal acts. Some circuses, however, such as Cirque du Soleil, don't feature animal acts, and Safiya continues to enjoy those. She's especially fond of magic acts; the art of illusion fascinates her.

Luckily, safiya didn't need to change her career, since oboes can be manufactured without harming animals. She did, however, review her IRA, to make sure she invested in no company that engages in overtly speciesist practices. She also stopped donating money for aids research, since aids researchers rely heavily on animal experiments. When I tell Safiya that, for the last seven years, I've been collecting money for cancer research, she suggests that, although my heart is no doubt in the right place, I might do better to support a less speciesist cause. I ask Safiya what causes she supports. A good many, she answers. She donates a tenth of her annual income to animal rights organizations, and another tenth to human rights organizations.

I admire Safiya for her generosity. I tell her, though, that I don't think I can afford to be as generous, because I'm not very wealthy. Donating twenty percent of my annual income would pose a significant hardship for me. Safiya replies that it's okay if some people give less than others. The important thing is to do the best one can. She adds that, as far as she can tell, adopting a vegan lifestyle has saved her money. Fur coats and leather couches, for example, are generally more expensive than faux fur coats and cloth couches, and many vegan foods, such as pasta and rice, are very inexpensive.

Each of the many things she does, Safiya is convinced, helps make a difference. She isn't sure how large the difference is, but she likes to think the difference she makes is more than marginal. Perhaps the most important thing she does—certainly the one thing she finds most rewarding—is to tell others about the animal rights philosophy that she has adopted. To be sure, she doesn't discuss animal rights with everyone she meets, since some people simply aren't ready to embrace the idea. Far from being persuaded, they'll only be turned off. No. There's no point trying to persuade someone who almost certainly won't be persuaded. But many people are curious about animal rights, and many become sympathetic once they learn more about it. These are the people Safiya enjoys talking to. She's glad that I'm one of them.

o o o

Thanking Safiya for her time, I start to get up from the picnic table. Safiya, however, doesn't let me go. Reaching across the table, she grasps my left hand with hers. "Wait," she says. "I'd like to ask you a question."

I sit down once more. "Certainly. Ask me anything you like."

Still holding my hand, Safiya says, "What got you interested in animal rights? Just last night, when we were having dinner, I'd never have guessed that you of all people, a lover of veal, would become an animal rights advocate."

My face reddens. I hesitate to tell Safiya about my adventures in Égalité, because they seem too incredible. Will Safiya believe me when I tell her that someone who claimed to be a daimon showed me a utopian society? Will she believe me when I tell her that the inhabitants of this utopian society bore a striking resemblance to people from my own society? Will she believe me when I tell her that I developed feelings for one of the Égalitéans, the very one who shared Safiya's name and physical appearance? Or will Safiya dismiss my story as the ravings of a lunatic?

In the end I take a chance. I tell Safiya my story. I tell it for a combination of reasons. First, I don't like hiding the truth. Second, Safiya seems genuinely interested. Third, I don't hear a reedy voice in my head saying, "No!"

Safiya hangs on to every word I tell her. Her hand squeezes mine. Her eyes sparkle with excitement. On several occasions she starts to interrupt, as if she has something of great importance to say, but then she bites her lip and remains silent. When I finally finish my story, she can contain herself no longer.

"I know how you can help animals!" she says. "Write down your story. Publish it. Let the world know about Égalité. Maybe Égalité doesn't exist. Maybe it'll never exist, at least not in every detail. But it's a beautiful ideal, and surely our society can adopt some of Égalité's practices. Your story can help change people's minds about animals. It can play a part, with any luck a more than minor part, in the ongoing efforts of the animal movement."

Again I hesitate. "I don't know," I say. "I'm not a good writer. I have only a high school education. I don't think I can pull it off."

"Don't worry," Safiya says. "I'm a fair writer. I can help you." She opens a Word document on her laptop. The cursor blinks on the blank page as Safiya thinks. Then she says, "I've got it! We can begin like this."

Safiya rapidly types a sentence, totaling twelve words. I look at the sentence. I like it. Safiya and I are going to make a good team.

o o o

"We hold these truths to be self-evident, that all animals are equal …"

Notes

Chapter 1

The "popular science fiction series, set in the twenty-fourth century," is *Star Trek: The Next Generation*. The episode showing on the TV is "Lonely Among Us."

The conditions under which food animals are raised and slaughtered are described in many places, including https://www.peta.org/issues/animals-used-for-food/factory-farming/. These conditions have in some respects improved modestly from ten years ago. For a comparison, see Peter Singer and Jim Mason's *The Ethics of What We Eat: Why Our Food Choices Matter* (2006). Singer and Mason discuss broilers in Chapter 2, laying hens in Chapter 3, pigs in Chapter 4 (pp. 43-54), and veal calves in Chapter 4 (pp. 58-59).

Chapter 2

The term "speciesism" was coined by Richard Ryder. Peter Singer compares speciesism with racism and sexism in Chapter 1 of *Animal Liberation* (1975, 1990, 2002, 2009).

Chapter 3

Peter Singer makes the case that all animals are equal in Chapter 1 of *Animal Liberation* (1975, 1990, 2002, 2009).

In *Ethics into Action: Henry Spira and the Animal Rights Movement* (1998), Peter Singer describes the Draize eye irritancy test and Henry Spira's campaign against its use by the cosmetics industry. See especially pp. 86-114.

The biblical verse that Brother Bell wrote on the blackboard is Matthew 6:26.

Tom Regan distinguishes between preference-interests and welfare-interests on p. 87 of *The Case for Animal Rights* (1983).

Chapter 4

The story about Socrates is told in Plato's *Symposium*. See 174d-175b.

The quotation from Aristotle can be found in Book I, Chapter 3 of the *Nicomachean Ethics*.

The example of the child falling into the swimming pool is taken, with minor modifications, from p. 199 of the third edition of Peter Singer's *Practical Ethics* (2011).

Phil's speculation that intelligence might be many things rather than one thing is developed by Howard Gardner in *Frames of Mind: The Theory of Multiple Intelligences* (1983).

Safiya's third argument for the principle of human equality is a variation of the argument Peter Singer advances in Chapter 1 of *Animal Liberation* (1975, 1990, 2002, 2009). On p. 6, Singer, too, gives the quote from Sojourner Truth. The quote is taken from her speech, "Ain't I a Woman?" The speech can be found on many websites, including http://www.fordham.edu/halsall/mod/sojtruth-woman.html.

Chapter 5

Safiya's argument for the principle of animal equality is a variation of the argument Peter Singer advances in Chapter 1 of *Animal Liberation* (1975, 1990, 2002, 2009).

On pp. 68-69 of *Empty Cages: Facing the Challenge of Animal Rights* (2004), Tom Regan objects much as Safiya does to the argument that speciesism is justified because, unlike animals, human beings have souls.

Chapter 6

For more information about the dissection of animals for educational purposes, see pp. 160-166 of Tom Regan's *Empty Cages: Facing the Challenge of Animal Rights* (2004). See also Jonathan Balcombe's *The Use of Animals in Higher Education: Problems, Alternatives, & Recommendations* (2000), as well as Andrew J. Petto and Karla D. Russell's "Humane Education: The Role of Animal-Based Learning," in the third edition of *The Animal Ethics Reader*, edited by Susan J. Armstrong and Richard G. Botzler (2016).

Chapter 7

For a defense of herbal remedies and a critique of pharmaceuticals, see Marti Kheel's "From Healing Herbs to Deadly Drugs: Western Medicine's War Against the Natural World," in *Healing the Wounds: The Promise of Ecofeminism*, edited by Judith Plant (1989).

"In your day, the pharmaceutical industry, worldwide, was more than a trillion dollar a year industry. Nearly half of that more than a trillion dollars came from the United States." For exact figures, see https://www.statista.com/topics/1764/global-pharmaceutical-industry/ and https://www.statista.com/topics/1719/pharmaceutical-industry/.

The "dish consisting of scrambled tofu, mixed vegetables, and herbs, with a hint of garlic and lemon" comes from a menu for Claire's Cornercopia, a popular vegetarian restaurant located in New Haven, Connecticut.

Xenotransplantation—the transplantation of an animal's organs into a human patient—is discussed by R. G. Frey in "Organs for Transplant: Animals, Moral Standing, and One View of the Ethics of Xenotransplantation" and by Gary L. Francione in "Xenografts and Animal Rights." Both articles are in the first edition of *The Animal Ethics Reader*, edited by Susan J. Armstrong and Richard G. Botzler (2003).

Some of the claims and arguments in the last section of Chapter 7 are taken from pp. 297-306 of Carl Cohen and Tom Regan's *The Animal Rights Debate* (2001).

Chapter 8

The quotation from Plato's *Republic* occurs at 372b-d.

The quotation from the Bible is Genesis 1:29.

The ending of the play that Phil and Safiya watch is taken, with slight modifications, from Timothy Eves' "Plato's Vegetarian Utopia," *Between the Species: An Electronic Journal for the Study of Philosophy and Animals*, Issue V, cla.calpoly.edu/~jlynch/05issue.html (2005).

Chapter 9

This chapter draws heavily on Peter Singer and Jim Mason's *The Ethics of What We Eat: Why Our Food Choices Matter* (2006).

"But a vegetarian society would discriminate against certain groups of people." Kathryn Paxton George advances this argument in "A Paradox of Ethical Vegetarianism: Unfairness to Women and Children," in *Food for Thought: The Debate over Eating Meat*, edited by Steve F. Sapontzis (2004).

Lists of vegetarian athletes abound on the Internet, including https://www.peta.org/features/vegetarian-athletes/.

I owe the example of the dandelion to Cindy Eves-Thomas.

"But plants feel pain too." Peter Singer refutes this argument on pp. 235-236 of the 2002 edition of *Animal Liberation* (1975, 1990, 2002, 2009).

"Which, then, kills fewer nonhuman animals: using our acre to grow crops, or using it to raise grass-fed cattle? One animal scientist from your era attempted to answer this question." The animal scientist is Steven L. Davis. He gives his answer in "The Least Harm Principle May Require that Humans Consume a Diet Containing Large Herbivores, not a Vegan Diet," *Journal of Agriculture and Environmental Ethics* 16:387-394 (2003).

"But God tells us we may eat meat." For a fuller discussion of this argument, see Timothy Eves' "Does the Bible Endorse Moral Vegetarianism?" *Between the Species: An Electronic Journal for the Study of Philosophy and Animals*, Issue VI, cla.calpoly.edu/~jlynch/06issue.html (2006).

Chapter 10

For more on the many ways companion animals are mistreated, see Bernard E. Rollin and Michael D. H. Rollin's "Dogmaticisms and Catechisms: Ethics and Companion Animals," in the second edition of *The Animal Ethics Reader*, edited by Susan J. Armstrong and Richard G. Botzler (2008).

For more information on puppy mills, see https://www.aspca.org/animal-cruelty/puppy-mills/closer-look-puppy-mills.

"Of the six and a half million cats and dogs taken to U.S. shelters each year, more than one and a half million were euthanized: about 670,000 dogs and 860,000 cats." These numbers are taken from https://www.aspca.org/animal-homelessness/shelter-intake-and-surrender/pet-statistics.

For more information on animal shelters, see Clare Palmer's "Killing Animals in Animal Shelters," in the third edition of *The Animal Ethics Reader*, edited by Susan J. Armstrong and Richard G. Botzler (2016). See also https://www.peta.org/issues/companion-animal-issues/animal-shelters/.

For two views on feeding cats and dogs a vegetarian or vegan diet, see http://pets.webmd.com/features/vegetarian-diet-dogs-cats#1 and https://www.peta.org/living/companion-animals/vegetarian-cats-dogs/.

For more information on assistance animals, see Tzachi Zamir's "The Moral Basis of Animal-Assisted Therapy," in the third edition of *The Animal Ethics Reader*, edited by Susan J. Armstrong and Richard G. Botzler (2016).

Chapter 11

This chapter draws on Chapter 7 of Tom Regan's *Empty Cages: Facing the Challenge of Animal Rights* (2004). See also http://www.peta.org/issues/Animals-Used-for-Clothing/default.aspx.

Chapter 12

For more on hunting, see pp. 142-150 of Tom Regan's *Empty Cages: Facing the Challenge of Animal Rights* (2004).

Charlie's ecofeminist critique of hunting draws on Marti Kheel's "The Killing Game: An Ecofeminist Critique of Hunting," in the third edition of *The Animal Ethics Reader*, edited by Susan J. Armstrong and Richard G. Botzler (2016). The quotation from Ortega y Gasset is taken from Kheel's essay.

The studies that suggest that fish can feel pain are described on pp. 130-131 of Peter Singer and Jim Mason's *The Ethics of What We Eat: Why Our Food Choices Matter* (2006).

Chapter 13

The case that this chapter makes against zoos draws on Dale Jamieson's "Against Zoos," in *In Defense of Animals: The Second Wave*, edited by Peter Singer (2006).

"In contrast, during the late 1980s and early 1990s, the infant mortality rate of polar bears who lived in the wild was thirty-five percent—though fifteen years later, as global warming increasingly impacted the Arctic Circle, infant mortality in the wild increased to fifty-seven percent." These numbers are taken from http://www.nbcnews.com/id/15747502/ns/us_news-environment/t/fewer-polar-bear-cubs-surviving-study-finds/#.WVkGDk0zXIU.

"The population increased to four hundred twenty-five, two hundred nineteen of which were living in the wild." These were the numbers of California condors as of October 31, 2014, according to www.sandiegozoo.org.

For more on greyhound racing and rodeos, see Chapter 9 of Tom Regan's *Empty Cages: Facing the Challenge of Animal Rights* (2004). For more on circuses, see Chapter 8 of the same book.

Chapter 14

The white dove that symbolizes peace is based on the Giant Peace Dove Puppets created by members of Roots & Shoots, a program sponsored by the Jane Goodall Institute.

The chess game that Blake and Phil play is a game that I played on March 10, 1976, at the University of Maine. I don't mean to suggest that my opponent in any way resembles either Blake or Phil.

Phil's response to Blake's objection to the principles of human and animal equality. Compare the views Peter Singer expresses in *The Expanding Circle: Ethics, Evolution, and Moral Progress* (1981, 2011).

"I can always take apart my PAD and figure out how it works. I'm sure it's a complicated device. It might take me years. But I'm a smart guy. I'll figure it out eventually. Then I'll start constructing PADs. I'll be the guy who invents them. This PAD will make me rich and famous." Compare an episode of *Star Trek: The Next Generation* called "A Matter of Time."

Chapter 15

Plato refers to Socrates' daimon in the *Apology*. See 31c-d.

Peter Singer and Jim Mason discuss cage-free eggs in Chapter 8 of *The Ethics of What We Eat: Why Our Food Choices Matter* (2006). They discuss dairy cows on pp. 55-60 in Chapter 4.

See https://www.peta.org/living/food/free-range-eggs/ for more on free-range eggs.